AN HEIR OF DISTINCTION

THE BAD HEIR DAY TALES

BOOK FIVE

GRACE BURROWES

GRACE BURROWES PUBLISHING

DEDICATION

To the fishes out of water.
Just keep swimming anyway.

CHAPTER ONE

"Lady Barclay is *Scottish*." Bernard Huxley paced the understated elegance of St. Didier's library as he flung that accusation. "His Grace did not bother to warn me that her ladyship is a Scottish, red-haired Amazonian and unfashionably devoted to her children."

"The last strikes me as a maternal virtue." St. Didier poured two brandies. "Do Lady Barclay's height, hair color, and antecedents truly matter?"

Bernard hesitated before accepting his drink. Strong spirits for other than medicinal purposes struck him as tending toward hedonism, but to refuse would be rude.

"My thanks. To your health." He sipped, unsure what to expect.

"I picked up a case of this vintage on my last jaunt to France." St. Didier settled into a wing chair that might have been related to a throne a few generations back. Commodious, deeply cushioned, generously proportioned, and beautifully upholstered in green brocade.

Not quite extravagant but powerfully inviting.

"Thank the celestial intercessors," St. Didier went on, "that

Napoleon didn't wreck the wineries, distilleries, and vineyards. He is said to be quite an appreciator of champagne."

Bernard took the proffered seat because manners required that as well. Then too, he was tired, and the chair was exquisitely comfortable.

"We wish *l'empereur* the joy of his epicurean tastes," Bernard replied, "as he endures his flea-infested purgatory in the South Atlantic. What am I to do about Lady Barclay?"

"You've met her?"

"That pleasure yet awaits me. I have *observed* her cavorting in the park with her offspring." Laughing loudly enough to turn heads, for pity's sake. Flying a kite. A bright *red* kite with a fantastical white creature in the middle—a winged unicorn or a dragon or some such. "One child each, male and female. Ages seven and six, respectively. Jordan and Bridget. His Grace of Chanderton claimed they are both quite bright, but then, the duke is their uncle. He would say that."

"You are their cousin. What do you say?"

"Chanderton is my uncle, too, else I should tell him that this little bit of family business is not *my* business. I have far too much else to contend with to be guardian of Lady Barclay's progeny."

"Bit of a shock, I'd guess, learning that your grandfather was the late Duke of Chanderton, and your biological papa was a courtesy lord."

St. Didier had a gift for understatement. Tallish, quiet, soft-spoken, and dark-haired, he also had a sense of self-possession that Bernard envied. Bernard had learned during his years in the Church to exercise self-restraint, but St. Didier had self-*possession*.

A different and more precious quality entirely.

"The real shock was learning that my mother was a fraud," Bernard said, taking another small sip of his drink. He knew next to nothing about brandy, but the libation in his glass was smooth, redolent of apples, and even boasted a touch of nutmeg in the finish.

Very pleasant, in moderation.

"Your mama," St. Didier said, "daughter of an earl, disported with a ducal scion, got with child, and then had to be hastily wed to the mere brother of a baron. Not that unusual a tale in polite society, but you only recently learned of your own antecedents. That cannot have been easy. Have you been told how much your papa's family added to her settlements?"

St. Didier also had an ability to discuss the most distressing subjects as if they counted for less than the weather. A vicar aspired to the same talent, and in that regard, Bernard had considered himself modestly successful.

When is the baby due? Do you know who the father is? Have you any relatives in Scotland or the Home Counties? Nothing on the scholarly road to ordination prepared a vicar for those conversations, and yet, they were necessary in even the most devout parishes—rather frequently.

"I am embarrassingly solvent," Bernard said. "My father apparently insisted that half the sum contributed to Mama's settlements be set aside for me and that annual contributions be added to it from his funds and from his estate. I was entitled to claim the whole when I turned five-and-twenty, but I had no notion the money was mine."

Had had no notion the funds existed, even as they kept racking up interest year by year.

"That had to hurt," St. Didier said, getting up to retrieve the decanter. "Your mother, leading light of the congregation, self-aggrandizing saint of the parish, and general meddlesome busybody, lied to you, tried to steal from you, and was more of a sinner than the whole rest of your flock put together. The Antipodes are welcome to her. How are you getting on with the present duke?"

"To be honest..." Bernard avoided honesty on most occasions. He was careful, kindly in the conservative fashion of an earnest churchman, and he tried to keep the Commandments. One could avoid bleating unhappy truths about without telling falsehoods. "Chanderton looks like me."

Tall, blond, and beaky. On the aging duke, those qualities were distinguished.

"How lucky for him, though you're too skinny and academic for most of Mayfair's matchmakers."

"I beg you, St. Didier, do not say that word. Do not whisper it. I have been in London a mere six months, and it's as if nobody thinks of anything else save matrimony and its preliminaries. Settlements, courting, understandings, vouchers, waltzes, and scandals. I am in Town to learn about and manage my cousin's commercial enterprises, not to appease the curiosity of Mayfair's numerous gossips. Where did you say you found this brandy?"

"Thought you'd like it. A little family operation in the Charente department, quite near the coast. I can give you their direction. As far as I know, they lack a British distributor."

Bernard nearly told him, *I could not possibly impose to that extent*, the polite version of *I could not possibly deal in the wickedness that is expensive, French spirits*.

No bishop was on hand, though, and brandy was merely a drink, no more wicked than ale or hard cider. Wickedness did not come aged in oak barrels. In Bernard's experience, evil usually pranced around on two human feet. Every bishop in the realm kept some brandy in his cellars.

"That would be appreciated." Bernard took another sip. "What can you tell me about Lady Barclay?"

St. Didier had invited Bernard to join him for supper at his club, where conversation had been mostly political—and surprisingly Whiggish. Bernard, as befit a loyal churchman, was more familiar with the Tory presentation of most issues. Seeing the realities of London life in all their squalid glory had invited a broadening of his perspective.

This nightcap, which St. Didier had suggested as an apparent afterthought, now struck Bernard as the point of the evening. Bernard's cousin Camden, who held the Lorne baronial title, had asked St. Didier to look in on the nursery, as it were.

Camden's businesses were prospering. Bernard was not sure the same could be said for Bernard himself as he learned to manage those businesses.

London stank, never slept, and was unrelentingly loud. London teemed with an unfathomable abundance of people from an unfathomably broad sampling of the world's locations and professions. Disease, prostitution, commerce, and gossip thrived in London.

Bernard had failed to divine how any sane soul could likewise prosper in the capital, and yet, hordes and scads and hundreds of thousands of people did.

Case in point: Lady Barclay, laughing like a dairymaid and flying her red kite in the yellowish gray skies over Hyde Park.

St. Didier set his drink aside. "I can tell you that Lady Barclay, like you, is only partly Scottish. Her grandmother was English, as your grandmother was Scottish. Her ladyship was well dowered, married quite young, and Lord Barclay left her well set-up. She will not purloin her children's means or fritter away her own. Barclay courted her in the usual fashion, the usual negotiations ensued, and the first child came along a decorous year after the wedding. The second followed a year later, and then Barclay's health began failing. He was quite a bit older than his bride, but nobody expected him to cock up his toes that soon."

"How will her ladyship take to having a guardian appointed for her children?"

"A successor guardian," St. Didier said. "The old duke was the guardian appointed in Lord Barclay's will, and he and her ladyship got on well. His Grace left her alone, and she's been raising the children quite without interference from her ducal in-laws. Your uncle now has the title, and he's petitioning to have you appointed as successor guardian to the old duke."

Bernard spoke aloud the question that had been haunting him since last week's summons from Chanderton. "Why me? I am a legitimate by-blow, a family secret, evidence of scandal, albeit scandal from years ago. I have no qualifications for the post of guardian. I have no children, and I was a poor excuse for a child. I was neither bright, nor charming, nor adorable."

"Perhaps," St. Didier said, "you were *normal*, and the present duke knows how rare and precious that experience can be for children raised under the penumbra of a title."

Penumbra. Shadow. Bernard's entire life had progressed under the penumbra of his mother's perfidy and meddling. Bernard sent up a short prayer, one of many, for the unfortunates soon to endure Mama's company in the Antipodes.

"Might you provide me an introduction to Lady Barclay?" Chanderton had not bestirred himself to see to that detail, and yet, even a red-haired, kite-flying, Scottish Amazon deserved the courtesies when meeting the proposed guardian of her children for the first time.

"I'd be happy to. Her ladyship hacks out in Hyde Park on the occasional fine morning, and I enjoy the odd horseback outing myself. Meet me by Tattersalls tomorrow at dawn."

Dawn. Dawn for one who communed with ledgers far into the night was inhumanly early. Needs must.

"Until tomorrow, then," Bernard said, finishing his drink and rising. "My thanks for a very pleasant evening."

"The pleasure was entirely mine, Huxley. Shall I send a footman with you, or would you prefer to take my coach?"

That question, like so much of Bernard's London experience, baffled him. "Neither will be necessary. I know my way. I'm three streets from my own quarters, but I thank you for the offer."

"Huxley, you are in *London*. At this hour, a pickpocket bides on every corner, two footpads lurk in most doorways, and an abundance of rats and stray dogs will menace the unsuspecting simply for entertainment. You will stroll along, mentally comparing Greek and Latin translations of some old prophet and find yourself relieved of your purse, cloak, top hat, and boots."

St. Didier was genuinely concerned. Bernard could not think why.

"You would expect a footman, anywhere from six inches to a foot shorter than my skinny, scholarly self, to make his way back alone here safely, when I—sword stick in hand, knife in my boot, and fists at the ready—am somehow unsafe without supervision. You need to breathe some fresh country air, St. Didier. The coal smoke is addling your wits."

"But you—"

Bernard held up a hand. "I know to carry little coin. The thieves are welcome to the small amount on my person, and I will not fight them over it. No honest work is available for most of them and, especially for our gallant former soldiers, that leaves only crime or starvation. I am no longer a churchman, but I still hope to claim a share of basic human decency."

A bit preachy, but St. Didier merely smiled and nodded. Like a good host, he accompanied Bernard to the door and helped him on with his coat. Wished him a pleasant evening and peaceful dreams...

Bernard walked out into the damp evening air feeling a little like he'd just escaped tea with the bishop and his wife. One bore up under the strain of duty and was permitted some relief when that duty had been faithfully executed.

As he strolled along in no particular hurry, footsteps sounded behind him in the same relaxed tempo. St. Didier had sent along an escort, no doubt, or might even be himself keeping pace with Bernard.

Not surprising. St. Didier was something of a nanny-for-hire where the peerage was concerned, though coin was probably never overtly discussed even with him. His specialty was shepherding reluctant heirs into their new duties and into Society's good graces.

Thankless notion, though Bernard, having been handed management of Cam's businesses and now guardianship of two half-Scottish children, appreciated the show of support.

"I miss Yorkshire." Bernard had put the sentiment in quiet Latin, a habit, along with preaching, that wasn't likely to leave him any time soon.

How would one say, *I am partly Scottish,* in Latin? *Partim Scotus sum,* or something of that nature. Partly Scottish, a duke for an uncle, very likely possessed of Scottish cousins.

Truly, pigs might be winging their way aloft somewhere high above London's dark and dreary skies.

"What can you tell me about Mr. Bernard Huxley?" Sorcha's mare stepped delicately around a pile of horse droppings steaming in dawn's early gloom. "Is he as stodgy as his name suggests?"

Stodgy would be bearable. When the late Lord Barclay had been stodgy, Sorcha had known how to deal with him. Walk softly, speak only when spoken to. Wear mauve and stitch dull samplers featuring boring platitudes and intricate floral borders.

A former vicar almost had a right to be stodgy.

"Huxley is..." Leopold St. Didier paused to navigate his gelding past a pothole in the cobbles. "He is at sea, I believe. The Church suited his intellectual appetites, though he has taken to commerce with astonishing aptitude. He's logical—always a good thing, in my estimation—and also cautious."

"Will he meddle?" The only question that really mattered.

"He will be a conscientious guardian to your children. If his assessment of their best interests differs from your own, you will at least have a fair hearing."

"Leopold, I do not want a fair hearing from some pious stranger whose aptitude for greed is excelled only by his ignorance of child-rearing. Why are you smirking?"

St. Didier comported himself at all times with decorum and discretion, but his dark eyes occasionally took on a sparkle that hinted at hidden merriment.

"You grow more Scottish when impassioned. You can always apply to me for aid should Huxley prove dunderheaded."

They reached the corner of the park occupied by Tattersalls

horse-trading establishment. No auction was to be held that morning, and Sorcha wouldn't have set a booted foot on the premises in any case. The activity nonetheless characterized the typical busy stable early in the day.

Barrows of pungent manure and damp straw came out of the shed rows, and fresh straw went in. Horses at the water troughs slurped noisily. Other steeds waited, saddled and bridled, for a morning hack.

Homesickness hit Sorcha with a vengeance. A longing for the mist rising over the Scottish hills, for the sharp springtime sunlight in Perthshire. An ache that yearned for impossibly tall pines and painfully fresh air.

"That's him," St. Didier said, gesturing discreetly with his chin. "On the gray at the corner."

Sorcha halted her mare, and St. Didier did likewise with his gelding.

Both Mr. Huxley and his horse needed some extra weight. The gray had the excuse of coming off winter rations.

"Mr. Huxley is woefully English-looking," Sorcha said. "English vicarish-looking, or he might be a headmaster at a particularly severe public school."

A disquieting thought.

"He was a vicar for years and well liked by his congregants. Given to brevity in the pulpit, from what I heard. Take heart, my lady. The guardianship has not yet been formally transferred, so Huxley is merely a family acquaintance at this point."

"Of the scandalous variety." Sorcha urged her mare forward.

"Lord Jerome has long since gone to his reward, the scandal was old news thirty years ago, and Jerome provided adequately for his offspring, even to the point of finding Huxley a decent fellow to serve as the legal papa. Smile, Sorcha. The evidence of my own experience tells me that you can be charming when you wish to be."

Sorcha. So few people called her that anymore. She mustered up the requisite cheerful expression and brought her mare to stand two yards from Mr. Huxley's ribby gray.

"Huxley," St. Didier said, "good morning. Lady Barclay, I am honored to introduce to you Mr. Bernard Huxley, whom you know to be a cousin to your children and a friend of mine. Huxley, Lady Barclay."

Sorcha held out her gloved hand. Introductions on horseback could be awkward, but she'd not wanted to put off an assessment of her foe—if a foe he was.

"My lady, I am at your service." Huxley took her hand briefly and nodded over it. "Shall we find a bridle path? I am still unfamiliar with all Hyde Park has to offer, having come to London as winter set in. Perhaps you might show me your favorite trail?"

He was correct to a fault. He sat his horse as if he were posing for a Stubbs portrait, *Gentleman Contemplating Philosophy Atop His Hunter*. The words were polite, the overture appropriate to the occasion. Huxley's attire was perfect for a morning hack in polite society's backyard.

"I keep to the quieter choices," Sorcha said. "The Season is upon us, and the popular paths can be congested with those interested in socializing rather than riding."

Mr. Huxley slanted her an unreadable look. "The quieter the path, the better. Lead on, your ladyship."

Sorcha set her mare on a tree-lined course on the northeast side of the Serpentine. "How do you find London, Mr. Huxley? Town does not show at its best in winter, though spring is a different proposition."

Thank heavens for the weather.

"I find London..." He glanced over his shoulder at St. Didier, toddling along to the rear like a bored groom. "I find London perplexing. What is the attraction of cramming so many people together in one place? Food and fuel must be brought in from greater and greater distances, refuse taken out. The river is hopelessly befouled by this great mass of people, the roads and turnpikes congested to impassability. I am at a loss to understand what happens in Town that could not happen in more healthful and appealing surrounds."

"You don't care for London?" The only question Sorcha could think to pose. Mr. Huxley's small talk was a bit peculiar, which made no sense. He'd been a vicar, and vicars should be the dukes of small talk.

"I do not *understand* London. I grasp that port cities are busy and that docks are a necessity. London is so much more complicated than a simple port. Would it be too forward of me to ask after your children?"

Yes, it was too forward. "Of course not. Jordan is seven, Bridget six. They get on well, enjoy good health, and can give a good account of themselves in the schoolroom." Sorcha made herself say the next part. "If you'd like to meet them, I will happily arrange that."

"I would very much like to meet them. They are my cousins."

That last part apparently discomfited him. He was new to London, and Sorcha grudgingly admitted that he was new to his ducal connections as well. Society would carefully avoid describing him as part of the ducal *family*, all the while acknowledging that Huxley's titled father had provided for him—the present duke had made that much plain to the gossips—and Huxley had been ordained and was technically legitimate.

As scandals went, Huxley only just qualified, and only in the outdated-nigh-to-irrelevance category.

"How are you and Chanderton getting along?" Sorcha asked.

"Politely. He invited me to dinner at his club, which I gather is some sort of rite of passage. I am in trade, ma'am. You must surely be aware of that fact. Given my status, my commercial activities are either ignored or acceptable. I have more or less inherited my business ventures from my cousin, Lord Lorne, who is newly wed and focused on estate matters."

His small talk definitely needed work. "You needn't apologize to any self-respecting Scot for doing an honest day's work for an honest day's pay, Mr. Huxley. One would think, though, that you'd kit yourself out with a mount more in keeping with a prosperous cit's image."

Mr. Huxley aimed *such* a look at her that Sorcha nearly sent her mare trotting across the grass. He was not angry with her so much as he scrutinized her with an intensity that went past rude to intrusive, to... oracular?

"I am a cit. You are correct. Interesting. Shall we canter the next bit? You note that my steed lacks conditioning, and I agree. He and I both need the exercise."

"A canter, then." One did not gallop neck or nothing in the park at dawn. Not unless one was a young, drunken lordling with more money than sense.

Sorcha set a sedate pace along a flat stretch, while Mr. Huxley's gelding kept pace. The beast was game for the first hundred yards or so, but quickly tired thereafter. Mr. Huxley pushed the horse on for another couple dozen yards, then cued the trot and, after another two dozen yards, the walk.

"He's not a hunter," Sorcha said as the gelding puffed along beside the mare. "Where did you find him?"

"The knacker's yard." Mr. Huxley patted the horse on the shoulder. "His conformation is excellent, his manners impeccable, but somebody did not want the bother of feeding him through the winter. Based on appearances, he wasn't enjoying much tucker in summer or autumn either."

Another inefficiency of city life—fodder for horses also had to be brought in from afar, and at considerable cost.

"He was a bargain, then?"

"Probably not. I have no idea what horses in London sell for, but he was a gentleman fallen on hard times, and deserved a second chance. I'm bringing him along slowly and will have him out on this path again, now that I know the direction."

The faster pace had put some color in Mr. Huxley's cheeks and a little more animation in his delivery. He had a beautiful voice, soothing, resonant, male without being strident or fussy.

Very English too, though. "What's his name?"

"Bounder."

"He jumps well?" *Bounder* was more often an insult in common parlance.

"I named him for Romans chapter 15, verse 13. Saint Paul exhorts his correspondents to 'abound in hope.' Seemed appropriate, given the straits the horse was in when I acquired him."

Where had St. Didier got off to? Sorcha adjusted her reins and took a casual inventory of the surrounds. Leopold had dropped back a good fifty feet and was idling along with some old fellow on an equally venerable bay.

"I am having trouble categorizing you, Mr. Huxley. You rescued a horse on a whim and named him for a bit of Scripture. You are a cit, but you were a vicar. You detest London, but you're apparently a natural talent with commerce. What sort of guardian will you make for my children?"

"I suppose that depends in part on what sort of children they are."

"No, it does not. Good children can fall into the hands of a very bad guardian, and a mere mother can do nothing about it."

Your temper is your besetting sin, madam wife. How often had Barclay said that before raising his own hand in ire? Even he had eventually been shamed by that blatant hypocrisy.

Mr. Huxley did not appear to take offense. "I beg leave to question your powerlessness, Lady Barclay. St. Didier speaks well of you, and anybody who claims that man's regard has at least one capable ally. From what I can deduce, this guardianship is a test of my worthiness to claim a Chanderton connection. If I bungle and cause trouble, you will report me to the authorities. If I fulfill the office adequately, I will be invited to Almack's or some boating party or another honor signaling my conditional acceptability."

He did not mince words or deal in innuendo, which was turning out to be a backward relief. "You might be right, though you don't sound very impressed with the prospect of yachting with the duchess." Her Grace was a good sort, despite the fact that keeping the duke content was the only meaningful imperative guiding her existence.

"I'm sure Her Grace is excellent company," Mr. Huxley said. "I have nonetheless struggled along adequately without her acquaintance for my entire life. I will manage somehow should she decide not to acknowledge me."

Either Mr. Huxley was an articulate bumpkin or he was socially dimwitted. "Will your businesses manage adequately if she cuts you?"

"They are not, strictly speaking, my businesses. I am slowly acquiring a controlling interest from Lorne, who has instincts I lack when it comes to trade. Even he, a famously errant younger son, would advise me to tread lightly around duchesses."

"Then if Chanderton tells you that Jordan must be sent off to Rugby next year, you'll send him off?"

"Not necessarily, for two reasons. First, Chanderton could well have had himself appointed guardian had he wanted ultimate authority over the children. The responsibility instead falls to me, and thus my judgment becomes determinative."

Sorcha did not like the sound of that at all. A bit too Old Testament, a bit too typical male of the Chanderton line ordering the universe to suit his every arrogant whim.

"The second reason?"

"I haven't even met the boy. If he's longing to depart for public school, that's a very different situation from a little fellow who's perfectly content to continue making excellent progress with his tutors at home. If you, as his mama, oppose the notion of public school, the matter takes on a different hue than if you support it. The tutors must be allowed to weigh in and an inspection made of the offerings at Rugby. Master Jordan should be included in that inspection, as should you. One does not sign a contract for goods or take on a curate without doing thorough research, your ladyship."

Whatever Sorcha had expected from Mr. Huxley, it wasn't a

homily on the management and education of a duke's grandson.

"Sorry," Mr. Huxley muttered. "The sermonizing habit is proving tenacious."

Sorcha halted her mare and sent a glower in St. Didier's direction. "I have a tenacious habit too, Mr. Huxley. I am plainspoken when tact and discretion would better suit my objectives."

"Say on, my lady."

Mr. Huxley again seemed only politely curious when another man might have turned up sniffy.

"If you think to impose your will on my children, and I am convinced that your judgment is contrary to their best interests, then I am your enemy. I will ruin your business prospects, poison the duchess against you, and steal your skinny horse before I let you interfere with the happiness or wellbeing of my children."

"My enemy, Lady Barclay?"

"They are my children."

"Very well. Bounder prefers apples to carrots, and he likes to have his hind feet picked out first. I learned that the hard way. St. Didier, did you lose your way?"

Leopold toddled up on his gelding, and some chat ensued about Colonel Weatherspoon's predictions for the St. Leger. Sorcha listened with half an ear from long habit, but also with growing puzzlement over her last exchange with Mr. Huxley.

She threatened his livelihood, his social standing, and his horse, and he came back with... drollery? Was he even capable of drollery? What manner of guardian had Chanderton chosen?

"I must let this fellow stretch his legs," St. Didier said, patting his gelding. "Huxley, can you escort her ladyship back to her groom?"

"My pleasure, of course. Shall we take a different path, my lady, or would you prefer to retrace our steps?"

"Retrace our steps." The more privately, the better. St. Didier completed his desertion by trotting off toward Rotten Row, where he doubtless knew half the assembled crowd and was spying on the other half.

Sorcha held her peace until she and Mr. Huxley were within sight of Park Lane and the grooms loitering at the gates.

"Thank you for accompanying me, Mr. Huxley. When would you like to meet the children?"

He drew his horse off the path and halted. "When would suit you and them?"

"Tomorrow. You and I can have an afternoon tea and then visit the nursery. You will want to interview the nurserymaid and tutor, I'm sure."

"Eventually. Tomorrow is for introducing me to my cousins. If you would let me explain my role as guardian, I would appreciate it."

She could hardly stop him. "Provided I am present when you do."

He tipped his hat. "Until tomorrow, then. A pleasure making your acquaintance, my lady."

No irony, no warmth, just correct words with the correct intonation. "I hope I can say the same, sir, but if you fail my children, we are enemies."

"Right, horse thievery to follow. Thank you for the warning."

He waved the groom over, touched a finger to his hat brim, and directed his gelding—Bounder—to Park Lane.

"I am utterly flummoxed," Sorcha muttered in the Erse, which her groom did not know. Bernard Huxley was complicated, and she had no patience, none at all, with complicated Englishmen and their convoluted male stratagems.

She rode home through the increasingly crowded streets while trying to decide if she liked him or disliked him and then realized that was an irrelevant inquiry. In a short, polite, slightly awkward exchange, Sorcha had learned that she'd best approach Bernard Huxley with respect. He wasn't stupid, silly, or vain, and neither was she.

They would never be allies, but they might not be enemies either, once she'd sorted him out properly.

CHAPTER TWO

"Tell me about my cousins," Bernard said, sipping a piping hot, rich China black from a plain blue porcelain cup. The drinking vessel was neither a mug nor a delicate little work of porcelain art.

Good workmanship, graceful lines, durable, if a bit plain. Middling households would prefer a service like this for everyday use, so what was Lady Barclay doing with it? Unicorns and dragons for her kites, but plain blue pottery on her tea trays? Did she mean to insult him, or was she simply not given to lavish displays of hospitality?

"I am from a large family," she said, offering Bernard a plate of cinnamon biscuits. "Compared to my own siblings, Jordan and Bridget seem sedate, but then, Jordan has no brothers, Bridget no sisters. Perhaps they have been a civilizing influence on each other."

"What about cousins?" Bernard set two still-warm biscuits on his saucer. The scent alone was luscious. "I understand that my late father was one of four brothers, and aristocrats generally preoccupy themselves with producing legitimate offspring."

Her ladyship took a moment too long choosing her own sweet. Perhaps one did not allude even indirectly to one's own bastardy.

"Jordy and Bridget have no male paternal cousins. I'm surprised you haven't memorized the family tree. Chanderton, the eldest, of course held the courtesy title until the old duke died. The given name of the present duke is Venable Hughes Marquette Christian Dolforth. The spare was Lord Cecil, who perished in the American wilderness as a young man. He left behind a daughter, Coraline, who married an earl's spare, the Honorable Tallister Greer. The extra spare was your late father, Lord Jerome. A hiatus followed the demise of the first duchess. We have the late second duchess to thank for Lord Barclay."

Familiarity with biblical-begats and son-ofs meant Bernard followed that recitation. "Lord Barclay was considerably your senior."

Her ladyship munched her biscuit. "He was. I was *his* second wife. Jordan takes after my side of the family, as does Bridget. They are both tall for their ages, and both have been blessedly healthy."

"Are your offspring happy, madam?" Lady Barclay struck Bernard as *un*happy. Restless, discontent, and easily agitated, despite occupying a large, elegant town house in the increasingly fashionable neighborhood between Knightsbridge and Buckingham Palace.

The appointments in her sitting room were neither fussy nor plain, but rather, in slightly outdated good taste. Pale *bleu de France* walls, white molding, touches of gilt on the pier glasses and windowsills, a bowl of pink tulips on the inlaid sideboard, and more pink, cream, and blue woven into the pattern of the Axminster carpet.

Tasteful. No faddish chinoiserie, Etruscan artifacts or fussy little japanned boxes.

Not a unicorn or a bold color in sight either.

No romantically symbolic bouquets.

"I hope my children are happy," she said. "Losing their father was hard on them, though Bridget barely recalls her papa. She misses the idea of him. Lord Barclay was fond of his children, regularly visited the nursery, and was genuinely interested in their welfare."

Lord Barclay, by Bernard's reckoning, had been gone for several years. The widow had apparently recovered from her loss, though appearances could be deceptive. Perhaps she'd doted on the old boy.

"Do you ever consider remarrying?"

Her ladyship paused mid-reach for the teapot. "What relevance has that question to the present topic?"

"If you were to remarry, your husband would be the logical resource to take on the guardianship of your children." The most logical resource was Chanderton, though His Grace was admittedly a busy man and getting on in years. The only other male mentioned thus far was Tallister Greer, who would be a cousin-by-marriage to the children.

"The notion of remarriage has not crossed my mind. What of you? Any matrimonial plans?"

Bernard demolished a biscuit that should have been slowly savored. "You will not tattle to the matchmakers?"

"I don't move much in Society, Mr. Huxley, and if I did, I would eschew the company of the gossips."

He believed her. Perhaps Lady Barclay hadn't declared herself the sworn foe of those gossips, but they would tread lightly in her presence.

"I would like to be married," Bernard said. "An unmarried vicar is a rarity, but until last year, I shared my dwelling with my mother, Lady Josephine Huxley. She has removed to foreign shores, where she will remain for all the rest of her days. She was an impediment to any union I might have contemplated."

Also an impediment to any joy Bernard might have contemplated, any peace, any real companionship. No point dwelling on the past.

"You aren't a vicar any longer, Mr. Huxley. I hope my children never consider me an impediment to their dreams. Shall we make our way to the nursery?"

"Might I finish my tea? It's quite good."

"You must buy direct from Twinings," she said. "Whoever makes your household purchases is likely budgeting for Twinings, but purchasing from the lesser shops that will mix anything with their tea to extend the product. Adulterated tea is an abomination against decency."

If rolled r's and crisp t's were any indication, Lady Barclay felt very strongly about her tea.

Bernard finished his serving and took his time with his second biscuit.

"Are you nervous about meeting the children?" Lady Barclay asked.

"A bit. One wants to make a good first impression, but without conveying any insecurity about one's status or welcome. If one cannot strike the right balance between authority and amiability, everything from choir rehearsals to pastoral committee meetings becomes so many pitched battles."

Her ladyship dusted her hands over the tea tray and rose. "Is this how you approach supervising your clerks? A combination of authority and amiability?"

"For the most part, yes." Bernard got to his feet, half of his second biscuit unfinished on his plate. "You disapprove?"

"I approve, though I hadn't put those terms to the strategy. No wonder your businesses prosper." She waited by the door until Bernard joined her.

"You will introduce me as Cousin Bernard, please."

"If that's your wish. Jordy isn't eligible for the courtesy title. He's not in the direct line."

As Bernard followed his hostess down the sunny, lemon-scented corridor and up the polished stairway, he translated her meaning.

Jordan was not a son, grandson, or great-grandson of the present titleholder. The duke also claimed lesser titles, probably a marquessate or an earldom along with a viscounty and a barony or two. By convention, only an heir in the direct line used the courtesy title. The age at which he adopted that title and the one he took were matters of family preference.

Title or no title, though, little Jordan Dolforth was likely to become the next Duke of Chanderton, and Bernard had been tasked with supervising the boy safely into manhood.

Not an easy job for any man. No wonder Lady Barclay was a bit prickly about the whole matter.

"Lessons are done for the day," Lady Barclay said, rounding the first-floor landing. "The children can be rambunctious when their studies are completed. We'd normally go to the park on such a fine day."

"My apologies for disturbing the routine. Shall we take them to the park, then?"

Her ladyship flicked a fulminating glance at Bernard as she continued her ascent. "Best not. I've told them you are coming to call when we'd normally have our outing. They do best if plans are kept to the greatest degree possible and last-minute disruptions are minimized."

"As do I."

Another fleeting inspection, this one a little annoyed. "One can have a surfeit of routine, Mr. Huxley. The mind grows dull when only the expected comes our way."

"I would have argued that point when I was vicaring in Yorkshire." Argued it at length. "Given the vicissitudes of rural life, I viewed a sedate progression of seasons, the liturgical calendar walking hand in hand with the agricultural year, as a refuge. I became part of that settled sameness for my congregation, and they appreciated me for it."

Another flight and another landing. "You weren't bored?"

"I did not know I was bored, but I did sense that the same families and feuds over and over, the same committees and even the same menus at the same Sunday suppers... What started off as a comfort took on some qualities of a penance."

Not something Bernard had admitted to even his own cousin. Why burden her ladyship with that realization? Perhaps because she knew a bit about gilded cages and duty becoming a burden?

They reached the uppermost story, which enjoyed good light

from abundant windows at either end of the corridor as well as from several alcoves. Light made learning possible.

"Did you become something of a penance for your parish?" Lady Barclay lobbed the question at him as they reached a plain, solid oak door. "Sermonizing on the bowling green, blessing every pint and pie, toting your *Book of Common Prayer* over hill and dale?"

Bernard was about to reply that the village had had no bowling green when it occurred to him that he was missing the point.

"Lady Barclay, are you teasing me?"

Her expression became saintly solemn. "You insult me, sir. I would never, on pain of my immortal soul, tease a former vicar."

Her expression was serious, but her eyes, the azure of a Scottish summer sky, danced.

"You are teasing me. Interesting. You likely excel at the sport because of all those siblings you mentioned. My clerks are similarly well versed in the art. They have fiendish talent with nicknames too."

She had her hand on the latch. "What nickname would you give me?"

"The matter wants thought. I would like to meet my cousins now, if you please." He would also like to stand in the slanting afternoon light and find names for the emotions chasing across Lady Barclay's face.

When she firmed those full lips, she looked positively Puritan. For the few moments when she'd been twitting him, she'd looked younger, sweeter, and confident in a way that the relict of Lord Barclay did not.

The widow, by contrast, was imposing, formidable, purposeful—

A shriek came from the other side of the door. Her ladyship rapped three times on the stout oak and thrust it open.

The scene that greeted Bernard was utter chaos. Toy soldiers lay everywhere amid blankets, dolls, books upended to resemble A-shaped tents, and a tray with a quarter inch of water in it on the bricks before the hearth. A girl was rocking furiously on a stuffed horse mounted on springs, while an adult female in maid's attire stood by a window, gazing out. A boy charged across a cushioned sofa onto a toy chest and looked to be eyeing a leap onto the mantel when Lady Barclay spoke.

"Children, I've brought your cousin, Mr. Bernard Huxley, to meet you."

"To the death, Sassenach!" The boy leaped off the toy chest, snatched the fireplace poker, and charged straight at Bernard.

Lady Barclay had described her children as unusually sedate. Perhaps she'd been teasing then too.

Please do not kill your prospective guardian.

Sorcha would have bellowed that order to her firstborn, except that Mr. Huxley, by the simple expedient of stepping aside, allowed Jordy's own momentum to send him hurtling across the room. The boy tripped on the flipped-up edge of the carpet and went down in a clattering heap while Bridget set up a wail from her horse.

"Jordy's dead, Mama! Jordy fell on his sword, and now he's dead!"

"He is not dead," Mr. Huxley said as calmly as if he were trying to decide whether he beheld a Gainsborough or a Lawrence at the Royal Exhibition. "He does appear to have split his lip, however."

Bridget dismounted and scowled at Mr. Huxley. "You are very big to be a cousin, sir. What's a split lip?"

A split lip was a regular occurrence where Jordan was concerned, along with skinned knees, bruised elbows, and banged shins.

"Split lips are minor lacerations," Mr. Huxley said, producing a plain white handkerchief. "They can bleed prodigiously, but usually heal in a few days. Master Jordan, I presume?" He hunkered down and offered his handkerchief to Jordy.

The boy grinned, blood trickling down his chin. "Is that a flag of surrender, Sassenach?"

Why did Jordy have to sound so convincingly Scottish?

"Let's call it a flag of truce." Mr. Huxley dropped the handkerchief on Jordy's tummy. "Direct pressure will slow the bleeding before you stain your mama's carpets." He rose and extended a hand to Sorcha's prostrate son.

The boy was on his feet in the next instant, the handkerchief pressed to his lip. "Am I supposed to make my bow? Mr. Entwhistle is always going on about a gentleman knows how to make his bow."

"A lady makes a curtsey," Bridget said, getting back on her horse. "I will not be a lady until I'm grown up, which won't be for years and years. I'm a Cossack now."

"For the sake of protocol," Mr. Huxley said, "let's dust off our manners, shall we? Master Jordan, let's see that bow."

Authoritative and amiable. Mr. Huxley had the balance down to an art.

"Jordan Dolforth, at your service." The boy flopped over from the waist, handkerchief in hand, and came up beaming. "You next, Bridge."

She dismounted by swinging her leg over the horse's hairy mane. "Miss Bridget Dolforth, sir. Pleased to make your acquaintance, though you are still tall to be a cousin. I don't have any boy cousins except in Scotland. Mama says they have red hair like me."

Bridget was cursed with flaming locks. Jordy, thank providence, sported auburn hair that might charitably be called brown in low light.

"Bernard Huxley, late of Yorkshire and Bloomsbury, pleased to make your acquaintance. Cousin Bernard will do nicely. Do I take it we've been fighting some battle after completing the day's studies?"

"The Battle of the Nations," Bridget said. "Everybody slaughters everybody else, and Napoleon won."

Jordy rounded on her. "He did not. Napoleon lost. He lost at Leipzig because his men were slaughtered, too, and he didn't have any horses left, and his cannon—"

"Regardless of who is the victor and who is the vanquished," Mr.

Huxley observed, "somebody has to clean up the mess. I nominate those who created it."

Oh dear. Gilchrist, who'd been minding the view of the mews from the window, turned. She was clearly agog at Mr. Huxley's suggestion.

As well she should be.

"Napoleon isn't here," Bridget said, flouncing over to her horse. "This is Copenhagen. He is named for a victory." She began braiding the mane of Wellington's favorite battle mount. "I must see to my horse."

"I have a split lip," Jordy said, assaying another smile. "Somebody should carry me to the infirmary."

Bridget excelled at changing the subject. Jordy's default tactic was charm. Sorcha preferred bribery—no trips to the park until, at the least, the books were restored to the shelf—while poor Gilchrist had adopted the habit of appeasement for the sake of her sanity.

"You are looking rather able-bodied to me," Mr. Huxley said. "Miss, please feel free to enjoy a cup of tea in the kitchen. Battles try the nerves of even noncombatants."

Gilchrist looked to Sorcha, who nodded.

"Gilly can't go," Jordy said, his good cheer fading. "She has to clean up. She should carry me to the infirmary first."

"Miss Gilly is excused to address a case of battle fatigue," Mr. Huxley said, "provided Lady Barclay agrees."

Amiable and authoritative. Sorcha motioned for the door, prepared to watch Cousin Bernard meet the force of nature that were her offspring in a stubborn mood. Not how she'd have preferred the first encounter to go, but then, she'd asked the children to be on their best behavior.

She should have known better. The legendarily horrific Battle of Leipzig hadn't made an appearance since the children had been cooped up for an entire week in January.

"Two cups of tea, Miss Gilly," Mr. Huxley said, "and when you come back, you may compliment the children on how effectively they have restored their domain to order."

Jordy might not have understood the words, but he understood that he was being challenged.

"Mama, I don't feel well. My lip hurts." He raised his arms, expecting Sorcha to offer him a maternal hug.

"Then perhaps," Mr. Huxley said, handing Jordy the poker, "you ought not to have charged so recklessly with your sword at the ready. Typical of the cavalry, though. You are no longer bleeding. You may keep my handkerchief as a memento of your valor. Find a fallen comrade or two, why don't you, and see them to the infirmary. That duck looks to be in a bad way."

Bridget had ceased any fiction of tending to her horse and frankly watched the combatants. Sorcha took a chair behind the desk by the window and waited for the next volley.

Jordy was in the act of replacing the poker in the stand when he apparently realized that simple act constituted a bit of cleaning up. He set the poker against the bricks, not among the implements in the hearth stand.

"That is Bridget's duck, and he's not injured. He's not real."

"He is a real stuffed duck," Bridget snapped.

"He is on the floor," Mr. Huxley said, "where he does not belong and would rather not spend the night." Mr. Huxley swiped a book from beside the duck and settled into the rocking chair beside the hearth. "A noble duck left to languish on the battlefield after doing his feathered best for king and country. A disheartening spectacle."

He opened the book and began at the beginning. "Once upon a time, there lived a dragon who loved to fly over Hyde Park."

"It doesn't say that."

Sorcha's thoughts marched exactly with Bridget's words.

"It says precisely that in dragon Latin," Mr. Huxley went on. "London's skies were so perpetually smoky that our winged friend could enjoy himself by the hour, and none of the people below knew he was above the clouds."

Jordy looked askance in Sorcha's direction. She gave him a bland smile. Mr. Huxley deserved to attempt whatever strategy he had up his sleeve. Sheer novelty might give him a temporary edge, and what a pleasant change that would make.

"What was the dragon's name?" Jordy asked.

Mr. Huxley produced a pair of spectacles and peered more closely at the page. Then he sent a pointed look at the poker leaning against the hearthstones two feet from the stand.

"I can't quite make it out. That poker is in my light."

It wasn't, of course. Bridget took the bait and moved it.

"Bridge..."

"What was his name?" Bridget asked.

"Socrates," Mr. Huxley replied. "His full name was Socrates Copenhagen MacTavish MacGillicuddy Lorne." Mr. Huxley turned a page. "Socks was his nickname. If you want to know what he saw way up in the smoky skies, you'd best take down all the tents cluttering up this carpet."

Jordy kicked a book flat. Mr. Huxley said nothing.

Sorcha remembered to breathe. Sitting in the rocking chair, spectacles perched on his nose, Mr. Huxley did not look like a dragon, but he surely had an ability to upend castles and leave the peasantry dumbstruck.

Bridget picked up a book and returned it to the shelf. "You shouldn't kick books, Jordy. I like books."

"I don't like you," Jordy said. "I think books are stupid."

Bridget went for a second book. "Tell me about the dragon, Cousin Mister."

"Socks? He wasn't very grown up, as dragons go, and he tended to break even the rules that were meant to keep him happy and safe. He did not, for example, remain above the clouds and the smoke when he went flying."

Jordy nudged the next tent-book over with his toe. "What did he do?"

"I know," Bridget said, picking up two more books. "He swooped so low, the people in the park saw him." She flew, arms outstretched, over to the bookshelf and stacked two more titles. "That's dangerous if you're a dragon. Somebody could shoot you right out of the sky. Bang!"

Jordy picked up a flattened book. "Is that what he did?"

"Socks committed many transgressions, alas for our young dragon friend. His mama despaired of him. He was blessed with a curious mind and simply did not see the harm in finding out for himself what lay beneath the clouds. He was also prone to singing, and for a dragon to sing where people could hear him was considered a very great breach of dragon law."

"I like to sing." Bridget collected six books at one go. "Jordy, put the book away, or we won't get our story."

Jordy stuck out his tongue at his sister and put the book away.

Mr. Huxley did not gloat. He did not lecture or preen. He made up a fantastic story involving winged dragons, hot-air balloons, a wind from the east named Circe, and thunder—"We humans hear thunder when the dragons are singing"—while the battlefield was gradually cleared and Sorcha tried to analyze how exactly that had happened.

Amiability and authority had been just the beginning. Bernard Huxley was also shrewd, imaginative, and tenacious. Sorcha was troubled by that conclusion and also, reluctantly, a little curious to know what other qualities he was keeping out of sight above the clouds and smoke of respectability.

"My horse is named Thunder," Bridget announced when the playroom was neat as a pin.

"Your horse is stupid," Jordy said, his grin back in evidence, complete with a small laceration on his upper lip. "I want a dragon instead of a horse."

"Then name your pony Dragon," Mr. Huxley said, rising from the rocking chair and returning the last book to the shelf.

"I haven't a pony," Jordy replied. "Bridget doesn't either. She just pretends with that thing."

"Thunder is not a thing. He's a real pretend horse."

"Then the two of you make up a story about a pony named Dragon," Mr. Huxley said. "Write it down, ask your mama for help with the big words, and I will happily read the tale when next I visit."

Which occasion, Sorcha devoutly hoped, might be months hence.

Gilchrist returned, peeking around the door when Mr. Huxley answered her knock with a hearty, "Here there be dragons. Enter at your own risk!"

Jordy and Bridget both mouthed the words silently.

"Goodness gracious," Gilchrist said. "I cannot believe my eyes. Not a fallen soldier in sight!"

"I put away most of the books," Bridget said. "Jordy helped."

"Master Jordan did an excellent job with the injured and fallen," Mr. Huxley said. "You did indeed handle the lion's share of the books, Miss Bridget. Very good work, the pair of you. Lady Barclay, I must not overstay my welcome. If you'd see me to the door, I'd appreciate it. Children, I am proud to call you my cousins. Never have I seen such an extensive battlefield so quickly put to rights. Your industry frankly amazes me."

He bowed to Bridget, who received the courtesy with shy consternation, and he offered his hand to Jordy, who shook with the same air of puzzled hesitance.

What manner of man is this cousin? they seemed to be asking, the same question that bothered Sorcha.

He offered Gilchrist a polite nod, completing the general befuddlement, and held the door for Sorcha.

"That didn't go too badly," he said. "When can I meet the governess and tutors?"

Sorcha considered dissembling and settled for a half-truth. "The most recent governess gave notice last week, and the tutor is on his half day."

The most recent governess had quit last month, after a single day. The less said about Entwhistle, the better.

"I see." Mr. Huxley began moving toward the stairs.

"What do you see, Mr. Huxley?"

"Cousin Bernard, please, or simply Bernard will do, given the family connection. I see that these children have yet to earn their ponies—very shrewd of you to withhold that boon—and that you need help."

He trotted down the first flight of stairs, while Sorcha followed more slowly.

"I beg your pardon, Mr. Huxley. What did you just say?"

He turned such that he and Sorcha were eye to eye because she stood one step up.

"You have coped wonderfully, managing a pair of very lively children, but the time has come to recruit worthy reinforcements. You need help, and I can see that you get it."

This pleased him, while he was alarming Sorcha.

Nobody helps me with my own children. Not quite true—bless Gilchrist—but true in spirit. "I admit that we just caught the children in the odd rambunctious mood and that they tested your authority, but we are contending well enough in the nursery for now."

The animation that had sent him bounding down the steps disappeared, like a dragon ascending into the clouds. Real, unexpected, and impressive, then invisible, as if it had never been there.

"Might I request, then, that I be allowed to interview prospective governesses with you, my lady?"

Sorcha could not antagonize him, and neither could she trust him. "Of course. I'll have the agency send over some candidates next week, if that would suit."

He resumed his progress down the steps. "I would prefer any time after three p.m. the day after tomorrow, and we are looking for a younger woman, one with plenty of energy, not too much book learning, and a good imagination."

He was looking. Sorcha would probably be permitted to behold his search, no more. "The agencies don't usually evaluate imagination, Mr. Huxley."

"Which leaves the job for us. A sense of humor wouldn't go amiss either. Bridget is a bit on the serious side."

While Jordy could be a clown. "The day after tomorrow, then. After three p.m."

They arrived at the front door in silence. Sorcha held Mr. Huxley's coat for him, which engendered some awkwardness as he fished for the sleeves. They got through that, and she handed him his hat and walking stick.

"Best hurry," she said, taking in the gray afternoon beyond the foyer window. "Looks like rain."

He tapped his hat onto his head. "We had rain in Yorkshire too. I liked it because nobody called at the vicarage on the sopping days. Bad of me."

Sorcha had no idea what to make of him, no idea what to make of his little story hour in the nursery. She attributed her next question to being completely at sixes and sevens and knowing that the upheaval Mr. Huxley would cause was just beginning.

"Mr. Huxley, weren't you ever lonely?" No wife, no children. Avoiding his callers, retreating into homilies where gossip and small talk should have been.

He stared out at the gloomy afternoon. "What an odd question. I will ponder my reply until next we meet. Perhaps I will put the same query to you. Please remember: Ponies must be earned, and my small cousins are miles and shires away from doing so."

"We are agreed. No ponies. Good day, Mr. Huxley."

He bowed, touched a finger to his hat brim, and jaunted down the front steps.

I do get lonely, if anybody's asking. Sorcha batted the thought away—the day had been a challenge—and went in search of the cinnamon biscuits that Mr. Huxley had eyed with such longing.

She was enjoying her third when a celestial rumbling sounded overhead, and for no reason at all, the thunder made her smile.

CHAPTER THREE

"What shall we do about Ipswich and Heevers?" Bernard asked, moving the coat stand from the corner of the room to a place about six feet from the office's hearth. He put his top hat on the highest hook, draped his greatcoat on the next hook down, and caught a familiar look of puzzlement on his oldest clerk's face. "What have I done now, Kessler?"

"The, um, damp will drip on the carpet if you leave the stand there, sir." Kessler was graying at the temples, passing from the prime of life into the sunset years, though he was spry, hardworking, and respected by his juniors. His appearance was modest, neither tall nor short, neither fussy nor plain. He attired himself much in the manner of a solicitor and knew more law off by heart than most solicitors could cite in a lifetime.

What defined the prime of a person's life, anyway? "The carpet will be a bit damp," Bernard said, "instead of the floor being damp. How is this a problem?"

"Not strictly a problem, sir, but anybody coming into your office will expect that stand to be in the corner, and there it is, like a tailor's dummy, right in the center of the room."

"In the center of the room, where the fire's heat can actually do some good with my sodden garments. Shall I move the stand back to the corner and consign myself to wearing wet wool when I walk home?"

"You shall not." Kessler linked his hands behind his back and cleared his throat. "You asked about Heevers and Ipswich."

"Yes. They were glowering at each other across the clerks' room, so I gather separating their desks has not calmed the hostilities."

"Ipswich took a notion to use a penny whistle to aim spitballs at Heevers's desk. Heevers retaliated by purchasing two penny whistles. The other clerks are spending more time placing bets and goading the combatants than working. I would say separating Ipswich and Heevers has had the opposite of the intended effect, Mr. Huxley. I do apologize."

Bernard gestured to the straight-backed chair opposite the desk. "Any suggestions?" Separating desks had been indirectly Kessler's idea, though he'd hemmed and perhaps'ed and what-would-you-think-sir'd at such length, Bernard realized that the idea was supposed to appear as Bernard's own.

"I could inquire if any other offices are hiring, sir, and send one of the boys to another post."

The warring parties were nine and ten years old, both late to be starting on apprenticeships.

"Word would get around?" Bernard asked. When a curate had a penchant for drink or causing upset among the parishioners, when he was overly fond of the ladies or overly long-winded in the pulpit, word certainly got around.

"Most assuredly, sir. They are bright boys. They both have significant potential." Kessler did not take the proffered seat, but braced a hand on the back, like a thespian posing for a soliloquy. "Ipswich is still new to his post and feels himself something of an underdog, being the youngest clerk. Heevers sees his status as threatened by a younger boy who is nearly as quick, even if he's not as experienced."

"And we cannot make one a bishop and the other a dean." The

Church knew a thing or two about productively channeling ambition. Give everybody a title—vestryman, deacon, chaplain, prebendary, prelate, canon—and give each man his own little fiefdom that might lead to a larger share of churchly glory.

In commerce, the titles were few—clerk, manager, director—and the opportunities for advancement fewer.

A hundred clerks knew that perhaps six of them, after years of toil, might become junior managers. Managers did not become directors, unless they married considerably up, looked the part, and offended no one over the course of decades.

"We are too aristocratic," Bernard said. "Too set in our ways and concerned with hierarchy. I will consider the matter."

Kessler sighed. "We could simply sack them, sir. I know you are reluctant to label young boys professional failures, but they refuse to give up their feud, and they are increasingly disruptive. His lordship might have some ideas. He dealt very well with the clerks."

His lordship in this context would only ever be Lord Lorne, whom Bernard had grown up knowing as Cousin Cam. To the surprise of all concerned, Bernard and Cam were unrelated by blood.

"We will not trouble the baron over a trivial irritant," Bernard said. "If they were choir boys, we could threaten each boy with a duet solo that involved a female partner of particularly dubious skill."

"We're to hire female clerks?" Kessler looked as if he had a megrim coming on, along with a gouty toe, a bout of melancholia, and an attack of nervous exhaustion.

"Females regularly occur in the clerking ranks on the Continent, Mr. Kessler. Commerce seems to weather the shock adequately in France and Germany."

Kessler studied the wooden chair at some length. "Meaning no disrespect, Mr. Huxley, the lot of young men you employ would not weather the shock. They would be so insulted, and so *distracted*, by the presence of females in the office that the little battle between Heevers and Ipswich would pale by comparison."

Besides which, *his lordship* would never have done such a thing.

Camden had sent his unruly younger clerks off to loiter on the docks of a morning, or in Hyde Park at the fashionable hour, and called it commercial reconnaissance.

"Let's have the day's latest correspondence, shall we, Kessler? I did not expect my outing to take quite so long, but needs must."

Kessler sighed again, which he did as eloquently as a violinist plied his fiddle. Kessler's sighs could convey relief, exasperation, acceptance, judgment... Many a curate could have learned the sighing art from Mr. Kessler.

Bernard dispatched the correspondence in less than two hours—he was getting better at it, and Kessler's ability to follow guidance with little elaboration was improving as well.

"And we will both be home very nearly in time for supper for a change," Bernard said, taking his dry greatcoat from the stand. A paper crackled in the pocket.

The few lines Bernard had jotted thereon were an address in France. "I almost forgot, Kessler. Please remind me that I'd like to pen an inquiry to a French distillery regarding some particularly fine cognac. Not urgent, but important."

"After the morning mail and before nooning, then, sir?"

"Exactly. I am having lunch with His Grace tomorrow. Please assist me to be punctual."

"Have you ever been late anywhere, sir?" Kessler removed his spectacles, folded them in the manner of a philosophically inclined headmaster, and let the question take on some subtle significance.

"I am certainly lagging in the matter of sorting out Ipswich and Heevers. Perhaps inspiration will come to me in the night."

"We live in hope, sir. We live in hope." Kessler bustled out, leaving assignments from the correspondence exercise for each clerk according to his ability and interest.

Bernard was enjoying a brisk stroll to the Lorne town house when it occurred to him that Lady Barclay might have some ideas for dealing with Heevers and Ipswich. Her children were lively to the point of unruliness, but Jordy and Bridget got along well. So well that when Bridget had told Jordy to put a book away, he'd done it.

Bernard tossed tuppence to the underfed crossing sweeper. "Good night, Enoch. Isn't it time for you to go home to your supper?" As the weather had moderated, Enoch's wardrobe had shifted from layers of rags bound around him with twine, to recognizable, if filthy, articles of clothing.

The boy ran a grubby finger under his nose and sniffed stoutly. "No going 'ome till the streets are quiet, Parson." He held up one of the coins Bernard had given him. "I'll eat good when I do, though!"

Probably a meat pie and tankard of watered ale. Not a bad meal. "Do you like your post, Enoch?"

Enoch surveyed the intersection, which was sadly devoid of horse droppings. "I like a clean street. If it wasn't for us sweeps, London would be a muck pit. I don't like being cold and wet nor hot and thirsty. I do like to eat."

His assessment of his station bore no rancor. The glory of London mattered to him. The glory of Huxley and Company did not matter to Ipswich and Heevers. Their modest pay packets didn't seem to matter to them either.

"Until tomorrow, Enoch. Don't stay out too late."

Enoch shook his head. "Right, Parson. Don't you be reading your Bible until the small hours neither."

"No worries there."

By the time Bernard reached his front door, a slight drizzle had started up. Perhaps that would send Enoch home, or to the nearest church doorway, where he'd be permitted to lurk for at least a short time.

"How did he do it?" Gilchrist, given name Tansy, set down the tea tray with an air of subdued pique. "How did Mr. Huxley make the children clean up that entire mess?"

Tansy took the plain chair near the hearth, her way of maintaining standards against the gross presumption of being asked to sit and take a cup of tea with her employer.

The presumption was Sorcha's, as was this small, informal parlor. She had chosen to take her tea in this room because it had no windows facing the street, and the walls and door were stout enough to ensure privacy.

"Mr. Huxley didn't threaten them, not directly." Sorcha poured two cups and drizzled honey in both before Tansy could object. "He did not wheedle. He did not try to order them about." She put two squares of cinnamon shortbread on each plate.

"What does that leave? Trickery? Mr. Huxley is from Yorkshire. They have some strange notions there. Backward notions."

Tansy was from Peeblesshire, but thanks to a father from the Isle of Mull, she was comfortable speaking the Erse. She was also patient beyond human comprehension and pretty in a comfortably plump, blond way.

"He charmed them," Sorcha said as steam rose from her cup. "Beguiled them. Made up a story about a naughty little dragon whose contrary nature caused all manner of mayhem." Not a simple moralist fable, but truly entertaining.

Tansy would not sip from her cup until Sorcha had, would not nibble her shortbread until Sorcha had partaken. Sorcha's clandestine rebellion against decorum was conducted along rules from which Tansy would never deviate.

"That's a form of trickery, to beguile," Tansy said. "My sister Patsy has been beguiled into another confinement."

Ye gods. The poor woman wasn't thirty years old. "Is this her eighth?" Sorcha sipped her tea, a jasmine-scented gunpowder.

"Seventh confinement, but four and five were twins. You have the sheep count correct. What will you do about this Mr. Huxley, my lady?"

The question of the day. "He and I are to interview governesses tomorrow afternoon."

"I'm sorry. It's only been a month."

Sorcha believed the sympathy was genuine, however tersely expressed. "We might have some luck this time. Mr. Huxley says we're looking for somebody with a good imagination and a sense of humor."

"Oh, aye. Every select academy for independent young ladies teaches fancifulness and silliness. Mazie said they beat her for giggling."

Patsy, the eldest sister, had been compromised by her father's curate. The reverend had promptly rectified the situation with an application of matrimonial vows. Mazie, the second-oldest sister, had been the lucky recipient of the sort of education that resulted in placement as a governess at a lesser household.

She dwelled in Glasgow and looked after four children for the wife of a ship's captain. Her penmanship was exquisite. Tansy had been left to try her luck in domestic service, a nursery post being a natural fit for somebody with five younger siblings.

Sorcha had the sense each sister envied the others, and all were bearing up in challenging situations.

"If we do hire a governess," Sorcha said, "you have leave coming to you, Tansy. Go home for the summer, see your family."

"My lady, I couldn't." She set down her tea cup, though the jasmine was Tansy's favorite. "What did you think of Mr. Huxley, when he wasn't spinning tales and being very tall?"

He was tall, but not loud with it. Barclay had worn two-inch heels on his boots and outlandishly high top hats.

"I don't know what to make of him, to be honest. He seems well intended. He kept referring to the children as his cousins."

"Odd," Tansy said, putting her cup and saucer on the tray, one piece of shortbread uneaten. "Though they are his cousins, I suppose." She sounded as if she begrudged him a connection to her charges. "He makes you nervous, doesn't he? He made me nervous. Never trust a man with faultless manners."

And how had Tansy learned that lesson? "He was a vicar for

more than a decade, Tansy. His manners had to be faultless." Almost as faultless as a Scottish widow's when she dwelled in Mayfair.

"'Vicar' doesn't mean anything, my lady. Trust me, I was raised by one. My sister is married to one. Too many of them are men first and vicars for a few hours on Sunday. I'd best get back to the nursery."

Tansy never lingered, never overstepped, and that was wise of her. At any moment, the door might open, and a footman bearing a bucket of coal would pretend he'd had no idea the parlor was occupied. Sorcha had taken far too long to realize that her exquisitely trained staff would never make such an error.

"We'll start the day in the park tomorrow," Sorcha said, "if the weather is fine. The children are always happier for some fresh air early in the day."

"My lady is happier for some fresh air at any hour." A slight smile leavened the observation. "I wish you luck with the governess interviews and with Mr. Huxley."

"Thank you."

She left, silently closing the door in her wake. Sorcha set aside the tea and shortbread, having lost her appetite for both.

Tansy was not quite the ally she'd been two years ago, but she was still a comfort. They conversed in Scottish Gaelic when private and also when private with the children, which meant Jordy and Bridget had rudimentary competence with the language.

Tansy had taken the job knowing neither child was an infant. In a widow's household, that meant the post would expire in a few years. Generous wages had been part of the inducement, but Sorcha suspected pity had been the rest.

Tansy was pragmatic, patient, and slightly bitter, also shrewd. She grasped that being a young, Scottish widow in the exalted ranks of the Dolforth ducal family was challenging. For Sorcha to hire Tansy instead of some little English mouse had caused a minor skirmish with the duke, but the duchess had dissuaded him from escalating the conflict outright.

See that you have no more Scots on your staff in future. My nephew must be surrounded by only appropriate influences.

Sorcha did not miss her husband, but his existence had simplified life in a few regards.

"Mr. Huxley is a complication," Sorcha muttered. "Whatever else he is—charming, mannerly, well intended—he is a complication."

Time for a call on the duchess. That thought would have inspired a wee nip from the flask Sorcha kept in the depths of her workbasket, but time did not allow for the indulgence. Then too, arriving at Her Grace's family parlor with spirits on the breath would not do *at all.*

"Why is it," Tallister Greer mused, "Sorcha is becoming more attractive, while my own dear Coraline has grown matronly?"

Lillian, Her Grace of Chanderton, turned a baleful eye on her guest, who was in actuality her nephew-by-marriage, despite being several years her senior.

"Keep your hands off Sorcha, sir." Tallister had kept his hands off Lilly, which suggested he wasn't a complete fool, despite being lazy, ambitious, and too comely for his own good.

"If Coraline has acquired some avoirdupois," the duchess went on, "she did so while presenting you with four daughters in close succession. She approaches the end of her childbearing years, and the passage of time takes a toll. That aside, a woman has more to do in this life than ornament her husband's existence."

Tallister struck a theatrical hand-to-the-heart pose. "The Lilly has thorns. I am wounded."

He was handsome enough for the stage. Tall, sable-haired, blue-eyed, and winsome. Tallister favored rare beefsteak for his meals, Byronic disarray for his dark curls, and mistresses half his age for sport. A fellow very near forty had no business being so attractive, much less attractive and charming. Even the threads of silver at his temples added to his appeal.

And yet, Lilly liked him, for the most part. "You are tedious, and you can stop pacing the carpet. Have a seat, decimate the tray, and report whatever news has brought you here."

Lilly received him in the formal family parlor, which looked out on the leafy street and the square beyond. For all his affability, Tallister was much taken with his own consequence. He would prefer to be seen calling upon his ducal in-laws rather than enjoy the cozier informal family parlor overlooking the garden.

"The news is all the same." With an elegant flip of his coattails, he settled into a wing chair. "The Wilson heiress has gone to the country for a repairing lease, which means she was plotting a jaunt to Gretna Green with some fortune hunter. The betting books claim Henry Duquette was leading the pack, but now he's off to some undisclosed foreign location with creditors howling for his blood."

"Duquette will not be missed." He was kicking his heels in the Low Countries, according to Lilly's sources. She fixed Tallister's tea as he liked it: two sugars, no milk. "A perpetual hanger-on. Duquette would have made Virginia Wilson miserable." Lilly passed Tallister the cup and an empty plate.

"Virginia Wilson would have made Duquette's creditors happy. Do the merchants of Bond Street deserve no consideration?" He sipped elegantly. "Nothing like a strong China black to lift the spirits. Where do you suppose the fortune hunters will turn now that La Wilson has retired from the lists?"

Lilly indulged him with a quarter hour of speculation, *on-dits*, and small talk as Tallister emptied his plate twice.

"Tell me, Lilly dearest. What is this I hear about Chanderton foisting Sorcha's little heathens on one of the family by-blows?"

He refilled his plate with tarts, tea cakes, and profiteroles, then dunked a tea cake in his tea and popped the whole sweet into his mouth. Tallister exuded good-natured ennui and looked the part of the man-about-Town making a pleasant social call.

His question regarding Jordy and Bridget was doubtless the point of the whole discussion.

Tallister was rather too interested in Lord Barclay's widow, like a spoiled boy is always more interested in another child's toys than in his own vast collection. Sorcha was either oblivious to Tallister's curiosity or knew better than to acknowledge it.

"Chanderton does as he pleases. He is the head of the family, and Mr. Bernard Huxley has until recently been serving in a vicarage up in Yorkshire. Huxley is connected to the Lorne barony by legal patrimony. His mother is the daughter of an earl, though she's apparently on an extended trip abroad. Huxley is willing to take on guardianship of the children, and you will acknowledge him socially when it becomes appropriate to do so."

Chanderton had been very clear on that score. Huxley was family, and the Dolforths did not snub family without cause. More to the point, Huxley had some independent means inherited from his Dolforth father. Huxley was not a poor relation of any sort. Chanderton owned tens of thousands of acres and claimed an impressive collection of heirlooms, family jewels, and properties, but he had very few relatives with real means.

"Bernard Huxley." Tallister dunked a second tea cake. "Sounds vicarish, or worse, headmasterish. I suppose he'll put the children on bread, water, and Bible verses. Sorcha won't care for that."

Which was none of Tallister's business. "How are your girls doing?"

"They grow. They giggle. They sigh over fashion plates and try their mother's patience. Coraline says they are pretty enough. To me, of course, they are all diamonds. Thank heavens Annette doesn't make her come out until next year, though it seems every moment of the next eleven months will be spent sewing a fabulous trousseau and polishing her French. Why French? I have no notion. French Society has no suitable *partis* left."

France had very few solvent *partis*, which should matter to any doting father. "And is Coraline assessing marital possibilities for Annette?"

"I gather you ladies are always assessing the bachelors, that matchmaking preoccupies you as horse racing preoccupies the turf crowd." He helped himself to a ham-and-watercress sandwich from the epergne and put it atop the pile of offerings already on his plate. "I want to see my daughters happy. I do acknowledge that one modestly agreeable fellow is much like another, but for his social standing."

Would Coraline consider her husband modestly agreeable? The marriage predated Lilly's union with Chanderton, but from what the duke had said, Coraline had found matrimony a difficult adjustment. She was a conscientious mama and never disloyal to Tallister in public, but neither did she adore him.

Fortunately, Tallister adored himself enough to suffice.

"I don't suppose this Huxfield fellow is modestly agreeable?" Tallister asked. "I realize he's Coraline's cousin and thus some sort of cousin to Annette. Cousins marry all the time."

They married occasionally, and Tallister knew Cousin Bernard's last name as surely as the Regent knew which titles were approaching escheat.

"Did Coraline send you here to investigate Mr. Huxley's prospects?" Lilly asked in bland tones.

Tallister assayed an innocent smile. "Coraline expressed a passing interest in this latest addition to the family tree, however attenuated and modest the branch he occupies. We both hope he is more settled than some other family connections I could mention. Tell me about Huxton, or whatever his name is."

"You are doing it too brown, Tallister. Bernard is on the mature side of thirty, nobody's fool, typically English, and one can understand his speech. He's not a Yorkshire bumpkin, and he is in trade. Chanderton says Huxley's businesses prosper, and Chanderton would know. I have no sense that Huxley is looking for a wife."

"Then Huxley is a fool." Another smile, this one a bit naughty. "It isn't good for a man to be alone. Didn't some prophet or other say that?"

"The sentiment is attributed to the Almighty Himself. One

wonders why, if female companionship is such a boon, we have no record of a heavenly spouse for the Creator."

Tallister looked astonished, then burst out laughing. "You must convey that question to Chanderton, Lilly dearest. You will confound him utterly."

Chanderton, who was a perfectly decent old fellow more than twice Lilly's age, and a serial husband, had found Lilly's question worth putting to a few bishops.

"Are you truly investigating Mr. Huxley as a potential suitor for Annette?" Lilly asked, topping up Tallister's cup. His ability to decimate a plate of food while gossiping nineteen to the dozen was truly amazing.

"I deny investigating anybody, though one always wants to be kept well informed regarding family. Annette is too young to marry. She was bouncing on my knee only a few short years ago. She outgrew her pony just last week, or so it seems. Coraline, though, and Annette herself, seem determined on putting some bachelor's boot firmly in parson's mousetrap, and Coraline is curious about Huxsetter. If he and Annette suit, why not consider him?"

Oh indeed. Why not save Tallister from the huge expense of a Mayfair Season? Why not form a connection with the financially healthy Lorne barony and with some earldom or other on the dam side? Then too, Huxley was acknowledged by Chanderton himself, and Tallister was always happy to strengthen ties with Coraline's ducal relations.

"Mr. Huxley would be nearly fifteen years Annette's senior, Tallister. I can tell you from experience that age differences can take a toll on a bride." Chanderton was all that was sweet and kind and considerate, but he was no Adonis. He wasn't Adonis's comely older brother either.

"Huxley is in his prime," Tallister said. "Much like myself. You've seen him. Is he acceptable?"

Bernard Huxley was not only handsome, he was *masculine*. Lilly had learned to distinguish between the two.

"He presents as well as the next gentleman in fine tailoring. A bit lean, tallish, polite to a fault." Huxley also did not fawn. He truly listened to what a lady said and had a subtle sense of humor. "You want me to invite him to an at home, don't you?"

"I come as Coraline's emissary. I can promise you that if you invite him, Annette will attend the same informal gathering. If she finds any fault with him at all, I will dissuade Coraline from further overtures. For my part, Huxley is family of a sort. Chanderton has decreed that we owe the former vicar a modest welcome, and Coraline and I are both ever respectful of His Grace's wishes."

All very noble on Tallister's part, except that Tallister probably knew Chanderton had dined with Mr. Huxley at White's. Tallister himself was lucky to enjoy that honor even once a year.

"Very well," Lilly said. "My next at home is a week from Thursday. Coraline and Annette are welcome, of course, and I will invite Mr. Huxley as well. I cannot compel him to attend, and I will thank you to remind Coraline of that fact."

Tallister rose, his plate somehow once again empty. "Coraline will account me the acme of husbands, the apex of all matrimonial partners. She will sing my praises for at least two days over breakfast, and all because of you, Lilly dearest."

"Stow it, Tally." Lilly endured a peck on the cheek and then got to her feet. "I will take a hand in Annette's situation if Coraline asks me to, but only then. Chanderton believes a union can be both cordial and practical, and I agree with him."

Lilly, in fact, made it a point to agree with His Grace in almost all matters and to keep the duke informed regarding any developments within the family. Tallister was doubtless concerned that Annette's settlements wouldn't attract much notice next spring. A quiet marriage to a family connection would spare Tallister, Coraline, and Annette embarrassment and leave that much more in the family coffers for the other three girls.

"You need not see me out," Tallister said. "I'm off to report to

Coraline, by way of a call on the tailors. Spring is such a *fashionable* time."

He jaunted off in great good spirits, leaving Lilly to wonder what exactly Coraline was up to. Sorcha might know. Lord Barclay's widow had been carefully gracious toward Lilly and was astute, as widows tended to be. Sorcha also had the benefit of direct dealings with Bernard Huxley and might have some useful information to share.

The butler stepped through the open door. Martin was a lovely old fellow whose parents had been born in Hispaniola. He ruled the staff with as much charm as authority, though to any caller, he was more dignified than Chanderton himself.

"Excuse me, Your Grace. Lady Barclay has come to call."

"Delightful. That saves me having to put the horses to. Did she bring the children, perchance?"

"She did not."

Chanderton took a particular interest in Bridget's and Jordy's wellbeing, and thus Lilly did as well.

"Let's adjourn to the informal family parlor, Martin. It's a wonder we have any food left in the larder after one of Tallister's visits."

Martin turned a puzzled eye on the decimated tea tray. "Mr. Greer's gustatory habits do resemble those of a young fortune hunter new to Town. One envies him such a robust physique."

What a delicate slur. "Doesn't one just? Will Chanderton be going out tonight?"

"His Grace has no plans that I know of. Cook has put a beef roast on the menu with raspberry fool for dessert."

The duke's favorites. They figured frequently on the menus that Lilly merely glanced at before approving. Chanderton was an uncomplicated man who put on airs only to the extent duty required them.

"Please inform the duke I shall be delighted to join him for an informal supper. Spring has supposedly arrived, but the nights are still too cold for proper socializing, if you ask me."

"According to my sainted mama, England is too cold for proper socializing, except for a fortnight in July or August."

Martin jaunted on his way, half employee, half confidant, and all understated expertise. His first loyalty was to Chanderton, of course. As long as Lilly's first loyalty lay in the same direction, she and Martin were the next thing to allies.

And Lilly's loyalty belonged to her husband, as it always would, even if she had to occasionally bend a rule, interpret a preference, or forget a piece of ducal guidance. Chanderton likely did the same where she was concerned, and thus the marriage, though childless, prospered.

Or had prospered thus far.

CHAPTER FOUR

"Fresh air in moderation is acceptable," Miss Babbington replied. "A weekly outing on the Sabbath, for example, provided the weather is fair and the children's conduct is limited to a sedate walk or sitting quietly on a bench before a pleasing prospect. Excited children learn little."

She smiled complacently at Sorcha as if waiting for agreement. To appearances, Miss Babbington was a favorite auntie in the making. Plump, graying, neatly attired, hair in a tidy bun.

She had thus far horrified Sorcha with successively more draconian views of childcare.

"And what of biblical instruction?" Mr. Huxley asked. "Do you include verses in the children's curriculum, or leave that for the tutors in later years?"

Miss Babbington scooted about on her chair like a hen preparing to lay an egg. "Sir, I might say in all modesty that I have found no greater instrument for imparting wisdom and discipline than Holy Scripture. Set a child to copy an hour or two of Proverbs, and that child will learn patience, persistence, and a good deal of durable wisdom. Include the exercise daily, year in and year out, and you will soon have a biddable scholar where an indifferent pupil had gone before. One can cure fidgets and daydreaming with Bible verses. In all modesty, I have done as much myself, several times over."

Miss Babbington apparently conducted most of her activities *in all modesty.*

"Languages?" Mr. Huxley asked.

"French for the girls, Latin for boys."

Sorcha bestirred herself to enter the conversation. "Have men no need of French and women no need of Latin?"

Miss Babbington all but smirked. "Here in England, my lady, we grasp that Latin is too complicated for female minds, while the male can easily absorb Latin, Greek, and Germanic tongues and then take on French as the social amenity it usually is. Girls are better advised to work on their needlepoint, watercolors, and pianoforte. If a young lady is particularly talented at the keyboard, she may be permitted to take up the flute or violin. In later years, she may be exposed to pastoral poetry as well."

Sorcha was supposed to say, *I see,* then nod, grateful for even this crumb of instruction. Instead, she rose and tugged the bell-pull.

"Thank you for your time, Miss Babbington. We will make a decision early next week. The footman will show you out."

Mr. Huxley rose and bowed. "Good day, miss, and thank you."

The footman, who'd kept a straight face throughout the proceedings, held the door for Miss Babbington. She sailed out, likely confident that she'd soon have Lady Barclay's children proceeding through the strait gate and along the narrow way, thus earning her universal approbation from the household and Mayfair generally.

"I clearly have a reputation at the agency," Sorcha said, returning to her wing chair when the footman had accompanied his charge through the door. "I am stupid, Scottish, and looking for somebody to torment my children."

Mr. Huxley took the second wing chair. Sorcha had chosen to interview potential governesses in the informal parlor. The house had a third parlor, almost an office, for meeting with tradesmen, prospective employees, and any social connection deserving of shame. Barclay had delighted in subjecting anybody who owed him money or to whom he owed money to the third parlor.

Sorcha refused to use it.

"Perhaps the agency is stupid," Mr. Huxley said, "and determined to torment your children. You specifically requested younger candidates this time, did you not?"

"Candidates accustomed to lively, active children. The agency apparently views liveliness as a fault to be cured."

"The agency is wrong." Said calmly enough that Sorcha's budding sense of frustration eased.

"Anybody can punish a child into miserable quiet," Mr. Huxley went on. "At least temporarily. The real teachers turn the liveliness into keen questions and informed curiosity. Let's take a break, shall we?"

"We aren't through the list."

He consulted a plain silver pocket watch. "We have twenty minutes before the next besom inflicts her backward thinking on us. I need a breath of fresh air and a sedate walk, or a not very sedate walk, and I am positive the view of the back garden will be more pleasing than the walls of this parlor."

He rose and extended a hand to Sorcha, which she accepted.

"Don't lose heart," he said, patting her knuckles. "I have a few ideas if this batch fails to fill the need."

Sorcha rose, all too willing to take a turn in the garden. "I use one of the best agencies in London, Mr. Huxley. Coraline will patronize no other, and she's hired a dozen governesses and nurserymaids over the years."

"Coraline Greer, daughter of my late uncle Cecil, now married to Tallister Greer, an earl's spare. Tell me, are there other by-blows?"

He asked this question while casually escorting Sorcha along the corridor.

"Yes, but you'd have to apply to Chanderton for the particulars. One is female—Chanderton's youthful indiscretion, who bides in

Dorset—and Lord Jerome's estate supports at least one other young man."

"I might have a half-brother?"

"You sound pleased. His name is Richard, and he also bears a resemblance to Chanderton."

They paused in the foyer to collect cloaks, the day being sunny but chilly. Sorcha decided against a bonnet, which was bad of her.

"I have a sibling," Mr. Huxley said. "That is indeed a happy development. Consider my position, Lady Barclay. My mother and her spouse had no other issue. I have but the one cousin extant, and Lord Lorne is a cousin in name only, though he would protest that characterization. I have no children and no wife and am far from the home I claimed for my entire life."

Was he admitting to loneliness? Lonely people were more apt to make regrettable choices.

Sorcha paused at the door to the back terrace. "May I tell you something?"

"Of course."

Bernard Huxley was so innocent. Blithely anticipating that he was the equal to any challenge she might describe. Believing implicitly that life was manageable, and every problem admitted of a solution. That he should have complete legal control of her children was as unfair as it probably was unavoidable.

"You are being considered as a potential spouse for Miss Annette Greer."

He held open the door. "I have not had the pleasure. I assume Miss Greer is Cousin Coraline's offspring. Should I be flattered, insulted, or terrified?"

He concluded that the situation could be merely troublesome when, in fact, Coraline's scheming might result in a lifetime of misery for two people and their offspring.

"You should be careful, Mr. Huxley. The duchess, Duchess Lilly, hinted at Coraline's interest in you, and Her Grace does not spread gossip for entertainment's sake."

"She was hoping you would warn me? Sporting of you both."

The brisk air in the garden was a tonic, though Mr. Huxley's company was proving oddly annoying. "Do you not understand that, for some people, Mr. Huxley, matrimony is a matter pursued in deadly earnest?"

He accompanied her onto the terrace, the breeze teasing at his blond locks. "I was a *vicar*, my lady. I have seen matrimony approached from every perspective: duty, joy, resentment, ignorance, cordial goodwill, and blind lust. Lorne warned me that Mayfair in spring is a scene of controlled madness. That a cousin I have yet to meet would consider me for her own daughter must be regarded as symptomatic of Society's collectively imbalanced humors."

He offered his arm. Sorcha ignored the courtesy and stalked off down the steps. Mr. Huxley followed more slowly.

What is wrong with me? The interminable interviews with the governesses, each of whom was more overbearing and smug than the last, would put any mother in a foul humor, but Sorcha was also specifically out of charity with Mr. Huxley.

She mostly liked him and mostly did not trust him. Vexing. "How do you stay so calm?" she asked when he caught up with her. "How do you not want to upend the tea tray, leap out the window, and run howling back to Yorkshire?"

"I forget," he said, "that you've been searching for a governess for months now, probably for years. They were a sorry lot, I grant you. Curiously so. If these are the elite exponents of the species, then Jordy and Bridget would be better off in any village dame school."

"Chanderton would have apoplexies at that suggestion, and he'd be justified. I dread the prospect of sending Jordy to public school, but those arrogant, righteous women with their Proverbs have a point. Children who fidget and daydream have a hard road ahead of them. Then I wonder if I am a bad mother because I believe daydreaming should be a child's right."

She ought not to have admitted that, and not to this man.

"You are a very good mother," Mr. Huxley said. "Unusually

devoted, given your station, and I offer that as a compliment. I do believe, though, that the children might benefit from spending time with you individually."

The compliment—*a very good mother, unusually devoted*—almost distracted her from the blow.

"To spend time with me individually, my children would have to spend time apart from each other. Jordy does pass two hours every afternoon with his tutor. Little scholarship is accomplished, but he's separated from his sister."

"I am curious about the tutor, though what of Bridget? What interests does she have that might allow her some freedom from her brother's company?"

"You are cozening me. Presenting the topic of separating the children as individual time with me, or time free of each other. You have concluded that they are too close to each other."

Mr. Huxley frowned at the daffodils bobbing along the south wall. "A child must develop some confidence in this life, and that is made more difficult if adults around the child imply that exploring the park, venturing out in a breeze, beholding drab vistas, or spending time without siblings is simply not done. The child will wonder, 'Why is it not done? Why is a perfectly sensible path closed to me? Am I somehow lacking, or are my minders a pack of dullards?'"

He swiveled his gaze to the aspens leafing out in the southern corner of the garden and then to Sorcha.

"Soon enough, the child either breaks the rules and gets in trouble or consigns himself to sedate walks on fair Sunday afternoons."

"Damn you." *I am not like those governesses.*

He smiled an astonishingly genial smile. "You take my point."

"I don't want to." Sorcha marched along toward the aspens, trying not to return that smile. "You aren't at all what I expected, Mr. Huxley." He was more than a parson come to Town to sponge off his family's investments. Much more.

"You cannot manage me, and I cannot intimidate you, you mean?

Your ladyship might be surprised to know that the average vicar cannot excommunicate a parishioner, cannot extort funds from the wealthier souls, and has little chance of intimidating even his curate, who can go whining to the bishop at any moment. I will spare you a recitation of the oppression the pastoral committee and vestrymen are capable of."

He kept stride with her easily.

In other words, Mr. Huxley had had to rely on native wit to achieve his ends. Sorcha well knew how that felt.

"What do you propose in terms of the children spending time separately?" And what was to be done about the lack of a governess?

"I can take them up one at a time with me when I hack out. One should have some horseback experience before acquiring a personal mount."

A sidesaddle did not allow for that sort of excursion. "If you are determined on this point, start with Bridget. Jordy took a tumble from a pony last summer when his Greer cousins were looking on. He'll be reluctant to try again unless Bridget goads him into it."

"How bad of a tumble was it?"

"Nothing awful. The saddle slipped to the side. The pony was very round, and the grooms said the girth was as tight as possible, but 'the young lad' hadn't acquired a balanced seat yet. Jordy felt foolish for being so alarmed, though—he came off in a crying heap. That he was clearly afraid probably stung more than the conk on the noggin and a few bruises."

"Very well, I will start with Bridget, and you and Jordy can amuse yourselves as you please. In my experience, no child can resist learning a card trick. Teach him one or two, and he will forget that Bridget has gone to the park."

They rounded the corner at the aspens, which put the breeze at their backs.

"You've raised many children, Mr. Huxley, that you've become a card sharp?"

"You don't know *any* card tricks, my lady, and you with a surfeit of siblings? I account myself appalled. What passes for childhood education in Scotland?"

"You are teasing me. Scottish children learn Latin, Greek, history, natural philosophy, literature, heaps of theology, and the like. No card sharping."

"Let's do our duty by the rest of the besoms, then, and I'll show you a few card tricks."

He linked arms with Sorcha, but she disentangled herself from him as soon as they had ascended the terrace steps.

"Mr. Huxley, do you never lose your temper, burst out laughing, or use profanity?"

"I have a temper," he said. "I was ready to strangle my mother."

He'd probably offered his dear mama a short lecture on financial restraint before she'd taken ship. "And the laughter and profanity?"

He paced off across the flagstones, and Sorcha followed him to the back door. Her question appeared to trouble him, which gratified her to an unladylike degree.

"I grow lonely and bored and resentful," he said. "I sometimes find commerce inexpressibly tedious, and I entertained untoward thoughts about the friendlier widows in the churchyard. I am as much a creature of animal spirits as the next fellow, Lady Barclay. I am no paragon, so you needn't fear I'll expect perfect deportment from your children. My objective is their lifetime happiness and their ability to make a meaningful contribution. Shall we return to the parlor?"

"I am not a paragon either," Sorcha said, which had nothing to do with anything. "Far from it. I do not expect perfection from anybody, Mr. Huxley."

He frowned down at her, not his usual thoughtful expression, but rather, a masculine, almost angry perusal. The expression was gone before Sorcha could properly describe it.

"Back to lists with us, my lady." He opened the door and bowed slightly.

Sorcha preceded him into the house, and they resumed the

thankless business of interviewing women wholly inappropriate for the post on offer. All the while, Sorcha was preoccupied with that last little exchange with Mr. Huxley.

He was lonely. He entertained untoward thoughts about the friendlier widows in the churchyard, and he was no paragon. Coraline's daft scheme to see him married to Annette might bear fruit after all, and that bothered Sorcha exceedingly.

~

"Lady Barclay is ferociously protective of her children," Bernard said. "They are at risk for becoming spoiled, in part as a result of their mother's influence in their lives."

"I cannot abide a spoiled child." St. Didier turned his horse off Park Lane into the quiet surrounds of Hyde Park at dawn. "I also find it difficult to see Lady Barclay allowing her offspring to be overindulged."

"I am unclear on the whole dynamic myself. The children are together the livelong day. They terrorize their nurse, who is no simpleton, and their studies have been neglected. Why Chanderton has allowed matters to come to such a pass, I do not know."

Bounder was in good spirits, while Bernard was... not in good spirits. Lady Barclay was a damsel in distress, though she did not seem to know it. Bernard was no knight in shining armor, and explaining to a mother that she must enforce some discipline in the nursery was hardly a noble quest.

More on the order of a doomed and thankless task when that mother viewed every offer of assistance as an attempt to interfere in her maternal demesne.

"Is Chanderton testing you?" St. Didier asked. "Seeing how you fare with a problem he can't solve by ducal fiat before he proposes to sponsor you in politics?"

"I have no ambition to stand for the hustings." Though illegitimate sons had been put to that use by many an influential family.

"You had no ambition to take up trade until Lorne started whispering in your ear."

"I had no vocation for the Church, according to you, though I was an exemplary parson, according to some. What am I to do with these children, St. Didier? Every governess we interviewed was a temple of rigidity and backwardness trussed up in bombazine and righteous certainty."

Bounder began to prance, a sure sign that Bernard's mood was communicating itself to his horse. He eased his grip on the reins, relaxed his legs, and exhaled. The horse settled.

"Which agency are you using?"

"Beardon's Select Service. Coraline Greer swears by them, and Cousin Coraline—who is apparently trying to marry me off to her eldest—is the family authority on all matters domestic."

"Beardon's has a reputation for uppishness, I'll grant you that. Try Swindon's Preferred. They aren't as venerable and aren't as high in the instep. Will you marry Miss Annette?"

"Have you memorized DeBrett's?"

"No. Tallister Greer has four daughters to fire off and no sons. He is an object of passing pity in the clubs and otherwise well liked. Even if his finances are very solid, four dowries going out, and none coming in, will be a challenge."

St. Didier, whose family had lost their title thanks to a paucity of legitimate sons, would know of other families similarly situated.

"The Dolforth succession rests on little Jordy's shoulders, doesn't it?" Perhaps that explained why the boy was overindulged.

"For now. Duchess Lillian isn't yet thirty. Coraline is hardly doddering. Either lady could produce a child who would bump Jordy out of contention for the title. Before Lady Barclay joined the family, Coraline would remind any who cared to listen that the earldom midway down the family's pile of titles can be preserved through the female line."

"The earldom is Scottish?"

"I believe so. What do you think of Lady Barclay when you aren't contemplating ripping her children from her loving embrace?"

"It won't come to that." Bernard could not let it come to that. Her ladyship would at the very least steal his horse should he even make the attempt. "She is formidable, intelligent, and..."

All manner of adjectives came to mind. Troublesome, vexatious, contentious, difficult, intense, distrustful, contrary... And yet, she had warned Bernard of Cousin Coraline's matrimonial nonsense, she listened to Bernard's concerns regarding the children, and she was right to be horrified by the parade of nursery wardens masquerading as governesses.

St. Didier tipped his hat to a pair of ladies in a low phaeton. "You were saying?"

"One finds descriptors for Lady Barclay both too numerous and insufficient. I gather her husband was not the doting sort."

"You gather correctly. Sorcha was the usual sacrificial young bride, more or less bought for her reproductive potential and blue blood. She held up her end of the bargain and mourned his lordship properly. She is and was dutiful."

"You call her Sorcha?" Roughly translated to mean *radiance* or *brightness*, and that struck Bernard as a little off. Her ladyship gave off the occasional blazing spark, but the true flame of her spirit burned behind manners, self-restraint, and maternal worries.

"She might grant you the privilege of familiar address," St. Didier said, "if you don't go all Archbishop of York on her. She has a wicked sense of humor when she's among friends."

St. Didier was her friend, apparently, which was surely fortunate. Surely not an indication of anything amatory or inappropriate.

Bounder began to prance again.

"We'd best let them have a gallop," Bernard said. "I am to collect Miss Bridget for a short outing when I've finished a proper hack. Bounder still hasn't much bottom, but we're making strides."

St. Didier tugged at his hat brim. "Keep up as best you can." He touched his heels to his horse's sides, and though Bounder gave it a good effort, he was no match for a fit youngster who'd had the best of care and conditioning.

"What will you do about Lady Barclay?" St. Didier asked as Bounder came down to the walk five minutes later, head low, sides heaving.

"I will see to the education of her children to the best of my ability. She hasn't said as much, but she seems to grasp that public school is an inevitability for Jordy."

"Sending him off sooner rather than later might be the kindest decision, Huxley. Little boys can establish a pecking order with less real viciousness than their elder brothers do."

"Those older boys often learn their cruelty at the hands of the headmasters in charge of the lower forms. Jordy is by no means ready for public school. His scholarship is sorely lacking."

"Sack the tutor."

"First, we will hire a governess. The tutor at least minds the boy for part of the afternoon."

They approached the gates, and Bernard was reluctant to leave the quiet, leafy surrounds of the park. The air was better here, the views green and growing. *I miss Yorkshire.*

"You never did answer my question, Huxley."

"Which question?"

"What will you do about Lady Barclay?"

"Why must I do anything about her? I am not her guardian." Though for a woman for whom Bernard had no responsibility, she was taking up rather a lot of Bernard's mental landscape. Not a pretty woman, but she moved with the sort of confidence that made watching her a pleasure. Comfortable in her skin, sure of her powers.

"You have *noticed* her," St. Didier said gently. "You could ignore every belle and bishop's daughter in Yorkshire. You've let the Mayfair hostesses look you over from teeth to tail, and you hardly turn a hair when you tell me that Coraline Greer, a veteran general of the ballrooms, has you in mind for her eldest. I use Lady Barclay's given name, and you are ready to challenge me to fists at dawn on Hampstead Heath."

Bernard drew his horse to a halt. One could admit the charges and look a fool, or deny the charges and look an utter dunce. An image came to mind, of Lady Barclay declaring herself to be no paragon *either*. She'd been so earnest about her admission and so utterly oblivious to where her words would lead the thoughts of a healthy, if flawed, male mind.

Such sincere blue eyes, such a fierce spirit.

Cease and desist. "I will comport myself as a gentleman," Bernard said. "In all matters, at all times."

"Precisely what I was afraid of. Enjoy your outing with Miss Bridget. She's partial to peppermint sticks."

"Stop twitting me, or it will be fists in the park at eight in the morning, St. Didier."

"I am aquiver with dread. Good day, Huxley." He trotted off and disappeared into the throng of morning traffic on Park Lane.

Bernard decided that, in a byzantine, backward manner, St. Didier had been trying to encourage the faint of heart, though Bernard was not faint of heart. He was perplexed, true, and in uncharted territory.

He stopped by a tobacconist's to buy a half-dozen peppermint sticks, then walked Bounder through the alleys the rest of the way to Lady Barclay's mews.

He had noticed Lady Barclay as a man notices a woman whom he both esteems and could desire. Absolutely nothing unusual about that.

She was worth noticing. The puzzle was how to earn her notice in return, and that was a quest Bernard was surprisingly willing to contemplate.

Interesting.

CHAPTER FIVE

"Bridget is quite comfortable on horseback," Mr. Huxley said. "She was particularly keen to canter all over the park, but alas, my steed wasn't up to that challenge. How did you and Jordy fare?"

The daffodils were still making a good show along the wall, the aspens were still a gauzy, hopeful green, but Sorcha was not as unsettled as when she and Mr. Huxley had most recently trod the garden path.

"We took a turn out here," Sorcha said, "though in Jordy's case, that meant pelting the whole circuit several times, and then we sat on the steps, and I showed him your card trick. He never did guess the secret, but when I explained it to him, he took the deck from me and was determined to learn how to shuffle without peeking."

"Shuffling cards is one of myriad masculine skills nobody warns a boy he should master."

"Like peeing a circle in the snow?" Truly, Sorcha's spirits were improving. "Sorry. Blame my brothers." Blame an incorrigible curiosity about what a flustered Bernard Huxley would look like.

"Or thank your brothers. If you are the parent of a son, particularly a son without a father, tolerance for masculine vulgarity can only be an asset. Bridget and I ran into an acquaintance of mine who also had a daughter or niece or connection of some sort in the saddle. The young ladies appeared to enjoy each other's company."

Perhaps the desire to fluster was mutual. "Who is your acquaintance?"

"Lord Greymoor. He's horse-mad and serves as his family's groom of the nursery. All the Alexander children begin their equestrian education with him. He also has an interest in ancient texts relating to horsemanship. He recalled that I'd taken firsts in Latin and Greek, though we missed being academic contemporaries by several years. He struck up a correspondence with me regarding some Greek translations."

Sorcha mentally turned pages on various Society guest lists. "Greymoor's brother is a marquess. Their lady cousin married a viscount. Greymoor's earldom appeared pretty much out of nowhere —meaning the marquess *lent* a fortune to the crown—and another viscount lurks among the in-laws. All of those men are married to women who move in Society. Be very mindful of your bachelorhood, Mr. Huxley."

"Greymoor was sent to inspect me?"

"Possibly. Given what I know of that family, he might have been sent to ensure you are being treated properly. Heathgate, the marquess, was something like sixth in line for the title. A boating accident took the lives of half the family, and the marquess came to Mayfair with a very dim view of polite society. He's accepted everywhere, and I'm told marriage has mellowed him somewhat, but he'll exert himself on behalf of unlikely heirs and outsiders. I've always found him charming."

"You know him?"

"He stood up with me twice when I was new to Town." Two kindnesses that let all and sundry know that Sorcha had allies. Barclay had been amused the first time and annoyed the second.

A pair of robins flitted to the top of the garden wall. Sidled a few steps this way and that, then flew off to perch on the balustrade. Mayfair mating games everywhere.

"I will assume," Mr. Huxley said, "that Greymoor was simply enjoying a hack with a daughter or niece in the saddle before him. Bridget declared her love of cantering, and the other girl—I forget her name—seconded the motion. They would still be debating the merits of grays and bays had not Greymoor declared that the horses needed to have their breakfast oats."

The outing had been a success, about which Sorcha was ambivalent. She paused to extract a pair of green leaves from the bowl of the shallow fountain at the foot of the garden.

"I cannot provide Bridget a pony before Jordy has earned his own mount."

"Oh, but you could, and Jordy might not even mind. Not every boy was born to sit a horse or enjoy sitting a horse. A gentleman should know how to ride, just as he should grasp the rudiments of fencing, shooting, smoking, sums, natural philosophy, sketching, history, languages, games of chance, cricket, current events, and flirtation. Jordy need not excel in the saddle."

Mr. Huxley passed over a handkerchief bearing a mess of embroidery in one corner that might have been some initials.

Sorcha wiped at her wet fingers. "Did you stitch this yourself?"

"Lorne and his lady are raising an enormous brood, and needlepoint is expected of even the youngest family members. I believe that one was done by a fellow named Toddman, who made a gift of it to me."

Sorcha folded up the linen and passed it back. "I do not foresee a career on Bond Street for young Toddman." And yet, as ridiculous as the monogram was, Mr. Huxley carried the handkerchief and used it before others.

He'd taken Bridget for her outing, not left the task to a groom, and he was inquiring about Jordy's progress toward the skills of a card sharp. He would make somebody a kind and considerate husband.

The next thought had Sorcha staring into the fountain as if it held the secrets of Delphi. Bernard Huxley would be a good *father*. Was that why Chanderton had cast him in the role of guardian?

"I have been invited to Her Grace's at home on Thursday," Mr. Huxley said. "Would I be imposing very greatly if I asked you to attend as well?"

As he asked, he studied the statue of Athena at the top of the garden. She bore her spear in her right hand. The robins were sitting on her left shoulder.

"I will not only attend as well, I will accept your escort, if that's what you're after. The duchess is in every way loyal to her husband. If you've been asked to attend, then Chanderton has decreed that you are to be accepted as a full-fledged member of the Dolforth lower ranks."

"We had dinner at his club a few weeks ago. The wine was indifferent, but the beefsteak was quite good. I suspected supper at the club was some rite of passage, and then he hosted me to lunch recently. There are others?"

"A few. After Thursday, the hostesses will be on notice that you are to be received. The invitations will start on Friday morning, and you should answer each one, accepting as many as you can manage."

He offered his arm, and Sorcha took it.

"I feel as I did in Paris last autumn. I've been reading French since I was in leading strings. I've spoken French, or an Englishman's version thereof, for at least twenty years, but for all I could comprehend upon setting foot on French soil, I might as well have been studying Ancient Norse. Everybody spoke too rapidly, and with a provincial accent, and using vernacular that wasn't in the lesson books."

"And then," Sorcha said, "they all pretended they could not comprehend your perfectly correct French."

He peered over at her. "Precisely. By the end of the second week, I was managing adequately, but the experience was lowering."

"Try being a Scottish bride in Mayfair, Mr. Huxley. Nobody can understand your English, and no matter which fork you use, you didn't use it correctly. You picked it up too soon, not soon enough, and your cutlery clattered when it touched your plate. Mortal sins, all."

"The English beauties were angry because you'd cut a ducal widower from the herd. I suppose I'd best avoid ducal daughters?"

"They won't trouble you. They'll dangle after German princes and Russian archdukes. The daughters of barons, viscounts, and courtesy lords will have their eyes on you. How did we get onto this dreary topic?"

"The at home, though Mayfair matchmaking is more a matter of irritation than dreariness for me. I have no time for gratuitous socializing simply to amuse the matchmakers. I am so far behind on my correspondence that my head clerk is likely considering retirement, while the junior ranks foment insurrection among the new recruits."

He took his business obligations seriously. Chanderton would approve of that.

Sorcha approved of that too. "Avoid linen closets and young ladies who claim to have pebbles in their slippers. Another common ploy is to fret miserably over a lost brooch, ring, or bracelet last seen in a secluded location. In the park, well-trained puppies run away with perplexing frequency. Next thing you know, the young lady will be searching your figurative pockets when the chaperones are likely to find her at her treasure hunt."

"You aren't trying to rattle me, are you?"

He *was* rattled, if his air of weary impatience was any indication. Discomfiting Mr. Huxley was not as gratifying as it should have been.

"Not this time. Be careful, Bernard."

He sat on the steps, a cold, hard bench, on which he looked utterly at ease. Sorcha took the place beside him.

"I ought not to need the warning," he said. "My mother thought to snabble Lord Jerome by sharing her favors with him. She neglected to account for her own family's appetite for coin. By mutual agreement, she was consigned to the arms of a baron's spare. The Dolforths augmented her settlements and made a generous provision for me in the bargain. Mama's relations were spared the expense of more Seasons and the scandal she courted. All very tidy and pragmatic."

As Mr. Huxley tried to keep his affairs tidy and pragmatic. He wasn't Scottish, but he did know what it was to dwell under an invisible cloud.

"Have you told anybody else that story?"

"Lorne certainly knows of my past, as does St. Didier, but no. I do not bruit ancient history about. Now we truly are on a dreary topic."

And yet, he'd told her. *Confided in her.* "Bernard, do you have friends up in Yorkshire?"

"I consider Lorne and his baroness my friends."

Such good friends that they'd consigned him to Paris, London, and the City, while they embarked on wedded bliss, somehow already complete with an enormous brood of offspring.

"Anybody else?"

He sat back, bracing his elbows on the next step up, and Sorcha was struck by his pure masculine appeal. A profile worthy of any Roman statesman, Yorkshire blue eyes, curling blond hair, and a complexion ever so slightly weathered by the elements.

The hostesses would pounce on him like house cats going after a loose canary.

"When I was with the Church," he said, "I enjoyed the company of the very old and the very young. The elders were not impressed by my station—they were closer to heaven than I was. The children were not intimidated by my calling. They, too, were closer to heaven than I was. I nevertheless miss Yorkshire. Anybody born and bred by the Dales would miss Yorkshire, but I no longer have a home there."

Sorcha sat forward and linked her arms around her knees. "I have avoided returning to Scotland for the same reason. I'm afraid I no longer have a home there."

"And everybody will say that you have acquired an English accent, and you walk like an Englishwoman, and your manners have become too fussy. I assure you, my lady, there is nothing whatsoever wrong with how you walk."

He squeezed her shoulder before she could ask for particulars, and she did want to ask. The next instant, he was standing and extending a hand to her.

"Let's interrogate the tutor, shall we? And St. Didier advises us to apply to Swindon's for the next batch of governesses. He claims Coraline's shop is uppish by reputation."

Sorcha rose easily and linked arms with Mr. Huxley. "Coraline specifically warned me away from Swindon's."

"We can try others, then. One doesn't want to offend Cousin Coraline."

Coraline would find fault with every other agency, save the one she'd chosen for her daughters. "Swindon's next, and we'll see how we fare."

"My lady has spoken."

Mr. Huxley was back on his mettle, ready to plow through the next task, two mountains of correspondence, and another half-dozen stuffy-governess interviews.

Sorcha was still pondering how he'd endured life in godforsaken Yorkshire without real friends, in the company of a mother haunted by scandal, and without family to cheer him through even an occasional friendly letter.

"Might you call me Sorcha when the situation is informal?" she asked as they mounted the steps. "You and I are some version of family. You will be involved with the children for the rest of their minorities, and I am no great advocate of pointless formality."

Or pointless enmity between people who had a surprising amount in common. Caution, yes. Sorcha would always regard her children's guardian with caution, but not enmity.

He looked, of all things, bashful. "You did honor me with the use of my given name. Twice."

"I will honor you with nicknames, a bit of strong language, and some muttered Gaelic if we're to get the children sorted. I will not see Jordy packed off to public school, Bernard. Not this year, not next."

"We are in accord, *Sorcha*, though he'll take his proper place among his peers when the time is right." The tone was brisk, the nod perfunctory, but Mr. Huxley—Bernard—was smiling at the door as if he beheld the Dales in all their springtime glory.

"The tutor is Mr. Entwhistle. He's terribly young and very serious."

"Jordy runs rings around him."

Sorcha was smiling, too, for no reason. "I leave them to their scholarship. Entwhistle came highly recommended."

"From Coraline's bosom bow or her vicar or some doddering ancient who was teaching Mayfair's daughters before the Flood. Very well, forewarned is forearmed."

He bowed her through the door, and Sorcha accompanied him up to the schoolroom lighter of heart than she could recall being since she'd come to London.

She viewed her own lightness of heart with as much caution as she could muster, which doubtless wasn't nearly enough.

"Mr. Huxley, may I make known to you Mr. Hermes Entwhistle, late of Kent. Mr. Entwhistle has had the privilege of tutoring Jordan for the past six months. Mr. Entwhistle, Mr. Huxley is to be appointed successor guardian to both children."

As Lady Barclay fell silent, Entwhistle scrambled to his feet, cleared his throat, and hauled down smartly on his somewhat worn lapels. The tome he'd been reading—*Sense and Sensibility*—fell from his lap to the floor.

Entwhistle blushed, bowed, stuck out a pale paw, then withdrew it.

Ye winged angels of academic disaster.

Bernard bowed and extended a hand. "Pleased to make your acquaintance, Entwhistle. You have my thanks for your continuing efforts with Master Jordan. My apologies for the delay in making your acquaintance."

Entwhistle wrung Bernard's hand. "One understands, sir. The press of business—that is to say, of other, erm, responsibilities and obligations and so forth."

"I'll leave you two gentlemen to get acquainted. Shall I have a tray sent up?"

Lady Barclay—Sorcha—impersonated the soul of guileless femininity as she jumped ship. Bernard was on the point of refusing a tray, but the loose fit of Entwhistle's clothing dissuaded him.

"My breakfast was hours ago," Bernard said. "Some sustenance would be appreciated."

"Of course." Sorcha curtseyed politely and withdrew, probably to indulge in a few snickers on the first landing.

Bernard closed the door in her wake. The tutor had been given an office that doubled as Jordy's schoolroom. An abacus was collecting dust on the mantel. Bookshelves held dozens of bound volumes, and a small desk by the window boasted a neat assortment of pens and pencils, an inkwell, paper, and sand.

The larger desk, where Entwhistle had been whiling away his morning, had a few scuff marks on one corner, where a fellow at his leisure might have been putting up his feet.

Bernard took inventory of the titles on the shelves. "I will rely on you, Entwistle, to acquaint me honestly with Master Jordy's situation. He appears to tyrannize the nurserymaid and has no compunction about bossing his sister—though, to her credit, she bosses him right back. Jordan is at risk to turn into an exact replica of his father."

Entwhistle stood rooted, clearly trying to ignore *Sense and Sensibility* at his feet. Bernard picked up the book and set it on the larger desk, which was also painfully well organized.

"Might you explain, Mr. Huxley? I'm told Lord Barclay was a paragon, an exemplar of all gentlemanly virtues, and a doting papa. Master Jordan would do well to follow his late father's example."

Sorcha would not have characterized her late spouse as any sort of paragon, of that Bernard was certain.

"Lord Barclay doubtless drank and debauched his way out of

public school and into university. He was no scholar at all, unless taking firsts in laziness and wagering count. I have no doubt he could be charming—he did win Lady Barclay's hand, and she is nobody's fool—but he was raised to hold himself in higher esteem than any other entity, save perhaps the Almighty. If Master Jordan was doted upon, that was because doting flattered the papa, not because the son benefited."

The indictment was a bit severe. Barclay had doubtless been fond of his offspring. The rest was Bernard's general sketch of the aristocracy's younger sons. They abounded in the Church and had been regular and generally inebriated fixtures at university.

"Mr. Huxley, if I might speak honestly?"

"Please do, in all situations when kindness doesn't forbid veracity."

"If you perceive that Master Jordan lacks scholarly inclinations, that he's behind in his studies, then you must apply to her ladyship to remedy the situation. She is a widow and without a husband's wise counsel, and thus allowances must be made. She nevertheless has undue influence over Master Jordan's studies. If I'm to ready him for public school in the next year or two, then she must cease distracting him with trips to the park, games in the garden, fairy tales, and *silliness*. Master Jordan might well be the family's next duke, and his education has been sorely neglected."

That was overstating the situation by half. "The boy is seven years old, Entwhistle. Many a lordling is educated at home until twelve or fourteen. Some rely on their tutors entirely until they reach university and then simply take their tutors with them."

Which raised the question: Who had put such a dire sense of responsibility on Entwhistle's bony shoulders? He looked to be barely beyond his own university years. His dark hair was ruthlessly pomaded, his cheeks gaunt, and his cravat going frayed at the seams.

He well understood, though, that Jordy's academic success could be the making of Entwhistle's career in the ranks of Mayfair tutors.

"I'm sure you will agree with me, Mr. Huxley, that Master Jordan must uphold ducal standards in all regards. Perhaps the view is different in Yorkshire, but in Mayfair, we expect scholarship of the peerage."

How utterly precious. In Mayfair, titled families expected fine tailoring, scandal, and fertility of their scions.

"Does my accent give me away?" Bernard asked, though he knew perfectly well the Yorkshire dialect had been birched right out of him at his dear mama's insistence. He understood the local speech up north, but did not indulge himself.

"Not your accent, sir, not precisely, but you are new to Town. I meant no insult."

"None taken."

The books were the usual aging assortment. Sermons, collected letters, histories, a few biographies. Philosophers. Tragic plays. Poetry. Racy old Shakespeare on an upper shelf, along with Sheridan. All six volumes of Mr. Gibbon's history of Rome, the pages of even the first volume—octavo size—still uncut. No fables, fairy tales, picture books, or illustrated Bible stories.

Though on a more encouraging note, Entwhistle had been amusing himself with a witty piece of extended satire in the guise of a novel.

"I would not be so plainspoken about Master Jordan's situation, Mr. Huxley, except that I am most concerned for my pupil. I hesitate to impart what does not flatter a lady, but you are the boy's guardian, and you have allowed me the courtesy of honesty."

Bernard had not condoned long-windedness. "Does some particular incident trouble you, Entwhistle?"

The tutor stalked to the window, which overlooked the terrace and the back garden. "I'll give you one example. This very day, sir, this morning, Lady Barclay appeared to instruct her own son in the matter of shuffling and dealing cards. She did this in plain sight, on the terrace steps, and if I am not mistaken, she taught him a simple card trick."

"A card trick, you say?" Entwhistle hadn't merely glanced out the window, he'd spied on his employer and her son.

"I do not engage in falsehoods, Mr. Huxley. Lady Barclay showed that boy how to casually glance at the card on the bottom of the deck as she shuffled and cut and chattered. She then instructed the boy to choose any card. One could demonstrate if one had a deck."

"I'm following so far."

"By dexterous manipulation, her ladyship would raise half the deck such that Master Jordy could see what appeared to be the card on the bottom of the exposed *half.* This, of course, had been drawn from the bottom of the entire deck. Her ladyship had earlier peeked at the card and well knew what it was. The boy was utterly baffled. Then she explained to him how the trickery was done, and nothing would serve except that he must learn to emulate her dubious skill. One shudders for the future of Scotland, sir, if Lady Barclay believes this to be an acceptable element of a boy's education."

Bernard joined Entwhistle at the window. A lovely spring morning was well under way below. An aging gardener watered potted salvia, snipped a few daffodils, and inspected a bed of tulips that had yet to bloom.

"How is it you know of this card trick yourself, Entwhistle?"

"I was at Warriner's Exclusive Academy for Gentleman Scholars for six years, Mr. Huxley. The occasional disgraced younger son found his way to our ranks and brought his inappropriate worldly knowledge with him."

Never heard of the place. "That is most fortunate for young Master Jordan. I'm certain you will use his interest in playing cards to enhance his mathematical skills, won't you? My duties at the vicarage included the education of a number of fidgety boys, and I know one must outwit them in order to educate them."

Entwhistle brushed him with a dismayed glance. "You cannot be suggesting that I teach any young boy the rudiments of gambling?"

Such shock. Entwhistle had been playing for farthing points before he'd memorized his first Latin verses.

"Certainly not. Do you play cribbage?"

A cautious nod.

"Then you grasp that much of the game is based on knowing which combinations of cards add to fifteen. Eight and seven. Ten and five, four plus two plus nine, that sort of thing. Another part of the game has the players alternating cards to try to add up to thirty-one without going over that number. You simply modify the rules. Add to fourteen, try to total thirty-seven points. If Jordan wants to try totaling to forty-seven or sixty-two, so much the better."

"But that is not cribbage."

No wonder Jordy's education was so lacking. "That is *sums*, Entwhistle. Sums in his head. The boy will do them with you all morning and without touching a pencil to paper. A week of that, and he'll be adding double digits easily."

Entwhistle looked thoughtful. "And what tactics did you employ in the vicarage for a child who had no interest in history?"

Matters were dire if Entwhistle made even history dull. "You tell stories while walking in the garden or the park, of course. Once upon a time, Napoleon thought he'd conquer Russia. He was very smart about military matters, but a roaring dunce about Russian winters. He was equally ill-informed about the diseases that rage through Poland in late summer. Terrible, ghastly disease with all sorts of symptoms to delight a small boy's ghoulish fancy. Boys in Yorkshire really aren't much different from boys in Mayfair, Entwhistle."

"I see. Diseases and disasters. Have you any advice for Latin?"

At least Entwhistle was asking. "Tell the boy to choose a personal motto. 'Ever brave.' 'Honor true.' Even 'no girls allowed' will do for a start. Then you show him how to translate it, how to add to it. Translate his favorite proverb, his favorite imprecation or insult. Explain declensions and conjugations through the side door, Entwhistle. Pedantry bored us both as boys. As teachers, we're cleverer than that, I hope."

"I am not devious by nature, sir."

Heaven bless the fellow. "Of course not, but you are intelligent, well-read, and resourceful. Jordan is one little boy a bit behindhand in his studies. Lure him into scholarship, Entwhistle, and get him using his mind. Sums through cribbage. Latin by way of mottos and battle cries. History in the garden. The world will thank you when that boy becomes a man."

Always end a sermon on a positive note—some of the best advice Bernard had ever been given.

"You've given me much to think about, sir. Much. Perhaps we might chat again when you have the time?"

Entwhistle was not beyond hope, which was a relief. "Of course. You would be appalled at the tribulations I endured trying to start my scholars on French. Thank goodness for cognates."

"Cognates, sir?"

"You know, Entwhistle. *Flatuler, uriner*, and every little boy's favorite, *déféquer*. Desperate measures, and all that. You won't tell her ladyship?"

"Certainly not, sir. Lady Barclay must be kept apprised of Master Jordan's curriculum generally. I've seen no need to trouble her ladyship with the details of Master Jordan's progress."

Because there had been so little? "We are in accord, then. Shall we plan on another chat in a week or so? Would Wednesday suit?"

Entwhistle linked his hands behind his back. "Wednesday is one of my half days, sir. I am engaged on Wednesday afternoons to assist the misses Greer with their French."

Bernard made a note to have a look at Entwhistle's wages. What he did with his half days—note the plural—was his business, but a tutor ought to put in more than a couple of hours with his charge every afternoon.

"A week from Friday, then. Best of luck until next we meet, Entwhistle."

"Thank you, sir. Thank you very much."

Bernard left Entwhistle at the desk, scribbling away at what was doubtless a list of French scatological verbs with similar English counterparts. Jordy would be shocking his mother in no time.

Or making her laugh. Bernard very much enjoyed the idea that Sorcha might have more reasons to laugh.

He nonetheless took a quick leave of her in a cozy back parlor, and nearly sprinted to the office, where the clerks' civil wars, insurrections, upheavals, and jealousies of the day were already well under way.

CHAPTER SIX

"Mama says I must begin to tap on Society's door, the better to take my place properly next year. A year is a long time to stand about on the stoop, Auntie Sorcha. I'm to accompany Mama to all the best shops, socialize at every opportunity with family, walk frequently in the square, and speak mostly French. I feel quite out of my depth already, and the Season is barely begun."

Sorcha adjusted her mount's pace to the plodding walk Annette's chestnut mare had adopted. Annette was no sort of equestrian, but she did make a fetching picture in a forest green riding habit and chocolate-colored toque with two pheasant feathers cocked over one shoulder.

"Coraline wants you to feel confident when next spring comes around," Sorcha said. "Impatient, even, to make your curtsey and have a look at the available bachelors."

"They are already looking at me." Annette shortened her reins, which resulted in the mare tossing her head. "I don't care to be examined like a heifer brought to the Wednesday market."

Annette had inherited her mother's forthright disposition rather than her father's charm. She was pretty enough, though her hair was a lustrous golden brown rather than blond, and her eyes were brown instead of blue. The poor girl had been subjected to years of lemon rinses in an effort to lighten her hair.

The result was a subtle citrus scent rather than the desired pale locks. She had lately taken to drenching herself with attar of roses, an unfortunate combination of aromas. More distinctive than pleasing.

Annette was also a trifle outspoken, as young ladies went. Not a bad thing, but not exactly fashionable either.

"You could look at the young men as if they are the livestock on offer," Sorcha said. "Then you will get a reputation for boldness, and the fussier specimens will leave you alone."

Annette smiled wanly. "Mama would put me on bread and water for a fortnight if I behaved like that. You didn't land a ducal son by being bold, Auntie."

Land him, as if Barclay had been some magnificent trout. "I was instructed to aim as high as possible, Annette, because my sisters' prospects rose and fell with my own." The same governess who'd explained that eternal verity had also warned Sorcha that diving first into the waters of matrimony was a thankless and grueling honor.

Choose carefully, if you're permitted to choose at all. Sorcha still heard those words in MacPhee's soft, precise Inverness accent.

"Mama is relentless on the topic of prospects," Annette went on, drumming a heel against the mare's side. "Mine, the family's, a husband's. I might marry the first eligible curate simply to get away from my dear mother. Why won't this dratted horse settle?"

"Because you are telling her to stop and to go at the same time. Ease up on the reins, Annette. Hold your foot still."

Annette frowned and gave the mare two inches of rein. "I wish Mama would ease up on me. If she's told me once, she's told me a thousand times. My grandpapa is an *earl*, my uncle is a *duke*. Chanderton's earldom can be preserved through the *female line*. I must comport myself with the dignity of a *queen* for the sake of my *sisters* and my yet-to-be-born *children.* None of the interesting bachelors want to marry a queen."

More to the point, none of Annette's peers would want to befriend a young woman conducting herself with what she hoped was regal dignity. That was especially the case if the young lady also happened to be Scottish, not all that pretty, or not so very well dowered.

What would MacPhee advise? "Unfortunately, Annette, your mother is at least half right. If you marry well, your sisters will benefit greatly. If you involve yourself in scandal, they will definitely suffer, and you love your sisters."

"I do, most of the time. Jessica can be ridiculous, but she's only eleven. She's the best rider among us."

"Marriage does not involve a great deal of horseback riding." Which was fortunate when a lady had as little skill in the saddle as Annette, but then, the purpose of a hack in the park was to look attractive, not to ride well.

"Did you love Uncle Barclay madly, Auntie?"

Not even a little. Sorcha had tried to like him and could still describe some of his personality as likable.

"I esteemed him insofar as his actions merited my respect. He was a winsome suitor and, because of his age, struck me as serious and poised, unlike the younger men buzzing about my settlements."

"I hate settlements." Annette gathered up her reins into fisted hands. "You are absolutely correct that my settlements are more interesting than I am. Papa says Uncle Chandy could do more to help the situation. Mama says that Grandpapa is not much use either."

Those old fellows were doing Annette a favor. "All the better to ensure you marry somebody who values you for yourself, Annette, and not for your fortune."

"Marry for love?" Annette snorted inelegantly. "Mama has no patience with that notion. To hear her tell it, I will be valued for my needlepoint, pianoforte, French, and deportment. At least I enjoy the pianoforte, and my French is coming along. My needlepoint is quite good."

But as for deportment... Annette still had some work to do. "Give a bit on the reins, or your mare will lose all patience with you."

Annette complied. "Sorry, Cinnamon. I am very cross today. Auntie, what am I to do? I feel as if I'm in a runaway coach plummeting toward a raging river. Mama will thrust me into the arms of some old baron, and he will want children, and... I cannot bear the thought."

Or, worse, he'd want *sons*. "I will tell you what my governess told me: In the course of a long and busy day, marital duties might take up a quarter hour after dark. For that quarter hour, you can tolerate your husband's attentions, knowing that conception necessitates your fortitude, and that your security and continued place in Society will depend upon having children."

Would Mr. Huxley call that a sermon? Sorcha had certainly sounded preachy to her own ears.

"Auntie, I don't even like children."

Probably because Annette was still, in some regards, childish herself. "You will like your own children. For a time, anyway. In the later years of the marriage, you will have more independence, if all goes well." If all did not go well, Annette might spend the later years of the marriage immured in an asylum for discarded wives. Barclay had rattled that sword only once and then looked as if he'd horrified even himself.

"Auntie, I am *afraid*. I am afraid I will be yoked to some awful old viscount with cold hands and fetid breath. He will dwell all year-round in a mildewed manor in Little Hogtrot, Backwardshire. My sisters will write to me out of pity, and his lordship will live forever while I bear him one daughter after another and lose what looks I have. He won't die until I am thirty-two at least, and he will leave me and my dozens of daughters penniless."

She was drumming her heel against the mare's side again, and the horse switched her tail in response.

Sorcha chose her words carefully, trying to balance honesty with reassurance. "You are right to be worried, Annette. Marriage is mortally serious business, and most of us get only one chance to decide. The Church will not allow a marriage if the bride is unwilling." Sorcha's older brother had told her that, may he be forever blessed. "This is well-established canon law, and you must not forget it. Remind your mother that you cannot be coerced. Remind the bachelors, if you must. You will have a place as my companion if needs must."

Making that offer risked all manner of family upheaval, but nobody had offered Sorcha any such haven. *Go to Mayfair and marry well.*

"Mama will never speak to me if I fail to find a good husband."

"And you will never be permitted to speak to your mother, your sisters, or me if you find a bad husband." Barclay had become increasingly possessive as the marriage had progressed, probably worried that Sorcha would play him false.

She hadn't been remotely tempted.

"You are telling me that the decision is mine. Why don't I believe—drat this mare."

"Stop kicking her. Stop hauling back on the reins. You are making that horse feel exactly as the prospect of next Season makes you feel. Harried and restrained and given a most unhappy job that you cannot avoid."

"Oh." Annette gave the reins forward and sat quietly in the saddle. "Poor Cinnamon."

Poor Annette, though if Sorcha could manage it, Annette would meet plenty of decent young fellows who had the maturity to look beyond a young lady's settlements. Annette was in good health, well connected, and—within the limits of her years and disposition—mostly sensible.

"The duchess will lend a hand," Sorcha said. "You will have good options, Annette, and thus your sisters will too."

An idea emerged into Sorcha's awareness, an idea that had been percolating through her awareness since Bernard Huxley had instructed her on the finer points of a simple card trick. He'd offered a precise, organized explanation for how to manipulate the deck and demonstrated the game with deft movements of his elegant hands.

The whole time Sorcha had been watching and listening and pretending to focus on the cards, she'd instead been focused on the vicar-turned-merchant-turned-guardian. He was far shrewder than he let on, shrewd enough not to emphasize aristocratic good looks, a protean intellect, and an unceasing appetite for challenges.

Bernard Huxley was becoming an ally, almost a friend. Sorcha allowed the emerging idea to bloom in her imagination: He'd be a generous and inventive *lover*.

"Will you be at Her Grace's at home?" Annette asked. "Mama says I am to appear under the ducal roof regularly from now on, and nothing against Her Grace, but everybody who calls upon her seems to be so old."

"Those old people have sons and nephews, Annette. They will mention the young Greer daughter who comported herself with such ease and confidence. These family outings do matter, and they will give you a chance to find your bearings."

"Mama said I am to hack out with you for the same reason." Annette apparently intended no insult with that disclosure. "To be seen in good company in a fashionable location. I have been bouncing around on one mare or another since well before I put up my hair, and all I'm perfecting is the ability to ignore feathers drooping incessantly on my shoulder."

The next instants unfolded as if Sorcha were reading them on a page, one action after another, when, in truth, reality blazed by faster than thought.

A rabbit darted across the path. Sorcha's mare skin-jumped and settled. The fair Cinnamon, however, having suffered long enough for the cause of fashionable public displays, got the bit between her teeth and took off across the grass. Like most horses, she had an exquisite sense of direction and bore down hard on the leafy path that led to the park's gates.

A gentleman arranged his lean gray gelding across the opening to the path and sat calmly while the mare approached at a fast canter. Annette, screaming like a banshee—no profanity, thank the heavenly intercessors—had given up any attempt at control and clutched wildly at the horse's mane, the reins flapping against the beast's neck.

Other riders had drawn to a halt, calling directions to the runaway.

"Take up the reins, woman!"

"Pull her head to your knee, for pity's sake."

"Stop screeching, young lady. Silence, and she'll slow down."

The gentleman sat on his gray, watching with a calm eye as the mare careened closer. Cinnamon, who seldom cantered for more than a few yards at a time, took note of the obstacle, dropped into a jarring trot, then came to a heaving halt a dozen feet from the path that would have led her to the gates.

Only then did the gentleman urge his horse close to the mare. He appropriated the reins to turn the mare in a half circle and accompanied Annette back to Sorcha's side.

"The grooms were apparently remiss," he said, "allowing the mare to go for an outing when she was still too fresh. Lady Barclay, perhaps you'd favor us with proper introductions?"

Annette regarded Bernard with a combination of wonder and disbelief. The groom was a good dozen yards back, doubtless trying to look invisible.

"Miss Greer," Sorcha said, "may I make known to you Mr. Bernard Huxley, who happens to be a cousin of yours in some fashion. Mr. Huxley, I have the honor to make known to you Miss Annette Greer."

"*You're* Cousin Bernard?"

He smiled slightly. "I have that honor, and you are something of a horsewoman, Miss Greer. How on earth did you stay aboard for that protracted display of naughtiness?"

Annette sat taller, adjusted her reins to a proper length, and returned his smile. "I did, didn't I? I stayed aboard across half the park. Auntie Sorcha, you saw me."

What Sorcha saw was that Bernard had worked whatever magic that came of years of vicaring in rural Yorkshire. Annette's view of herself, which might have landed in the ditch, had just improved in some critical fashion, and Bernard had done that with a few words and a small smile.

He was a gentleman to his bones, and that, more than his card tricks or self-possession or subtle humor, turned the thought in Sorcha's mind, about Bernard's intimate appeal, in the direction of a wish.

Perhaps even in the direction of a hope.

"Heaven, defend me," Bernard muttered as he surveyed three dozen of Mayfair's finest lounging about Her Grace's vast formal parlor. Two beldames seated by the potted palms raised lorgnettes, the better to peer at him.

Sorcha took a firmer grip of his elbow. "They are here to socialize with the duchess and have a look at Annette. You are merely a passing curiosity."

The duchess, literally cornered by a pair of what looked like German royals, did not so much as glance up. The luminaries ranged about the room studied the passing curiosity as if he were a new hyena at the royal menagerie.

He's not one of us. Worth an inspection and a tad on the exotic side, but never one of us. Public schoolyard judgments writ large across both genders, though Bernard—with a titled grandfather—had not suffered the worst the puerile pecking order could have meted out.

Was this what a younger Sorcha had faced when she'd come to London in search of a husband?

"Lady Barclay, Mr. Bernard Huxley," the footman-cum-herald announced. The hubbub of conversation ebbed to a whispering hum.

The duchess glanced over her shoulder, extricated herself from her captors, and came forward. "Lady Barclay, Cousin Bernard, how lovely of you to drop by. His Grace will be so pleased."

The hubbub resumed and soon approached a roar.

"Apologies," the duchess said quietly. "The duke was insistent that Society be given clear orders. I will never refer to you as Cousin Bernard again if it offends you, Mr. Huxley."

She smiled warmly through the apology, and Bernard felt once again as if he were the new fellow at the vicarage, the new fellow at the office. Everybody else spoke the local dialect. Everybody else knew one another and well understood what role he was expected to fulfill.

He, himself, was clueless.

"Any polite address will do, Your Grace." He bowed correctly over her hand. "We are not, in fact, cousins, are we?"

"Chanderton is your uncle, making me your auntie by marriage. No accounting for Mayfair marriages. Sorcha, how are the children?"

Sorcha, who still had a comfortingly firm grip on Bernard's arm, smiled just as convincingly. "Thank you for asking. I actually have some reason to be hopeful where Jordy's scholarship is concerned. He's taken to doing sums with the sort of glee my mother exhibited on the same topic. Bridget has begun sketching with the same enthusiasm."

Bridget was drawing everything she saw because her new little friend from the park was an enthusiastic artist. That some of her masterpieces were unrecognizable, and most of them had manes and tails, was no less reason to admire her efforts.

"And what of the great governess hunt?" Her Grace asked. "Any progress?"

"Why, yes," Sorcha replied. "We're re-interviewing the two best candidates from a dozen sent over by Swindon's. By this time next week, we should have new talent in the nursery."

"Delightful news. I heard about Annette's little adventure in the park, you two. Well done, the both of you, not making a mishap into a disaster, but what are we to do with a girl who cannot ride even an aging mare?"

Marry her off, apparently. The German princesses were eyeing Bernard speculatively, as were half the older women and men chatting around the drawing room. The ceiling was at least twelve feet above Bernard's head, painted with a fresco involving angels, toga-clad figures, and billowing clouds that provided the occasional touch of modesty to voluptuous nymphs.

The angels and gods seemed to be watching his every move as well.

"Annette's horsemanship will likely improve going forward," Sorcha said. "She kept her seat, and half of Hyde Park came up to congratulate her on that feat."

Oh right. In the alternative, they had trotted over to have a look at the curiosity on the skinny gray gelding.

"Let me introduce you to Lord and Lady Fitzcarruthers," the duchess said. "They have holdings in York, and they will be most pleased to meet a former neighbor."

Yorkshire being more than ten thousand square miles, of course.

Sorcha towed Bernard along. He bowed, he chatted, he missed York when it was appropriate to do so, he enjoyed Paris when that half-truth seemed called for. All the while, he was wishing himself back at the office, where Kessler had taken to muttering about his daughter's cottage in Dorset.

And Bernard was wishing himself alone with Sorcha even more.

"We have done what's required," she said after the second circuit of the room. "The buffet is across the corridor if you'd like a snack before we leave."

A snack. Well, yes. Bernard had been wishing for sustenance too. "I am famished, now that you mention it. Have I passed muster?"

"Time will tell. You spoke the King's English. You did not leer, even when you were all but invited to do so. You merited the duchess's best, most personable smile and her most familiar address. Mayfair cannot take you into dislike now without genuine provocation."

"Isn't being in trade such a provocation?"

"You are managing the Lorne family investments, according to what I overheard, and that sort of behavior is all but expected from the more obscure denizens of titled Society. The food is this way."

The food was a feast fit for princes, if not kings. The offerings included myriad sandwiches—no crusts, white bread—and tarts of every description. Sliced oranges with currants, cinnamon, walnuts, and some sort of wine sauce. Puddings, cold sliced ham, cold sliced beef, and four different cheeses. The sweets were as varied and abundant, including chocolates that might well have been imported from France.

"Don't," Sorcha said, handing him a plate.

They had the gallery to themselves.

"Don't?"

"You are thinking of every hungry child, begging soldier, and streetwalker you passed on the way here."

"And on the way to the office. They are more numerous along that route." Though the poor, the injured former soldiers, the orphans, and women trading their bodies for bread were ubiquitous in the metropolis.

"Her Grace sends the leftovers to a church in St. Giles, and she makes sure there are always abundant leftovers. Everything but the oranges can be eaten without utensils, and she'll send over a crate of oranges with the peel still on, if I'm not mistaken."

"Good to know." A relief to know. In addition to London's social and commercial puzzles, Town also posed moral conundrums. "Shall we fill you a plate?"

"See to yourself, and I'll manage on my own. The punch is safe."

Bernard selected mostly ham and cheese tarts, which had been flavored with basil and a hint of pepper. For his sweet, he took two of the chocolates. He avoided the oranges, though they looked delicious, and asked the footman to ladle him half a serving of punch.

Safe did not mean *palatable*, as any veteran of rural quarterly assemblies knew.

"Let's admire His Grace's library, shall we?" Sorcha led the way, velvet skirts swishing briskly. She'd donned an ensemble of dark green trimmed with aubergine piping and aubergine lace. The result flattered her coloring and did not in any regard resemble mourning.

The library was, above all, quiet. A rumble of conversation echoed from down the corridor, like distant cannons or thunder, but once inside the library itself, all other sounds were muted. Tall windows flanked by blue velvet curtains, thick Axminster carpets, and furniture upholstered in deep blue brocades helped deaden sound, while light suffused the whole.

Bound books in their thousands stood along darkly gleaming mahogany shelves, and a reading table of the same wood occupied the center of the room. Above, another fresco of mythical grandeur adorned the ceiling, and gilt molding encircled the whole.

More light. More incalculable wealth.

"Are we permitted to eat in such elegant surrounds?" Bernard asked.

"His Grace regularly takes a tray here when he's reading late at night. The chairs at the reading table are surprisingly comfortable."

"I will feel as if Apollo and Zeus are watching me. Might we use the alcove?"

Sorcha again led the way, and Bernard found it difficult to limit his admiration to her wardrobe choices. He positively adored her stride from any perspective. She half prowled, half conquered with each step and neither hurried nor tarried en route.

"I love the light here," Sorcha said, taking a seat in a wing chair.

"Proximity to the parks means the air isn't as sooty even in winter. I saw this room and understood Barclay a little better."

Bernard took the second chair. The alcove was out of sight of the door and of the gods flying aloft.

"You wanted *me* to see this place," he said. "The formal drawing room, the corridors with their Gainsboroughs and Lawrences, the golden molding, and gods."

Sorcha took up a tart. "Your father was raised to think this was his due, Bernard. My husband had the same expectations. Chanderton doesn't seem to take it all that seriously, but then, he's the duke, not the younger son living on an allowance and investments. Eat something."

Bernard tried the punch, which was a pleasant, cidery, spicy affair that managed to be not too awfully sweet.

"I should be at my office."

Sorcha passed him a tart from his own plate. "You should be enjoying this excellent fare. What could possibly be so troubling at the office that it distracts you from one of the grandest homes in Mayfair?"

Bernard accepted the tart. "One of the junior clerks, Heevers..." Bernard wished they'd closed the door. "*Heevers a uriné dans les bottes d'Ipswich.*"

Sorcha regarded him over her tart, and he saw the moment when she'd completed the translation. Her dark brows knit, rose, and settled.

"He *peed* on another junior clerk's boots?"

"*In* them. And the retaliation involved that evidence of canine street life referred to in the vernacular as *pure*." In Heevers's overcoat pockets.

Sorcha put down her tart, fought a visible though fleeting battle for composure, and went off into whoops.

Seeing her laugh, joy stole through Bernard. The pleasure of having lightened Lady Barclay's practical, careful Scottish heart was subtle and sweet, and he was soon smiling as well. They could laugh together, and this wondrous state of affairs convinced him, as trotting in the park and card tricks and governess interviews could not, that he had finally found the woman he was meant to love.

And perhaps, given the luminous sense of mischief in Sorcha's gaze, she could love him back, if he was very lucky, very persistent, and a little bit daring in his wooing.

CHAPTER SEVEN

Bernard Huxley flummoxed and charmed Sorcha in equal measures. Fretting about his clerks when he ought to have been rhapsodizing about some of James Thornhill's most impressive frescoes, worrying for the beggars while half of Society tried to puzzle out exactly how polite to be to the Dolforth family oddity.

The young ladies and some of the not-so-young ladies had goggled behind their fans, though Bernard had been severely oblivious to their admiring glances. He'd listened with every evidence of fascination while Lord Fitzcarruthers had maundered on about mangel-wurzels and turnips. Bernard looked politely fascinated with Lady Bloomton's advice on when a gentleman new to Town should presume to attempt the waltz.

She knew the most *excellent* dancing master, if Bernard cared to inquire of her...?

Bernard had instead made admiring comments about a bust of the present duke, whom Bernard clearly resembled. Subtle, but not so subtle that Lady Bloomton could miss the point.

"You think I have criminal tendencies?" Bernard asked, his

admiring gaze now fastened on a flaky ham-and-cheese tart. "In what regard?"

"I did not say that," Sorcha replied. "I said that Society is fortunate that you are not drawn to criminal enterprises, because you have such outstanding managerial tendencies. You are calculating, ruthless, terribly self-disciplined, and frightfully intelligent. Lady Bloomton nearly had a fit of the vapors when you so gently pointed out that you could pass for a younger version of Chanderton. She kept her dancing-master comments to herself after that."

"She was trying to be helpful. These tarts are scrumptious."

They were also disappearing at a great rate. Sorcha chose a cheese tart from her own plate. "She was trying to put you ever so subtly in her debt, such that when you did waltz, which I assume you do competently, she could take credit for your accomplishment."

"I have two functional legs, thank the generosity of heaven. Waltzing isn't complicated."

He took a sip of his punch and studied the view of the garden beyond the alcove's windows. Roses were not yet budding, though beds of purple and yellow irises made a cheerful display.

"Whatever shall I do about Heevers and Ipswich, my lady? My head clerk has given up on the boys. If we turn them off, with or without a character, we might well doom them to hopeless penury and worse. They are capable of learning the clerking trade, capable of more than that, too, very likely, but the purpose of the enterprise is not to sort out a pair of overly stubborn children as they sorely disrupt the entire business."

Bernard was not especially absorbed with having earned the favor of Her Grace of Chanderton, though Sorcha was certain he appreciated the duchess's gracious welcome. He was *worried* about his clerks, worried enough to ask for Sorcha's help.

"Tell me more about these boys. Where do they hail from?"

As the food disappeared, Bernard sketched a situation where two boys, both at the bottom of a rigid office hierarchy, both with few skills other than penmanship and ciphering, had decided to be rivals rather than allies.

"My children love each other," Sorcha said slowly. "Siblings aren't always so fortunate. One of my sisters affirmatively loathes one of our brothers. He's not overwhelmingly bright about people, though he's well-read. He's also the oldest and quite comely. He's a good sort on the whole, unless he feels attacked. Then he's insufferable."

Bernard resumed studying the irises. "I was raised mostly with a cousin for company—the late baron—and we decided early on that it was more important to be friends..." His gaze came back to Sorcha. "I see what you're saying. Lorne and I, Bridget and Jordy were thrown on each other's exclusive company. If Lorne hadn't wanted me about, or if I'd taken him into dislike, we would have had no company our own age. You are saying I should isolate Ipswich and Heevers from the other clerks."

Sorcha had not reasoned quite that far. "This is part of why I am so reluctant to consign Jordy to the tutors and public schools. Who else does Bridget have to boss about, spat with, and be challenged by? Who else does Jordy have?"

Perhaps she ought not to have admitted that, but Bernard's suggestion, that the children should spend time apart, still troubled her. He hadn't forced the issue—yet—but it was a step on the road to sending Jordy to public school, and Sorcha didn't care for that path at all.

Bernard had demolished his food, but for the two chocolates. He put one on Sorcha's plate.

"You are suggesting that I place Ipswich and Heevers in a situation that encourages a strategic alliance. I've tried separating them. That tactic resulted in widening the zone of hostilities, so to speak. Kessler—my chief clerk and commercial finishing governess—suggested a competition, but I cannot see that ending well."

"Nor can I. What is a commercial finishing governess?"

"Lorne—the present baron and younger brother of the previous titleholder—bequeathed Kessler to me when I became responsible for the businesses. Kessler explains with whom I am to have lunch, with whom I am to schedule meetings, and whether the time and place of the meeting are my choice or the other party's. Kessler knows mercantile law as no Lord Justice ever did, and he's ready to quit over the situation with the junior clerks."

"Quit? That sounds drastic."

"Retire, rather. Kessler has served loyally and well, but he never banked on having to turn a vicar into a merchant."

"As you never banked on having to turn unhappy little boys into productive clerks."

Bernard eyed the sweet left on his plate. "Or myself into a ducal relation, however—what word did you use?—obscure. To be honest, I wish I could be a bit more obscure." He popped the chocolate into his mouth and closed his eyes. "Delicious. These have to be French."

Sorcha bit into her own sweet, which managed to be buttery, rich, intensely chocolate, and creamy.

"I haven't tried these before," she said. "Do you suppose we might go back for seconds?"

"Fancy them?"

I fancy you. The thought was larger than the sort of impulsive, passing desire a chocolate drop of any sort would engender. For Sorcha, Bernard's attraction encompassed his seriousness of purpose, his kindness, his imagination, and his integrity. He *listened*, he set aside his own biases as best he could, he sought common good wherever possible. He had self-respect but no vanity, and he could laugh at himself.

If only Barclay had been able to manage the same feat.

Sorcha could respect Bernard, desire him, and—this notion accounted for much of what flummoxed her about him—*like him.* She enjoyed his company, enjoyed matching wits with him, and enjoyed simply watching him deftly navigate social shoals that had taken her years to learn.

That he would be the children's guardian was a complication, or would be once that authority had been officially vested in him.

Which might be never, given how slowly the courts moved. "Bernard?"

"Hmm?"

Sorcha kissed him. Her lips landed on the corner of his mouth, an equivocal location, resulting from a lack of practice on her part. She hadn't the confidence to move closer to the mark, though, so for a moment, nobody moved.

Then Bernard turned his head ever so slightly, cupped Sorcha's nape with a warm hand, and kissed her back. Chocolate had never tasted so marvelous.

He started off-center as well and adjusted his aim with a maddening, leisurely approach that had Sorcha on the edge of her chair, one fist anchored in his golden locks. She was melting and igniting and sparkling inside as joy and desire collided with wonder.

They bumped knees, and Sorcha felt Bernard smiling. Then he resumed his addresses in a more focused manner. She was contemplating straddling his lap when she became aware of some alteration in the world beyond the intoxicating pleasure of kissing Bernard Huxley.

She shifted back and rested her forehead on his shoulder. "Something..."

"If you apologize, I will protest in loud, broad Yorkshire. I've been wanting to do this for eons and hadn't lit upon a strategy adequate for the challenge of... Blessed botherations. Big sentences are beyond me. Please don't apologize. I adore kissing you."

Sorcha mentally batted aside a fog of equally appreciative short sentences. "I like kissing you, too, though the door..." Something about the door.

"Right." Bernard sat up. "Open. What is that racket?"

Sorcha sat up as well and sat back. Bernard had divined the disturbance Sorcha had only vaguely perceived.

"I know that racket. If you haven't met your cousin Coraline, the oversight is about to be rectified."

Bernard touched a finger to Sorcha's lips. "Cousin Coraline has miserable timing, but I suppose I should thank her. Might we discuss the weather or the price of whale oil or something equally dull?"

He was in a state. From a few kisses and caresses.

Sorcha was in a state, too, and the last thing—the very last thing—she wanted to do was part with such a delicious welter of sensations and emotions. Poetry failed, panegyrics paled.

But Bernard had asked... "We will soon need rain, though one does enjoy the sunny stretches exceedingly."

"And then," Bernard said, "one enjoys the leisure of a good old English rainy day, for lazing about and... reading newspapers."

He looked so determined.

Sorcha guffawed. "You've never lazed about and read newspapers in your life."

Bernard collected up the plates. "Perhaps you'd best fetch us some more chocolates, my lady. Even the weather isn't sufficient to return my mind to paths fit for a social outing." He sounded uncharacteristically disgruntled.

Sorcha patted his hand, rose, and quit the room, feeling equal parts smug and silly. She and Bernard had put each other in a state. He was as flummoxed as she was, and even that thought pleased her inordinately.

~

Cousin Coraline was a particular type, and Bernard did not make the mistake of underestimating her. She was tall and pretty, in a robust, blond, matronly fashion. Her coiffure was an arrangement of looping plaits, and she wore an ensemble of a flattering pale blue also adorned with gold braids.

Annette looked like the petite schoolgirl she was beside her elegant mama. Bernard suspected that result was calculated on Coraline's part: Annette was not yet *out*. To have appeared at a ducal function, however informal, sporting the latest fashion, poised and preening would have been to earn the ire of every matchmaker and hopeful young lady in Mayfair.

One played by the rules, and Coraline would well understand the rules of her fiefdom. She was like a cathedral dean or a bishop. Outside her native purlieus, she might appear supercilious or awkward, but in Mayfair's elegant drawing rooms, her dozen shining plaits and matching gold trim were of a piece with confidence and competence.

Bernard much preferred Sorcha's plainer ensemble, with its more severe cut and simpler piping. She stood beside him quietly, for which he sent up a quick, sincere prayer of gratitude.

"Cousin Bernard." Coraline offered a gloved hand, over which Bernard bowed politely. "Such a pleasure to meet you at last. Her Grace has spoken so highly of you, and Chanderton has as well."

Bernard felt Sorcha's amusement at that sally. Chanderton likely hadn't spoken directly to Coraline since Yuletide—and then only pleasantries—but Coraline would have onlookers believe she was in the duke's confidence. At the same time, she'd communicated that ducal by-blows, even legitimate ducal by-blows, had not previously figured on her guest lists.

"You flatter me, madam," Bernard said. "Delighted to make your acquaintance. Miss Greer, good day. You wear that shade of lilac quite well. Puts me in mind of spring at its best. Lady Barclay, might you complete the introductions?"

A tallish, pleasant-looking gentleman going a touch gray at the temples stood on Annette's other side. She resembled him about the eyes and mouth. The papa, no doubt, come to complete the picture of close family ties with the titled patriarch. Showing the colors to support his firstborn and to be commended for the display. He'd doubtless been a handsome blade in his youth, and he was attractive still.

"No need for formalities between familial associations," the fellow said, sticking out a hand. "Tallister Greer, Tally to friends and family, an Honorable if the hostesses are in a stickling mood."

If Annette ever learned to beam in her father's genial manner, she'd conquer Mayfair at the next formal ball.

"Bernard Huxley at your service. A pleasure, Mr. Greer."

"Call me Tally. If we were still at university, I'd be Tally-ho, of course, but that epithet was fortunately lost in the sobering mists of fatherhood. Allow me to introduce you around a bit, and if we are very clever,"—Greer leaned a few conspiratorial inches closer, and treated Bernard to a sharp whiff of rosemary shaving soap—"we can make the acquaintance of the buffet in the next quarter hour."

Bernard had no intention of being dragged into another circuit of mangel-wurzels and matchmakers, nor would he risk informalities that might result in any references to Cousin Bernie, Bern, Huxtle-berry, or the like.

"I must decline your generous offer, Greer. Lady Barclay has introduced me to the assemblage and to the magnificent buffet, and the hour advances. One has other obligations, and they do not allow one to tarry, even in such delightful company."

"I cannot hear of you leaving so soon," Coraline said. "Surely you can spare another few minutes at a casual family gathering?"

No. No, and no again. Bernard was well aware of what a lot of unsupervised clerks could get up to on a mild spring afternoon. Then too, he wanted to part from these people, the better to savor what had just passed between him and Sorcha.

She'd kissed him. Made a thorough job of the business, beguiled him witless, and given him much to think about.

Much—most of it wonderful. Then too, with the Coralines of the world, one began as one intended to go on. To accede to her direction—stay, trot dutifully around the room again, speak when directed—would be to set a pattern Bernard could not allow.

"I truly am sorry," he said. "I must be getting on. My time is not always my own, but I am usually at my leisure on Sunday afternoons

—an old habit and a pleasant one." A habit such as *former vicars* might enjoy. Former vicars who held a place of at least spiritual authority in most communities. "Might I call upon you then?"

Sorcha found it necessary to consult the watch pinned to her sleeve.

"We must have Cousin Bernard to supper on Sunday, Coraline," Greer said. "Fatted calf, all the trimmings. Sorcha dearest, you must come as well and bring the children. A true family gathering, and I will have some masculine reinforcements about the table, as well as the beauteous company of the ladies."

"Do come, Cousin," Coraline said, taking up the chorus. "Mr. Greer has made an excellent suggestion, and the girls always enjoy time spent with their younger cousins."

"I would be delighted," Bernard said. "Lady Barclay, shall I collect you and the children on my way?"

"Why not walk with us?" Sorcha said. "We're all of three streets from the Greers' abode. Jordy and Bridget will be better behaved for having a little exercise. If the weather is disobliging, the coach will serve, but let's plan on walking."

Coraline established the time, Annette took her papa's arm, and off they went to shepherd their daughter through the gauntlet of polite society's inspection.

Bernard and Sorcha took a quick leave of their hostess, gathered wraps from a strikingly handsome footman, and were soon out in the relatively fresh air.

"Shall you share my coach as far as your office?" Sorcha asked.

"I ought to walk. My thoughts are in disarray, and heaven knows what havoc Ipswich and Heevers have got up to in my absence. Do you mind very much attending Sunday supper with the Greers?"

Sorcha's coach came clip-clopping around the corner, matched chestnuts in the traces. The liveried footman hopped off the boot and set down the steps, then resumed his post a discreet dozen paces away.

"Coraline would rather I didn't intrude," Sorcha said. "Tally was just being polite for form's sake. My children are younger than hers, more boisterous. She'll want to interrogate you without me on hand to report particulars to the duchess."

Well, botheration. "You'll plead a headache?"

"Let me give you a ride to the office, Bernard. We'll turn the crests, if that's your concern."

The crests, on the coach, which identified the vehicle as belonging to Lord Barclay's widow. Those crests.

"If I get in that coach," he said quietly, "I will want to pull the shades down. For no earthly reason would I want the crests turned. I would happily let all of London know that Bernard Huxley and Lady Barclay are on very comfortable terms. We can send a few pigeons to the provinces with the same news."

Lest he carry on in a similarly bold fashion, Bernard made a production out of glancing assessingly at the sky, the grand edifices across the street, the crows strutting on the walkway.

Sorcha looked gratifyingly bashful at his declarations. Better still, she had no protests or remonstrations to offer.

"If I get into that coach," Bernard went on, "I will hope that traffic is infernally congested and that the horses can manage only an intermittent plod in the direction of my responsibilities, and still the journey will go too quickly."

He was doing his paltry best to flirt, and his efforts did not result in a naughty smile or a laughing departure. Sorcha's eyes glinted as if she was close to tears.

"Get in the coach, you dratted man. Get in the coach, and I will count the hours until Sunday afternoon."

Bernard handed Sorcha up. He followed and pulled the shades. By some gift of fate, traffic was indeed horrendously thick.

Sorcha's kisses, by contrast, were revelations wrapped in miracles, tied up with glories too astounding for mere words, even in Latin.

"That went well," Coraline said, arranging her skirts as she took her place on the coach's forward-facing seat. "Annette, you struck the perfect balance between humility to be in such august surrounds and ease among family and friends at an informal event. We must find you topics other than the weather to raise with the elders, though. They always use changing temperatures as an excuse to bring up their ailments."

"I like the elders." Annette fluffed her skirts in the exact same fashion as her mother. "They usually laugh at their ailments. They don't laugh at me."

Tallister took the backward-facing bench, though he did not care for it. He did not care for the duchess's at homes, and he was also disinclined to like the latest family sensation, Mr. Bernard Huxley.

"Cousin Bernard was quite at ease in those same august surrounds," Annette went on. "And he's not a fribble. Cousin Richard used to be a fribble, but he's put that behind him."

Tallister's oldest daughter still had one foot in the innocence of the schoolroom, for all that she occasionally came up with adult insights. The less said about Cousin Richard, who was actually a half-brother to Huxley, the better.

"At Huxley's age," Tally muttered, "playing the fribble would be quite a challenge."

"And yet," Coraline said mildly, "so many men do, from infancy, to boyhood, to fribbling in earnest, to inebriation, to senility. Mr. Huxley is cut from more admirable cloth."

He'd been cut from an altar cloth, the kind made luminous with gold threads of aristocracy, propriety, and education, if Tally's sources were to be believed. The Dolforth family good looks hadn't done the former vicar a disservice either.

"He can sit a horse," Annette said. "A real horse, not one of those prancing ninnyhammer Thoroughbreds that's happy only at a dead run."

Coraline smiled, and Tally recalled the younger version of his wife, the one who'd smiled more often and smiled *at him*. The girl he'd courted had been quietly pretty, well aware of her ducal connections, and refreshingly sensible. She'd not pored over ledgers and fashion magazines with an intensity that should have been saved for intimate moments with her spouse.

"You've become quite the equestrienne," Coraline said. "That's all to the good, of course, but do recall that the turf crowd venerates their blood horses, and plenty of dukes and earls own racing stables."

Royal dukes had nigh bankrupted themselves with their bloodstock, as had the Regent in his younger days.

"Papa, will I still be riding Cinnamon when I make my come out next year? She is getting on, and Eglantine will need to begin learning her way about the park."

The question was so earnest. "I will buy you a winged unicorn for your very own, darling girl. Apollo himself will envy you your mount."

"Papa, be serious."

"He is being serious," Coraline said. "If a new mount is necessary to see you properly launched, we'll procure one, but the question might well come down to seed pearls for the bodice of your presentation ensemble or a new mare. Those are decisions for another day, my dear. For now, be pleased with today's accomplishments. You acquitted yourself well."

Coraline had acquitted herself well too. Tally waited to compliment his wife until Annette had gone skipping up the garden's flagstone walkway like the schoolgirl she still was.

"Well done, my dear. Annette did us proud, and all because you have prepared her for these next steps."

The day was fine. The outing had gone well. Tally genuinely respected Coraline's maternal devotion and understood how serious the business of launching Annette was. He also respected the need to remain apprised of his dear wife's machinations.

"What did you think of Mr. Huxley?" Coraline asked, slipping a hand around Tally's arm and leading him toward the bench beside the sundial. The garden was small, with high walls on all sides. The air was perfumed with irises, and the quince tree in the bottom corner was just beginning to blossom.

A lovely day, and yet, Tally wished for a larger garden in which to stroll with his wife. He wished to be able to buy each of his daughters a new mare—a matched quartet, like Sorcha's matched chestnuts—and he wished Coraline was as determined on his happiness as she was on Annette's success.

"Huxley struck me," Tally said, "as a vicar whose exquisite manners are aiding him to manage a shift in circumstances that would defeat most men. He's not only left the Church, he's in trade, and his provenance is dubious. Sorcha's doing her bit for him, but then, she's nobody's fool. Huxley will soon stand in authority over her children, and she does dote on them both."

"You don't like him," Coraline said.

How had she divined the truth from a few factual sentences? "I don't know him well enough to have formed a valid opinion, but he vexes me anyway."

"He refused to adopt familiar address with you."

Tally thought back. "He called me Greer—that's informal—but you cite an example of his... superiority, I suppose. He is related to you by blood, we are family, and, setting aside his true patrimony, he is merely a baron's heir presumptive. Why not accept a friendly overture?"

Coraline plucked a sprig of blooming blue speedwell, twisted the stem off two inches below the flowers, and tucked the posey into Tally's lapel.

"Illegitimacy and that peculiar transition you mention might make him cling to decorum, or he might just be shy. Provincials can be more fixed in their manners than their sophisticated Town cousins are. Do I take it you'd object to Huxley as a suitor for Annette?"

Tally tolerated the display of wifely attention, though speedwell could leave stains as they wilted, and the only audience for her little show of domestic fealty would be the children and staff.

"Nobody is good enough for our Annette."

"Tally, I am asking because I want an honest answer. If you have taken Huxley into dislike, then I must not raise Annette's hopes where he is concerned. He is eligible, and Annette is impressed with him."

Annette was impressed with this week's fashion plates as well. "We cannot alienate him, Coraline. He is family, and Chanderton has decreed that we acknowledge him cordially."

Coraline studied the flower and nudged it more upright with a single gloved finger. "And?"

"And Vicar Huxley paid Annette a compliment because he knew we'd approve of him for that. He also knows that all of Mayfair is aware of his previous calling and will be predisposed to think well of him because of his churchly background."

"I do think well of him," Coraline said. "He was a perfect gentleman, and Annette has sense enough to recognize him as such. I was prepared for Mr. Huxley to be a very different sort of man."

Coraline's liking was a complicated gift, usually entailing some benefit to Coraline, or a lot of benefit.

"Be careful, Coraline. By rights, I should be the guardian of Sorcha's children if Chanderton doesn't want the job. I am an experienced parent. I am family. I know everybody and am accepted everywhere. I'm not some vicar-come-lately from the wrong side of the blanket and in trade as well, but the vicar was deemed worthy to supervise the upbringing of Chanderton's niece and nephew."

While I was found wanting. The conclusion stung, and Chanderton hadn't shown Tally the courtesy of offering any explanation. Age was a possibility. Huxley was nearly a decade Tally's junior, though experience as a parent ought to count for more than relative youth.

Coraline patted Tally's sleeve, a particularly annoying presumption. "Chanderton means you no insult, Husband. We have our hands full with our daughters. When suitors start cluttering up your study next spring, each of them convinced he will expire for lack of Annette's hand, you will be glad you don't also have Sorcha's little hellions to manage. The pair of them are entirely incorrigible. Barclay must be spinning in his grave."

Sorcha had given birth to a son, and sons were different from daughters. Daughters who had brothers were different from daughters who did not. Coraline, for all her many fine qualities, knew only the joys of parenting her own four princesses. Tally could not raise the point without indirectly alluding to his rambunctious indiscretions, both boys, both being raised by cousins north of the border in nurseries that included girl cousins.

Both boys were likely to be as handsome as their papa and twice as impecunious, at the rate matters were progressing.

"Dearest wife, if I must buy Annette a snow-white mare who boasts exquisite manners and an equine royal lineage, then Annette's sisters will insist on equal consideration, and that will have *me* spinning in an early grave, and a pauper's grave at that. We will be cordial to Huxley. His nominal cousin was said to be doing quite comfortably in trade, and now Huxley helms the same enterprises. He's a contriving sort. A noticing sort. I never cared for noticing sorts. They leave one no privacy."

Coraline paced off halfway to the gate and back. "You have likely landed on Chanderton's reasons for appointing Huxley guardian of those children. Lord Jerome would have made generous provisions for any son, any son at all, out of duty and pride. He certainly didn't leave Richard without means. Chanderton is pragmatic. Offending a former vicar who now has means... Chanderton would avoid that. Then too, Huxley might have left his holy post, but the Church will still acknowledge him, especially if he's well fixed. Chanderton will not offend the bishops."

Sound reasoning, though little comfort to Tally's pride. "The Church is likely pleased with Huxley—heir to a barony, tacitly received by a duke as family, of sound mind and sound finances, and he has all of his teeth." No wonder Tally disliked him. "I still can't say he's my idea of a match for Annette."

"Dearest husband, do you have any idea how much seed pearls cost? And do not think for one moment that Annette's presentation gown can be made over for Elise, Jessica, or Eglantine. Each girl must have an ensemble that shows her off to her best advantage."

Tally recognized a veiled threat when he heard one. "We are not made of money, Coraline. Far from it."

"All the more reason why we must make a very favorable impression on Cousin Bernard this Sunday."

She curtseyed, came up smiling graciously, and put Tally in the frustrating position of having been handed what he wished for. Coraline was smiling at him, but still... it wasn't the right smile. She looked, in fact, smug at her own cleverness.

"You be careful, darling wife. All of Mayfair is watching Huxley, and he's not the only bachelor in the ballroom."

"But he was the bachelor on the bridle path who saved our daughter from ridicule, he paid Annette a lovely and public compliment, and he all but invited himself to Sunday supper *en famille*, Tally. Make of that what you will."

She sashayed into the house, and Tally, as usual, let her have the last word.

The problem was, Tally wanted guardianship of at least Jordy—and thus supervisory responsibility for Jordy's funds. The solicitors would not allow him to personally touch the money, of course, but clerks could be bribed and accounts juggled when one held a position of authority. Huxley was not yet legally established as the guardian, and thus Tally still had time to maneuver.

And yet... to discredit Huxley as a guardian would mean discrediting him as a suitor as well, and Coraline showed every sign of having fixed upon the notion that Huxley was intended for Annette.

The situation called for a few hands of cards at the club, perhaps many hands. Somebody would have heard something unflattering about Huxley, more unflattering than mere illegitimacy. Tally needed to lose just the right amount to get just the right gossip so that he learned all the unflattering details lurking behind Huxley's fine tailoring and finer manners.

He jaunted back to the mews, his mood improved for having decided upon next steps that would lead to happier days for him—and for his womenfolk, too, of course.

CHAPTER EIGHT

"When Lord Lorne went north," Bernard said, "his lordship being 'the other Mr. Huxley' to you lot, he took with him all of our most experienced junior clerks."

"Himself is a baron now." Heevers rocked back and forth on his heels, clearly eager to impress Bernard with his knowledge. "He shook my hand when he left for Yorkshire and told me to guard the garrison."

"Because you had just been hired," Bernard pointed out, "and have family in London. A remove to Yorkshire would have been difficult for you."

Ipswich, hands behind his back, looked mutinous but held his peace. He was junior to Heevers in seniority and years both. Of the two, Bernard would attribute more strategy to the younger boy and more sheer bloody-mindedness to the elder. Heevers's pride had been offended, probably when Lorne hadn't included him in the batch of urchins and orphans taken north "to receive a clerk's proper education" and had then replenished the ranks with only the likes of Ipswich to help carry the load.

Nothing about an education at the vast and stately Lorne Hall, surrounded by tutors and governesses and nannies and ponies, would be considered proper for aspiring "clerks" from the gutter. Lord and Lady Lorne intended to give their dubious charges every possible advantage, including a large and genuinely loving, if highly unconventional, family.

"I can't spare either of you," Bernard said, "so you can forget about quitting Town for Yorkshire any time soon."

Two little sets of eyes eased about the corners. Two pairs of skinny shoulders relaxed. Interesting.

"I am also reluctant to part with coin the livelong day to hire porters and messengers to see to our business. The weather has relented. Both of you are London born and bred. You are to add to your duties the tasks of handling our local deliveries and collections."

Heevers scowled up at him. "We're messenger boys now?"

Give the lad credit, he was trying to look critical of the notion of spending the day more or less at liberty, scampering about London's safer districts on the company's business.

"I'm articled," Ipswich said. "You gotta train me up to clerk, not to be no messenger."

"Valid point." Bernard propped a hip against his desk and folded his arms. "What city on the whole, entire planet sees more commerce than any other three cities combined?"

"London!" Both boys answered at once.

"Which clerk is more useful to his employer—the one who knows only his own street and neighborhood, or the one who knows how far the docks are from the shops, how large a competitor's warehouse is, or how much Twinings just raised its prices for tea? Would you rather employ the fellow who knows where the stevedores, porters, joiners, or bricklayers enjoy their pints, or the man who, after five years at his desk, knows only a few pals at his local pub and plays bowls with a few more on Saturday afternoons?"

Ipswich took the bait. "Joiners favor the Brown Dog. Porters like the Hare and Harp."

"Bricklayers," Heevers added, "like the Rose and Thorns."

Bernard had exhausted his list of trade haunts in the immediate surrounds. "You take my point. A competent general knows the whole terrain, in addition to his enemies, allies, and quartermaster's stores. Lord Lorne gutted our regiment of its scouts, and you two are left to fill the whole job."

Both boys stood a little taller.

"I know London," Heevers said, chin coming up. "Town born and bred, like you said, guv'nor."

"He's *Mister Huxley.*" Ipswich punctuated the correction with an elbow to Heevers's ribs. "And I know London *and* Southwark."

"You board in Southwark 'cause it's cheaper," Heevers retorted, elbow a fraction too late to connect with its target. "The best clerks bide on this side of the river so we don't have to hike the bridges like a lot of shopgirls and dailies."

"I have always admired the quality of thrift," Bernard observed. "I have an assignment for the pair of you."

"I write faster than he does," Ipswich said.

"I write neater than him," Heevers countered.

"Then you both still have room for improvement when it comes to your penmanship, don't you? This is not a writing assignment. This is reconnaissance."

"Scouting?" Ipswich asked.

"It's French," Heevers said. "For reconnoitering."

How did Heevers know that? "This job has to do with French chocolates," Bernard said, "and lest you scoff at the subject, French chocolates are much coveted by polite society. I had some at Her Grace of Chanderton's at home earlier today, the most ambrosial little sweets you can imagine. They were the talk of the gathering, the only item on the buffet for which demand exceeded supply."

Some fine day, the terms *supply* and *demand* might loom as powerful incantations to these two. That day was apparently far in the future. Mr. Smith's *The Wealth of Nations* had yet to pique their interest, alas.

"Huxley's is planning to sell chocolates?" Heevers, who had

likely never seen, much less tasted, a chocolate drop, sounded as if the notion was ridiculous past all bearing.

Bernard adopted his most episcopal scowl. "For pity's sake, young man, keep your voice down. If the idea is profitable, and I suspect it will be, then every shop owner on the Strand will soon be selling French chocolate drops, and we'll lose any advantage our initiative might gain us."

"So what's the job?" Ipswich asked.

Bernard produced two pieces of paper on which he'd written the names of the four sweetshops most commonly patronized by Mayfair families.

"You swagger into these shops like truant schoolboys who have yet to spend your allowances. Ask for two of their most popular sweet. If the first and second shop both suggest the raspberry tart, you ask for their next most popular treat. You will sample four different sweets, do you understand?"

"We're to *eat sweets*?" Ipswich asked, sending Heevers a perplexed glance.

Yes, the guv'nor was dicked in the nob. As long as Bernard achieved a point of agreement between the warring parties, the discussion was a success.

"You are to *evaluate the competition*," Bernard replied. "Of course, the appearance of the product will carry some weight, but to render a truly informed opinion, you will have to consume the goods."

"Eat sweets," Heevers murmured. "On a Thursday."

"Only the top four sweets in all of London, forming a careful impression of each one. I will ask for your detailed assessments, gentlemen. Your final stop will be the home of the Duchess of Chanderton, and you are to deliver to Her Grace this note. You might have to wait for an answer."

They'd be shown to the servants' hall and plied with ale and sandwiches. The pair of them were too skinny by half, and tramping about Town would give them an appetite.

"We go to the sweetshops, then deliver a note," Heevers said. "That's it?"

"We *eat the sweets*," Ipswich added. "We wait for a reply."

If the duchess read the note, she'd see that each boy was given a single chocolate drop as well.

"You keep an accounting of expenditures," Bernard added, producing a few shillings. "Fancy sweets are dear. You'll have to work out the shortest route if you're to complete the whole task before the streets are thronged and the shops are sold out. We'll discuss results first thing tomorrow."

"We're to eat the sweets?" Heevers asked. "Like Ipswich said?"

"You are to evaluate the sweets, which includes consuming them when you have thoroughly inspected them for visual appeal, scent, freshness, and so forth. Any other questions?"

Not an elbow twitched.

"Then I have one final point. Any dishonor to an employee of Huxley's will be taken very seriously. I am sending you out as a pair because your safety matters to this firm. I will not be put to the inconvenience of hiring and training more junior clerks because some gang of little thugs took a notion to steal your clothes. You sally forth as a twosome for safety and because two heads are better than one. Should either one of you come to harm, get lost, or run afoul of the miscreants lurking all over this metropolis, the other is to notify me immediately."

"Get help?"

"Set up the hue and cry, summon the watch. Champion your fallen comrade as if he's the last of the regiment and you his only hope."

Both boys turned baffled expressions on Bernard. Perhaps the military metaphors had limits.

"*You look out for your mate*," Bernard thundered, in his Wrath of Yorkshire voice, which generally only impressed children between the ages of four and six. "London is dangerous. Keep your eyes and ears open, get the job done without frolics or detours, and no matter what, *stick together*."

Heevers nodded. "And eat the sweets. Got it, guv. C'mon, Switch. We'll start off on Park Lane." He grabbed Ipswich by the elbow and headed for the door.

Ipswich snatched his arm back. "We'll start on Oxford Street. That's closer, and we can do Park Lane second."

They argued their way off the premises, though no blows were exchanged, while Bernard watched them bustling out onto the busy street.

"Will we see them again?" Kessler asked, bringing a stack of correspondence to Bernard's desk.

"Most assuredly, and they might even settle down to some productive work," Bernard said. "They were afraid."

"Afraid of being sacked?"

"That, too, but mostly afraid of being sent north, far from everything they know and anybody who loves them, like all the other junior clerks. They are under articles. We could have sent them anywhere we pleased, and they'd have had to go. I suppose, in their boyish minds, being sacked was better than being banished two hundred miles into the countryside. Or maybe they figured that poor performance would spare them the honor of a trip to Lorne Hall."

Kessler frowned at the pile of letters, which measured at least three inches in height. "Logical, I grant you. Farfetched, but logical, in the manner that boys aspire to logic. Shall we begin on the letters?"

"I'll make notes, and you can start on them in the morning. What's your favorite sweet, Kessler?"

His rheumy eyes became animated. "I do fancy my daughter's currant buns, sir. She makes them with this honey-butter glaze and lets the dough rise twice. You taste heavenly fare when you bite into one, and I vow, they are half the reason her spouse begged me for her hand."

"Ask her to bake up a few batches for the clerks," Bernard said. "We'll compensate her for her time and the ingredients. A Monday morning treat to start the week off on a nutritious note, and she's not to spare the spices."

Kessler's bushy brows rose. "If you say so, sir."

"Ask her. She's doubtless a busy lady, but we must find some way to keep our clerks thinking of their jobs and not of springtime's other distractions."

"True, sir. Unusual perspective, but true. Might I inquire as to your favorite treat, Mr. Huxley?"

Bernard returned to his desk and to the pile of letters. "I'd have to give the matter some thought. Until tomorrow, Kessler."

Kessler paused in the doorway. "Sir, I would never have deduced why Heevers and Ipswich were behaving so badly. You must not chastise yourself for needing some time to puzzle it out."

"Thank you, Kessler, but it's also true all the evidence was right before my eyes, and I simply did not put it together. We won't have immediate peace on all fronts, but the pair of them should soon be content with verbal sniping and insults going forth. Ipswich has a nickname—Switch—and that's a start."

"Very good, sir."

Bernard was halfway through his letters before he permitted himself a break. Darkness was on the way—the daylight was lengthening week by week, and the hour was no longer early.

He'd been less than honest with Kessler. Bernard knew exactly what his favorite sweet was. He'd also given *the matter* a very great deal of thought.

A kiss shared with Sorcha, flavored with chocolate, joy, desire, and hope. That was his favorite treat in the whole world, and he suspected it always would be.

"If this coach goes any slower, I shall scream." Sorcha spoke in French to avoid alarming the children.

"The coachman doesn't want to make the situation any worse," Bernard replied in the same language. "*Si les enfants vomissent...*"

If the children vomit... "They might feel better." Sorcha finished the thought as Bridget moaned beside her. "I cannot imagine them feeling worse. Ask John Coachman for the trot, please."

The coach was well sprung, but the increased movement did, indeed, inspire Jordy to cast up his accounts. Fortunately, Bernard had lifted the boy from the bench and out onto the walkway before the coach had even halted.

Jordy returned to the coach as white as apple blossoms, Bernard's handkerchief in his hand.

"I am never eating raspberry fool again." He climbed onto the seat and budged up to Sorcha's free side. "Vile, hateful business. Nobody should eat it."

"I'm not eating it either." Bridget's voice was barely above a whisper.

Bernard took the backward-facing bench as the coach rolled forward. "More for me, then. I ate a large helping, and I'm not ill. Your mother is quite in the pink as well. What else did you eat besides the raspberry fool?"

"Ham," Jordy said. "Too salty. Potatoes. Not enough butter. Those ghastly beans that stink like wine. I ate two bites because Mama says I must. The beans were awful, and I don't want to talk about food."

"Mama." Bridget's hand flew to her mouth.

Bernard reacted before Sorcha could. He thumped the coach roof with his right fist, gathered Bridget up under his left arm, and once again vaulted to the walkway with a heaving child.

"Will Bridget get better, Mama?" Jordy sounded very small and scared.

"You will both recover. Did you and Bridget eat something you shouldn't have? Licorice drops in the nursery, perhaps?" A whole bag of licorice drops?

"No, Mama. We were polite. We wanted Cousin Bernard to see

our good manners. Even when stupid Eglantine started reciting her stupid poetry, we were polite."

The poetry had been ridiculous, but then, it had been written by a fanciful girl who was watching her even more fanciful older sister become the center of the family's entire orbit.

Bernard stuck his head in the door. "Have we another handkerchief?"

Sorcha passed hers over. "Thank you."

"Happy to be of service."

He meant that. He was nearly cheerful under circumstances that would have sent Barclay howling to his club. The children had done well upon arriving at the Greer residence, first disappearing up to the schoolroom with Jessica, the cousin for whom Sorcha took the most genuine liking. Jessica was neither vain nor foolish, though she was occasionally plainspoken to a fault.

Jordy and Bridget had made a good show at the table, too, until the dessert course.

Bernard handed a pale Bridget into the coach.

"Mama, I want to die. Everybody saw me be sick."

"They saw me too." Jordy was clearly trying to be helpful. "We *are* sick, Bridge. We can't help it if Cousin Coraline's cook should be sacked."

"Coraline said we got overexcited," Bridget retorted. "Annette said so, too, and so did Cousin Tally. I am not excited. I am especially, doubly, *not* overexcited."

Bernard took the backward bench, and Bridget did as well. She scooted and fussed and wiggled until she'd affixed herself to Bernard's side. He tucked an arm around her shoulders, and she settled on a sigh.

"Have we any water in this vehicle?" Bernard asked. "A few sips apiece for the afflicted wouldn't go amiss."

"I'm thirsty." Jordy rubbed his eyes with his fists. "And I hate raspberry fool."

Sorcha opened a panel beneath the coach window. "Water. Sips only, children, or the neighbors will be treated to more digestive drama *en plein air*."

She handed Bernard the flask. He uncorked it and offered a drink to Bridget.

"Three sips only, Miss Dolforth, or there will be consequences."

Bridget smiled weakly, sipped, and passed him back the flask. He wiped the mouth with Sorcha's handkerchief and extended the vessel to Jordy.

"Why do I have to drink after Bridget?"

"Because you are a gentleman," Bernard said, "and the ladies go first. You can decline to drink, if you'd rather not."

Said so blandly that it *almost* wasn't a challenge. Jordy drank.

"Would my lady care for something stronger?" Bernard had produced another flask, pewter, dented, not exactly sparkling.

"No, thank you, but feel free to indulge. We can set you down at your house, if you like." She made the offer reluctantly. The children had become so ill so suddenly, and Bernard had simply... coped. Called for the coach, thanked the Greers for their hospitality, declared the meal superb and the company delightful, and then he'd handed Sorcha and the children into the coach.

And climbed right in with them.

"No need to take me home. I will see the invalids to the infirmary, if you don't mind. You're still feeling quite the thing?"

"In the pink, as noted. You?"

"Same. Do the children often take ill this way?"

"We don't," Bridget replied. "We are healthy as horses. Gilchrist says so all the time."

"We were sick at Mirobello, Bridge. You first, then me. We vomited then too. Gilchrist said we ate too many sweets, but we didn't. Cousin Tally called us shoats, and that means pigs, and it's not a nice name."

Bridget turned her face against Bernard's arm. "I'm tired."

"Almost home," Sorcha said as Jordy yawned. His color was

coming back, but both he and Bridget would probably benefit from a nap.

Bernard scooped Bridget into his lap, and when the coach clattered into the mews, he simply carried her into the house and up the steps to the nursery.

"Can you carry me, Mama?" Jordy asked, trundling into the house hand in hand with Sorcha.

Sorcha could, but truth be told, she wasn't exactly, entirely in the pink after all. "I'd drop you on the steps, and then you'd have bruises to go with your sour tummy. You have had the audacity to grow up on me. Not well done of you, sir."

"I'm not *all* grown up."

But you will be soon. "When you are *all* grown up, you will carry me up the steps, because I will be a little old lady wobbling about with my canes."

"You might be old, Mama, but you cannot be little again. That part is over."

Sorcha would have said several parts of her life were over, and yet...

They reached the nursery floor, the climb more taxing than Sorcha preferred to admit. Bernard and Bridget were already in the playroom, which, in honor of the Sabbath, was as neat as Sorcha imagined Bernard's dressing closet would be.

"I shall have a lie-down," Bridget said, sounding exactly like Annette in a missish moment. "I'm exhausted. Where's Gilchrist?"

"It's Sunday." Sorcha untied the bow at the back of Bridget's pinafore and undid half a dozen buttons. "Gilchrist is enjoying a well-deserved afternoon of rest. Jordy, a short nap will do you good too."

Jordy got down a book from the shelves by the window. "I'm not tired."

Bernard plucked the volume from Jordy's hand. "The patient is recovering. Get into your nightshirt, young man, and I will read a few pages of this stirring volume while you prove to us how not tired you are."

"Those are just fables."

Bernard made a face. "So I see. Not a naughty dragon in the lot. We will somehow contrive nonetheless. Nightshirt, sir, and use your toothpowder for good measure."

Just like that, Jordy trooped off to his room, Bridget disappeared into hers, and Sorcha was left alone with Bernard.

He wrapped his arms around her, kissed her forehead, and let her simply rest in his embrace. The sheer comfort, the pleasure... and she hadn't even had to ask.

"Fear not, my lady. They will be shooting about the nursery like Congreve rockets after a short rest."

"They probably did get overly excited. They like Jessica. She'll play hide-and-seek with them, and she tells them tales of haunted ruins. Why am I so tired?"

"Because you didn't sleep well last night, fretting over the stupid Sunday dinner, as did I. Now I sound like Jordy."

He stepped back, and Sorcha let him go. "I'll read to Bridget," she said, "if you'll read to Jordy. My impromptu dragons pale compared to yours."

"Three pages, no more, and then we are having a digestif to settle our nerves."

"Two pages," Sorcha said, "and a wee dram." Or not so wee.

They shared a smile that was partly humor and partly mutual fortification. Not the sort of smile Sorcha had ever shared with Barclay, or with anybody else, for that matter.

She arrived at her assigned post in Bridget's room to find the child half asleep atop the covers. Bridget went unresisting into her nightgown and from there to the arms of Morpheus. Sorcha poured a glass of water and set it on the bedside table, then returned to the playroom, where she could hear Bernard expounding on the days when even jungles had had a proper complement of dragons.

The urge to weep ambushed her as she dropped into the wing chair, though no immediate cause for sadness came to mind.

Bernard's voice grew quieter, a masculine murmur calculated to soothe an upset boy to sleep.

I could fall in love with that sound. Somebody should have fallen in love with it, and with the selflessness of a man who'd make up tales for the amusement of small children and spend his Sunday afternoon playing nursemaid simply because that was the helpful thing to do.

He sauntered into the playroom, shelved the book, and took the second wing chair. "Bridget's asleep?" he asked.

"Sound asleep. Jordy?"

"Same. Are they prone to these sorts of ailments?"

"Probably no more than any other pair of lively children. Sunday supper at the Greers' is heady stuff for them. Thank you."

He peered at her. "For?"

"For being a better nanny than their own nursemaid can sometimes be. For leaping in when another man, even another mother, would likely have left me to deal as best I could."

"You would have coped splendidly."

"I am tired of coping splendidly." Tired enough to not guard her words apparently. "Perhaps I need a nap. I find the Greers something of a challenge myself." Though how much of that challenge was because, for the past several years, Sorcha had been the widowed auntie rather than Lord Barclay's wife? The family dinners hadn't started until after Barclay's demise.

"Coraline enjoys great confidence in her opinions," Bernard observed, "and the three oldest daughters appear to take after their mama. One has some sympathy for Tallister, being surrounded by all that feminine expertise. He was a very helpful host, though. I recall my own father making a little production out of bringing the ham forth from the kitchen. Imagine what their Sunday suppers will be like in ten years."

The same overly salted meat, the same bungled French sauce for the beans. Hairy-cot vairts, to hear Eglantine's version. Coraline instructing her daughters on how to manage her granddaughters...

"The mind boggles. I suppose I'd best apprise Gilchrist of the day's developments." The wing chair was growing seductively comfortable, and the urge to weep was fading.

The Sunday suppers were a fairly recent development because Barclay would have never consented to Sunday supper *en famille* with the Greers. He would have insisted on Gilchrist accompanying the children to any destination, even on the Sabbath. He would have found every reason to hold Sorcha responsible when the children were under the weather.

He'd been a nasty, insecure husband once Jordy had arrived, unworthy of the vows Sorcha had taken in all good faith.

"You look vexed," Bernard said. "I can find Gilchrist on my way out, and you can grab forty winks in that ever-so-comfy chair."

Sorcha was vexed, and to simply acknowledge that was a curious relief. "I am vexed by the memories of past disappointments. Why are you so nice?" Even Barclay had been able to manufacture agreeableness while playing the part of a suitor.

"I am not so nice. Vicars are supposed to be kindly because compassion is a virtue. In truth, comporting oneself with some consideration for others tends to make for fewer fistfights and duels, even of the churchyard and committee meeting variety. Lorne would say taking the decent path is good for business, and he'd be right in almost any context."

"If more men adhered to that view, there would also be a deuced sight fewer unhappy brides, Mr. Huxley." *I should have never married Lord Barclay Dolforth.* Sorcha managed to keep that part to herself, but the sentiment—long suppressed, never expressed—now felt like a simple statement of fact.

"You speak from experience. I'm sorry."

Sorcha pushed to her feet. "Let's find that wee dram, shall we? I'll ask Gilchrist to wake the children in an hour or so. We can use that hour to toast Coraline's faultless expertise regarding every possible topic and Annette's stated desire to take Mayfair by storm."

Bernard rose. "A fine plan, appealing in every particular, but might I kiss you first?"

Lord Barclay had never had the basic gentlemanly sense to ask a question like that, ever. "We'll kiss each other, and to borrow from the Scottish play, damned be him who first cries, 'Enough.'"

CHAPTER NINE

"The children fell ill," Chanderton said, pouring out two cups. "Tummy troubles. One is inclined to blame the company at the Greer table, but then one would sound churlish. Brandy, my dear?"

"Please, and two chocolate drops." They were Lilly's guilty pleasure—one of her several guilty pleasures. "Have the children recovered?"

"Apparently so. Gilchrist reports no cause for alarm." His Grace poured two servings at the sideboard, brought them over to the hearth, and returned with a plate of chocolate drops. "One hopes Coraline hasn't been reduced to hiring an incompetent cook."

He took his chair heavily, in the manner of an older man feeling the weight of another long week in the offing after a series of long weeks. Why Parliament had to sit during the busiest social season of the year was a mystery no Mayfair hostess had solved.

"Coraline's cook is no more French than I am," Lilly said, "but she's been on the job for at least five years and never a whisper about her capabilities. Young children do not handle rich fare easily, I'm told."

Chanderton passed her the brandy glass. "To your health, Madam Duchess."

"And yours, Your Grace." She nosed her drink as Chanderton had taught her to. Apples, nutmeg, honey, perhaps. A cidery, autumnal combination, but suitable for a spring evening going chilly.

"What is your impression of Mr. Huxley, Duchess?"

A complicated matter, like the fragrance of the brandy. "He is nobody's fool. One suspects that he's somehow already capable of handling Mayfair ballrooms, though his education to date has been exclusively in Yorkshire churchyards."

"And Oxford, where he took firsts." Chanderton sipped. "Not afraid to apply his mind."

Lilly would have bet her workbasket that His Grace was refraining from one of his most heartfelt laments. *Young men today. Lazy, pleasure-seeking, overindulged dimwits, the lot of them, interested only in vice and wagering.*

That most of the young men Chandy knew had come from long lines of lazy, pleasure-seeking dimwits was Lilly's usual retort.

"Do you like Mr. Huxley?" Chanderton asked, holding up the plate of chocolate drops.

Lilly took one. "I can't say I like him, precisely. He's like a handsome racing colt. Delightful to watch when exerting himself in pursuit of victory, a testament to the Creator's skill and all that, but the other jockeys will resent him, and then speed alone won't save him."

"Right. He'll need guile and guts. Lorne has both, and Lorne loves those businesses like a cat with one kitten loves her offspring. Camden Huxley would not have entrusted his mercantile kittens to a fool."

The chocolate was just right. Smooth, rich, sweet, and ever so slightly abrasive. "But what sort of vicar steps into busy commercial concerns like that and acquits himself knowledgeably?"

"One who pays attention, asks questions, and relies on old Kessler to steer him straight. Where did we get this brandy?"

"Huxley sent it over on Friday, a thank-you for my hospitality. I like it. He also made inquiries regarding the chocolate drops and asked that I treat his messengers to one sample each."

Chanderton popped a sweet into his mouth. "Odd behavior. Messengers, plural?"

"According to Martin, two skinny, albeit clean, boys. They ate everything Cook put in front of them, down to the last crumb."

"Keeping up the Huxley tradition, then." Chanderton chased his treat with a sip of brandy. "Do you *trust* Huxley, Lillian?"

Chanderton so rarely used her name. *My dear, Duchess, darling wife...* The question was serious.

"I do. He plays the handsome-bachelor part, but he can sort motives and tactics all while bowing over a lady's hand. He is currying favor with the Greers, and they with him, but he's keeping Sorcha at his side to ensure the whole business remains on family footing. Sorcha, who does not suffer fools or the near occasion thereof, is abetting him."

"Ye devils in training. Has Annette set her cap for Huxley already? I heard about that business in the park with her mare."

"Better to ask if Coraline or Tally have set Annette's cap for him. Annette is growing into exactly the sort of young lady I dread."

Chanderton rose to toss another square of peat on the fire. If Lilly loved anything about him—and she loved much about her husband—it was his lack of pretension. Chanderton could play the duke and even enjoyed playing the duke on public occasions, but he was at heart just a man trying to safeguard a family legacy, and do his bit to safeguard Merry Olde, while being a friend to his wife and mankind.

His sorrows were private, his dignity never allowed to lapse into arrogance. He was considered old-fashioned rather than stodgy. Respected, pragmatic, and even genial within the limits of his station.

"Please, dear duchess, do not tell me Annette is planning to become an original? Even for Coraline, that would be ambitious."

Lilly thought back to Thursday, to Annette giggling at Count von

Hauptman, simpering before Lord Peaskip, and listening with a rapturous gaze to Lady Daunton's description of a new bonnet.

"Annette is a spoiled little schemer," Lillian said at length. "She comes by her traits honestly on both sides. If that's the worst charge I can lay at her feet, she'll manage splendidly next spring. How is your hip?"

"My hip protests the idiot benches in Parliament, but I will be damned if I will bring myself extra cushions while old Moreland sits in the next row up as spry as an organ grinder's monkey."

Lilly lifted her glass in her husband's direction. "The honor of the house and all that."

The pride of the Dolforths, rather. His Grace of Moreland was not only of an age with Chanderton, and possessed of an older title, he had also sired ten children. Eight were extant, three of them strapping sons, albeit one on the wrong side of the blanket. The succession was in better repair by the year, and Esther, Her Grace of Moreland, was said to wield more influence in Society than her husband did in any realm.

"Shall I suggest that Moreland's duchess include Bernard on a guest list or two?" Lilly asked.

"I like that idea. If he's to be Jordy's guardian, then we mustn't spare the horses."

Why? What was so imperative about putting Bernard Huxley in charge of two small children?

"Chanderton, is there something you haven't told me that you should tell me?" Something relating to chest pains or worsening megrims or relentless indigestion? The Dolforth men were not particularly long-lived.

He patted her hand. "You mustn't worry. My perspective always grows jaundiced when Almack's opens its doors. Will you have another chocolate?"

He was changing the subject and not even bothering to be subtle about it. "You don't care for Tally, do you?"

"Never have, and that's no secret. He's Scottish by birth and trying to pass for English. Why do that? The Scots have a long, proud heritage, and plaid is becoming all the rage. Tally is lazy, charming, and awash in daughters he cannot properly dower. His solution to this problem so far has been to allow Coraline to bankrupt him while trying to launch Annette in hopes she will marry money."

Well, yes, but what else was Tally to do? "He puts on Englishness because Coraline expects it of him. She doesn't want Annette marrying some bumpkin lord of Parliament down from the Western Isles." Lilly took a second chocolate from the proffered plate. "What do we hear from Richard?"

"Kicking his heels out in Hampshire, dodging matchmakers, no doubt. Better than dodging creditors or angry papas, I suppose. Hard to believe he and Huxley are half-brothers."

"They bear a resemblance, though. A family resemblance. You should alert Richard to Huxley's arrival in Town."

Chanderton sighed and leaned his head back against the upholstery. "Suppose I ought. A courtesy. Does Huxley know he has a half-brother?"

"You should ask him. He hacks out on fine mornings and prefers Hyde Park's more obscure bridle paths."

Chanderton fetched the decanter and refreshed his drink. He wasn't moving with any particular stiffness yet, but by June, he'd be nearly hobbling.

"You write to Richard," he said. "Remind him that Duchess's Day is in the offing. I will contrive to meet Bernard at an ungodly hour to exchange pleasantries out of earshot of the gossips. Gilchrist said Mr. Huxley was the soul of assistance when the children were ailing earlier today. Upset tummies are not for the faint of heart."

"Vicars spend endless hours in sickrooms. One would not have thought that a useful skill for a Mayfair merchant. Shall I leave you to your newspapers?"

"If you must. You'll write to Richard soon?"

Chanderton was worried about something having to do with

Lord Jerome's offspring, Sorcha's children, or Tally's finances. *Uneasy lies the head...*

"I will write to Richard before I retire and leave the note on your blotter in case you want to add the ducal imprimatur. I will invite both Richard and Bernard to Duchess's Day and see that they cross paths on friendly terrain."

"Doubtless a sound notion, lest the gossips get their oars in first. I do adore you, Duchess."

Lilly rose, kissed her husband's cheek, and smoothed a hand over his shoulder. "The feeling is mutual. The best day of my life was the day I accepted your suit." Also the saddest day, which ripped at her still.

"You are too kind. Sweet dreams, my dear. I will give your regards to Huxley when next he and I meet, no matter how ridiculously early the hour."

Lilly took her leave of His Grace, knowing he would be awake until the small hours with newspapers, draft bills, and correspondence. A few short hours of sleep, and he'd be in the park, pretending that time on horseback had no impact on a dodgy hip.

Men, and dukes in particular, were a vexatious lot on a good day.

~

A vicar learned to live with fatigue.

Between sickrooms, Sunday services, funerals, baptisms, weddings, and the squabbles and travels engendered by all those holy undertakings, any parson's schedule was often characterized by little sleep and too many miles out in the elements.

Bernard would have given much to resume the mere tiredness known to clergy. Keeping matters in the office moving forward, accepting invitations for this ridotto or that card party, and managing the occasional letter to Lorne Hall seemed to require twenty-seven hours a day.

To say nothing of hacks in the park, beefsteak dinners with this or that business associate, meetings that had no apparent point or end...

The business required vast amounts of time and energy, when the only place Bernard truly wanted to be was with Sorcha.

"Her Grace of Moreland has invited me to a Venetian breakfast," he said, joining Sorcha on her coach's forward-facing bench. "What, I ask you, is so lacking about a good old English meal of steak, eggs, and toast that we must take the meal out of doors and garnish the occasion with fashionable attire, a groaning board where the buffet should be, as well as gossip and a string quartet?"

Sorcha took off his hat and put it on the opposite bench. "Her Grace of Moreland sits atop Mayfair's version of Olympus, Bernard. You will attend her breakfast, be your amiable self in every direction, and take your leave only after others of higher rank have begun the exodus."

Bernard pulled off his gloves and draped them over the brim of his hat. "I never sought to break bread with goddesses. How long will you allow the children to ride up on the box?" They had merely waved to him, too excited on their lofty perch to observe social niceties.

And may dear John Coachman be rewarded with a long and happy life too.

Sorcha was looking luscious in a walking dress of some raspberry-colored lightweight material. Her bonnet sat on the opposite bench as well, a simple straw hat suitable for the afternoon's outing to the countryside.

"I am remiss," Bernard said, taking her hand. "Lady Barclay, greetings. I have been looking very much forward to this excursion." Because the shades were up, he did not kiss her.

But, oh, he wanted to. Wanted to kiss her until he forgot all about the dunning notice from Ruskin and Peach invoicing an enormous sum for goods that had never arrived at the Huxley warehouse. Forgot about the fragile truce between Ipswich and Heevers. Forgot about a meeting Kessler had arranged with a Monsieur

Fournier, the London expert on all French libations—the legal ones, anyway.

"I always look forward to time spent at Mirobello," Sorcha replied, slipping an arm around Bernard's waist. "The children will stay on the box until we're through most of the turnpikes. They don't care to be beside John Coachman when we cross the bridge. To be that high above the water makes them uneasy."

Bernard pulled down the shades, looped an arm around Sorcha's shoulders, and sent up a prayer of thanksgiving. Just to be beside her, to hear her voice, quieted a tension that inevitably followed him from the offices of Huxley and Company. The first little orison was shortly followed by a request to a benevolent Deity for stamina.

"I lack the bottom for London hours," he said, resting his cheek against her crown and breathing in the scent of jasmine. Such a light scent for such a formidable woman. "Apologies if the result is poor company and dull conversation. Kessler assures me the Season always exhausted Camden, too, and June will see the pace slow considerably."

"Town will turn blessedly dull as the weather grows warm. Go ahead and nap, Bernard. You look all in, and you can't enjoy an afternoon in the country if you're dead on your feet."

"I have missed you terribly." He'd seen her three nights ago, at some card party or other, but they'd exchanged no more than pleasantries, and that still bothered him. "The children continue to enjoy good health?"

The sour tummies had been five days ago. Bernard had barely enjoyed a proper meal since.

"Exceedingly good health. Entwhistle reports that Jordy is a genius with sums, and the new governess starts Monday. Gilchrist tries to appear indifferent, but she nonetheless exudes a hopeful air."

"You are hopeful." Luminous with private joy.

"I am, and now we are to have the whole afternoon in the quiet and fresh air at Mirobello. I always enjoy time spent here, and the children do too."

The children had earned this outing with good behavior. Bernard had earned the respite by almost catching up on his correspondence, rescheduling two meetings, and sending regrets to Lady Bloomton's soiree.

"Do you own Mirobello outright?" he asked.

"The property came to me as part of my settlements. I own it now, though the finances for it all run through a trust of some sort. I maintain the property for any in the family who'd like a rural respite. Her Grace occasionally entertains at Mirobello because of its proximity to London."

"And the Greers enjoy Mirobello's hospitality."

"You say that as if they're becoming something of a problem."

Bernard kissed Sorcha's knuckles. "I believe it to be the province of family to dwell in the space between blessing and burden. Annette and one or the other of her parents are apparently fascinated with my morning hacks. She fails to accost me only if rain is threatening."

"Oh dear."

"You laugh, but Greer himself has turned up at a club I thought was reserved for Society's marginal bachelors, and my ears might be deceiving me, but I suspect Greer is seeking investment advice. The other fellows at The Marches seem to think so, too, if their pitying glances are any indication."

"Four daughters, Bernard. Have mercy upon the man. Compassion is a virtue, I'm told."

For that remark, and for the smirk accompanying it, Bernard kissed her. What started off as a buss to the cheek soon became a tussle of wills, and at least one part of Bernard threw off the shackles of exhaustion in anticipation of vigorous and delightful activity.

"I am so naughty," Sorcha said, easing away and sounding delighted with herself. "I have plans for you, Mr. Huxley, and they threaten to part me from common sense."

Between desire ready to riot, Bridget bellowing, "Stand and deliver," at the top of her lungs, and residual befuddlement from too many hours at his desk, Bernard plucked an item that had been hovering at the top of his mental agenda.

"You seek to have your way with me?" he asked.

Sorcha's glee dimmed. "I hope the way-having is a mutual undertaking, but yes. If the afternoon goes as planned, we'll have some privacy, and I do harbor aspirations."

Bernard had been hoping, too, in a distracted, abstracted, how-does-one-actually sort of way.

"What is it my lady hopes for, besides the obvious?"

Sorcha sat up and raised the shade on her side, which revealed a sparkling view of the river between increasingly sparse buildings.

"Bernard, are you asking my intentions toward you?"

Direct speech. Also brave speech. "I am. I have been so smitten that I have not taken the time to ensure our intentions lead to the same destination." Had not wanted to take that time.

Bernard was tired to the point of incoherence, the moment was all wrong for a philosophical digression, and Sorcha was looking peevish instead of pleased.

"Forget I said anything." He laced his fingers with hers. "My thinking is muddled, and I am on unfamiliar ground on every hand. We will have the pleasant afternoon you've wished for us, and..."

"And?"

And he did not want to be a widow's tawdry little diversion. Sorcha had given him no indication his role would be limited to a frolic, but neither had they discussed the future. The vicar had been taken out of the Church, but...

Frolicking appealed, strongly, though Bernard was sure in his bones that mere frolicking would come with regrets, too, for him at least.

Carpe momentum. "And I am asking your ladyship's permission to embark on a courtship. We are growing close in the manner of friends, kissing in a manner that goes beyond friendly, and I esteem you mightily. Do I have your permission to pursue an engagement to be married to you?"

St. Didier would tell him he was getting above his illegitimate, commercial, bumpkin station. Camden, though, would applaud a path supported by instinct and ambition, and also by the yearnings of Bernard's heart.

"You wish to marry me?" Sorcha gave away nothing with the question. Not amusement, offense, curiosity. Nothing.

"I believe we would suit. I am asking for your permission to investigate the possibility."

"I did not see this coming." And the lady was clearly less than delighted with the prospect of a courtship.

"Neither did I." Bernard had thought about a life with Sorcha and the children, dreamed about it, and let his wishes grow wings and fill his imagination, but the matter wanted frank talk and clear understandings.

"Barclay never asked me," Sorcha said, studying their joined hands. "The solicitors started meeting, the documents were drawn up, and I was not consulted."

"I am not consulting you either," Bernard said slowly. "I am making a request, and you must answer in whatever honest fashion suits you. The decision, my lady, is yours."

She was silent for so long that Bernard wondered if she was about to order John Coachman to turn the vehicle around. Then she subsided against Bernard, her posture having nothing of flirtation about it.

"Courtship," she said, relaxing against him as one very weary sank against a safe haven. "Courtship. Only you, Bernard, and my answer is a tentative yes. I make no promises—the besotted fog has been blowing in my direction as well—but to courtship, I can say yes."

Tentative wasn't good. "Despite winning free of Lord Barclay, memories of a sour marriage still haunt you."

"Barclay threatened at one point to have me committed to an asylum. I needed more time after Jordy was born. Barclay was insistent. I tried to be insistent, too, and I failed to carry my point. He gave me a fortnight longer, grudgingly. In hindsight, I suspect Barclay's urgency was driven by harbingers of failing health.

"Bridget's delivery was hellish," Sorcha went on. "She came out in the wrong position, and I thought the bleeding would never stop. I've wondered if that was because she was conceived too soon after Jordy. The midwives say not, but I still have my doubts."

Sorcha wasn't merely angry at her late husband, the damned man had frightened her, physically disrespected her, and utterly broken her trust.

The damned man had also gone to his eternal reward.

"And yet, you have given me permission to court you."

"Tentatively. Please be reminded that I am not all that keen on having you for the children's guardian. That is not an objection to you personally, but to anybody else having control over my offspring. If I marry you, you will become even more of an authority over me than if you were *my* guardian. I don't like that part at all, Bernard."

What woman of sense would willingly agree to become her husband's chattel? Rather than attempt that thicket, Bernard chose figurative retreat.

"Why not defer your decision until later?" he asked. "Take your time, think the matter over, and withhold judgment for now?"

He was not a horse on offer at Tatts, and yet... Sorcha had been badly thrown by Lord Barclay's inconsideration.

"You wouldn't approve of a passing dalliance," she said. "Neither would I. You have permission to court me, Bernard. Just don't assume we are engaged, or that we have an understanding, or that I'm merely delaying an inevitable capitulation."

Was she protesting too much? While the coach rattled onward, Bernard recalled that Sorcha had come to London as a girl, been more or less thrust into Lord Barclay's unloving arms, and endured a marriage to a man who'd expected her to risk her life for his family's succession.

Since then, she'd been circumspect, if not quite reclusive. She was entitled to her skepticism. Bernard, by contrast, felt entitled to his optimism.

They would suit. They *did* suit. She'd had plans for him even before they'd embarked on this awkward conversation.

"We are courting, then," he said. "That's... that's marvelous." A relief, really, putting Bernard on the path to the most wondrous sort of new terrain.

He kissed her, tasting tentative pleasure from his intended. They were not engaged—yet. He'd made his intentions clear to her. She was allowing him to proceed.

The rest was a matter of being patient—he was good at that—and *not bungling.*

When Sorcha sighed and snuggled up against him, Bernard fell into a sort of reverie. Not sleep—more like waking dreams. Happy years, a noisy house, ponies, trips north...

He was mentally composing his proposal speech—brief, a touch of wit, a generous helping of sincerity—when a pair of juvenile highwaymen invaded the coach. They brandished fearsome finger pistols and threatened their hapless victims with riotous giggles.

"Your sweet buns or your life!"

Refreshed by his respite, and by the prospect of a thoroughly enjoyable afternoon, Bernard subdued the brigands with an impromptu story about a swimming unicorn who could tickle unsuspecting mermaids with his horn.

Bridget was soon expressing a determination to learn to swim, while Jordy preferred to learn to fly. Sorcha endured two coughing fits while Bernard spun his narrative blather.

For his part, he wished he had more facility with poetry and pretty words, though maybe, with Sorcha, it wouldn't be that sort of courtship.

A man truly could hope, after all. Hope and dream.

CHAPTER TEN

As soon as Bernard had climbed into the coach, Sorcha had wanted to pull the shades, seize him in an embrace, and suggest they run away together to Scotland. She had *missed* him, and even a retiring widow grew bored with Society's entertainments. Even a settled mother of two could be lonely, and...

And *besotted.* Bernard had used the word *honest*, and now they were to court. Of course they were. Sorcha had needed some time to adjust her thoughts—to have coherent thoughts at all—but Bernard had dared to posit what would likely have been obvious to any lady who'd never endured marriage to Lord Barclay Dolforth.

I have fallen in love with him. A mannerly, English, slightly shy bachelor who'd been hiding in an obscure Yorkshire parish and was now trying to hide in his commercial endeavors while doing the pretty for his ducal connections, while helping Sorcha sort out her nursery.

I have fallen in love with him, and he has... She did not dare think the rest of that notion.

"Are we there yet?" Bridget asked, gaze on the landscape beyond the window.

"Not yet, Bridge," Jordy replied. "If we were there, we'd be out of this coach. I want to be a coachman when I grow up."

Bridget stuck her tongue out at him. "I want to be a unicorn."

Sorcha wanted to be private with Bernard in a large and comfy bed. She'd planned that much of their afternoon before Bernard's request to court her. Her ambitions had been driven by a combination of desire, curiosity—how much of the vicar still dictated to the man?—and a growing case of nerves.

She'd never been a merry widow and hadn't quite reconciled herself to embarking on that career with Bernard. He wasn't the merry-widowing sort, though he was apparently the marrying sort.

From the backward-facing bench, Bernard sent her a commiserating smile.

"Those are our gateposts!" Bridget pointed out the window. "We're *here*. I was right, and you were wrong, Jordy Dolforth. We're here, and we are not out of the coach, so there."

"Gloating becomes no one," Sorcha said. "We will also be at Mirobello when the coach stops and we join your cousins, so you were both right."

The Greer girls would travel out from Town with their mama, making the outing a sort of family garden party.

"We'll play battledore," Jordy said, "and Gilchrist will be on our team, and she will wallop stupid Annette with the shuttlecock."

"A gentleman does not speak ill of a lady," Bernard said, though Sorcha heard humor in the platitude. "Particularly not a lady in his own family."

"Annette isn't a lady yet," Bridget observed as the coach tooled up the drive. "She isn't *out*, and she will not be out until next year. Jordy should be allowed to speak ill of her until next year, even though he's only saying the truth. Annette is very silly. She says she could marry a prince, and then we would not be allowed to turn our backs to her."

"Her prediction is theoretically possible," Bernard said. "You'd best conduct yourselves accordingly toward your lady cousins. They might all be princesses-in-waiting."

"Then I will be a king!" Jordy grinned at his own faultless reasoning, stood, saluted, bowed, and toppled to the seat behind him when the coach rocked to a halt.

"A day in the country was apparently overdue for all concerned," Sorcha observed ten minutes later. She and Bernard stood on the sunny back terrace as the children went racing around the formal parterres, which some genius had laid out in a perfect pattern to accommodate a game of fox and geese.

Coraline's brood had arrived a quarter hour earlier, along with their governess. Gilchrist, who'd chosen to ride with the hampers in the second coach, took the first shift as referee.

"A day in the country was a wonderful idea." Bernard winged his arm. "One forgets just how gratifying bright sunshine can be."

One forgot how gratifying good company could be. Sorcha let her mind wander along the prospect of years with Bernard—his wickedly subtle humor, his inherent sense of calm, his decency and affection. Why, oh, why, had she settled for a strutting, self-important lordling when men like Bernard were to be found instead?

Because she'd been told to settle for the lordling, of course. Told that Barclay was the only option for a girl who had any sense of duty toward her family or her future.

And because men like Bernard were more precious than rubies and twice as rare. The more she knew of him, the more he fell into the too-good-to-be-true category, and MacPhee had had very terse words for fellows of that ilk.

Poor, dear MacPhee.

"I'll show you the house," Sorcha said, wrapping a hand around Bernard's arm. "Mirobello isn't half so grand as some of its neighbors, but I'll be able to heat the place should I ever need to dwell here."

"You haven't considered renting it out?"

"I did rent it out occasionally until this year. Coraline asked me not to let it. The family might need it to host events over the next several years."

"The family. Right. Do you like Coraline?"

They passed into the house, a newish edifice that had been enlarged along with many others in the neighborhood during the past century. As London had grown smokier and more squalid, Richmond had arisen as a patch of countryside within frolicking distance of Town. Market gardens had sprung up, as had the occasional country showplace and rural retreat.

"I don't truly *know* Coraline," Sorcha replied. "I respect that she's had her hands full with Tallister and four girls, but she seems to relish the challenges. The library is this way, and I suspect you will want to see that first."

The library was a cozy study by ducal standards, about twenty-four feet by eighteen feet. The outer wall was graced with tall windows, as befit a space where light would be at a premium, but the ceiling was a mere ten feet, making the room feel more domestic and less grand.

Books were shelved along most of the inside wall, and two hearths—one at the far end, one halfway down the outside wall—would provide sufficient warmth even in winter. The carpets were cheerfully floral Axminsters, the art a series of bucolic landscapes. The obligatory set of French doors opened directly onto the terrace.

The furniture was both elegant and comfortable. Sorcha liked the color scheme—burgundy and amethyst appointments against sapphire blue walls and eggshell trim. The palette was pretty, did not show dirt, and avoided the trite pastels common in the public spaces of grander houses.

"Window seats," Bernard said. "I have long admired the utility of window seats and spent much of my boyhood occupying them."

"You hid from your tutors behind the curtains?" Sorcha certainly had.

"I was not a hiding-from-my-tutors sort of child. I was studious. From a young age, I was told I was meant for the Church, and churchmen are to be studious."

The windows faced the back terrace, where governesses, footmen, or other spectators might bide. Sorcha was abruptly seized with the impulse to close the drapes and hug the stuffing out of Bernard. He was all that was manly and desirable and wondrous, but from a young age, he'd also been expected to uphold duty at the expense of his own capacity for joy.

What a dreary patch of common ground. "Let's have a look around upstairs," she said. "From the east side of the house, we have a lovely view of the Thames."

The most commodious bedrooms occupied that wing, and the views were the best the house had to offer.

I am dithering.

If what Sorcha had heard in any number of retiring rooms was true, a widow would approach a tryst with confidence, humor, and honest lust, but what, exactly, did those attributes look like on a fine spring afternoon?

"The original house became the western half of the present edifice," she said as they climbed the curving main staircase. "The eastern half is the modern addition. The kitchens and pantries lie on the east side, while the western foundation holds the wine cellar, root cellar, coal cellar, and so forth. A great-great-uncle of the present duke did a marvelous job with the expansion."

"The house makes a lovely impression," Bernard said as they passed an alcove with the requisite Roman bust, thriving fern, and reading chair. "Sorcha, are you nervous?"

"Yes." With Bernard, only honesty would do. "Also determined. I have been a paragon, Bernard. A paragon of ignorance and propriety. The role grows tedious and lonely."

"Lonely. In recent years, I have begun to feel as if the inner and outer man live at a greater and greater distance from each other. I'd watch myself partaking of somebody's overcooked roast at yet another Sunday supper, all the talk of harvest or plowing or planting, and there I'd be, holding up my portion of the conversation, complimenting the kitchen, while mentally..."

"You were suffocating?"

"Hibernating, let's say. Watching and wondering, 'Is this what the next forty years of my life will entail, this polite lie, this little performance? Do no harm. Be a friend to all. Want for nothing. Have no expressed discontents or ambitions beyond keep Mama as content as she could be.' All the while, I knew that such maunderings were in themselves evidence of vast privilege."

"At least you were pondering your situation over a dried-up roast. I'd ruminate like that while my husband..." Sorcha fell silent, not out of loyalty to Barclay, but rather, out of pity for Barclay's very young wife.

Bernard took her in his arms, and Sorcha hugged him back.

"I have missed you, Bernard. I did not know who you were, or where you were, but you should have been in my life, and now you are, and I fear the day when that's no longer the case."

"You have me to keep, if that's your wish, and I am delighted to think you might be mine to keep as well."

Sorcha hadn't seriously considered remarrying, and yet, she was increasingly unable to envision a future without Bernard in it. Rather than admit as much—cautious habits died hard—she led him to the apartment she favored for herself. The sitting room was small and sunny, the bedroom airy and ample, and a wide balcony spanned both. The view looked out over the springtime verdure of the home wood to the silvery ribbon of the Thames half a mile away.

The tang of turned earth and early haying scented the air. A bouquet of purple irises on the sideboard added a note of sweetness and accented the lilac-and-cream appointments.

"The irises symbolize dignity," Sorcha said, cuddling closer. "My dignity matters to me, Bernard."

"Your dignity matters to me as well, and so does your pleasure." With that, he commenced kissing her, sweetly at first, but with the sort of relentless patience Sorcha had seen him exhibit so often.

His hands explored her back, then her waist and hips and, finally, the contours of her derriere.

His kisses, tame initially, became increasingly carnal, until Sorcha was ready to drag him by the cravat into the bedroom.

His smile, a curving of lips she felt rather than saw, became a diabolically knowing expression he turned on her as she panted between amatory skirmishes and went on a few exploratory forays of her own.

A shaft of regret pierced Sorcha's growing desire. Damn Barclay. He'd been a bungling, blundering oaf. A clueless, hopeless bumbler, and he'd probably known it. All his posturing and strutting and lording about... and he hadn't been able to kiss worth a tinker's curse. He was nearly to be pitied.

"I am not your late husband," Bernard said, perhaps feeling the shift in her emotions, "but I would dearly like to be your next husband. Might we move the discussion to the next room?"

The words were polite. The invitation promised anything but fine manners and decorum.

Sorcha eased away from him, locked the door to the corridor, and led the way into the bedroom.

~

The whole house appealed to Bernard. Solid foundation, elegant neoclassical lines, spotless housekeeping. To all appearances, a pleasant, unpretentious country retreat. Closer examination revealed care and thought in every detail. The alcoves were not directly across from one another, but rather, alternating, so an entire corridor was blessed with light.

Cushioned window seats, abundant wall sconces, burgundy carpet on the main staircase to protect the marble and quiet footsteps in the otherwise grand white marble foyer.

Flowers—irises in my lady's sitting room, tulips in the library, salvia potted on the back terrace. Why did the offices of Huxley and Company boast not a single bloom on any occasion?

"What does that look portend?" Sorcha asked, drawing the bedroom drapes.

"Might we leave them open?" Bernard asked. "The view is

magnificent. I was contemplating flowers for the front steps of my commercial establishment. An extravagance, I'm sure, but a thriving enterprise can afford the occasional small extravagances."

Sorcha grinned at him with such mischief and tenderness that Bernard was felled by a wave of sheer affection for her. She was like this house—solid, unaffected, and, upon closer examination, utterly endearing. Full of delightful surprises and ingenious touches.

She ceased fussing with the drapes and prowled across the room, coming to a halt two feet away. "Are *you* nervous, Bernard?"

Her ladyship was also full of devilment. "I am suitably in awe of the opportunity before me."

"I am an opportunity?" The word clearly did not sit well with her.

"The chance to make love with you is an opportunity to please you. Best foot forward and all that." He'd be babbling in French next.

"No offense, Bernard, but your foot comes well down the list of anatomical items of interest."

He stepped around behind her and returned fire by starting on the hooks at the back of her dress.

"Then caresses to your feet won't be needed?" he asked, speaking close to her ear. "I confess I'm disappointed, but I will console myself with other explorations."

He'd meant the comment flirtatiously, but Sorcha turned and wrapped her arms around his waist and then rested her forehead against his chest.

Not a moment for more kisses, Bernard understood that much.

"Bernard, there is much I don't know. You were serious about my feet, weren't you?"

Thus begins the loving. The true loving. Bernard delivered a short sermon to himself on the topic of male insecurity and gathered his lady close.

"You asked if I am nervous, Sorcha, and I evaded the truth." Tried to evade it in the one context where few men could convincingly lie. "I am so desperately worried that I will fail to meet your expectations that mere nerves would be a relief. I am out of practice, to take refuge in euphemisms. Like you, there is much I don't know. I was marked for the Church, as you are aware, and thus the usual university entertainments were available to me in only the most discreet manner."

She peeked up at him. "University was years ago, Bernard. You've been celibate ever since?"

"Not quite. Once a quarter, the bishop would hail me into York for a polite chat about trivialities. I lodged on those occasions at a boardinghouse frequented by half the unmarried clergy on the Dales—one recommended by the bishop himself, oddly enough. The proprietress was friendly."

Sorcha's fingers kneaded the nape of Bernard's neck. "She must miss you."

"She married two years ago. I was honestly relieved. The encounters were pleasant, but also pointless."

"The pointlessness has stopped me," Sorcha said, "on the few occasions I've been tempted. The usual rogues and roues have offered, but..."

"They were the usual and doubtless adept at the mechanics, but you deserve better than the usual anything, and you have sense enough to know it." Since when had the nape of a man's neck held the key to his dignity? "If I were a dog, my back leg would be twitching with bliss."

The next few minutes were spent exploring exactly how pleasurable a caress to the human nape and surrounds could be. Bernard bore up as best he could, though the experience inspired a few soft groans and more than one sigh.

"Barclay was the usual," Sorcha said, stepping away and giving Bernard her back. "He was the usual lordling past his prime. He'd never had to exert himself to please anybody else, and when he might have wished to be a little impressive, a little special, he'd no idea how to go on. It's a relief to pity him, Bernard. An enormous relief."

"Like when the boardinghouse widow married. A door that

wanted closing could finally be shut for good." Bernard suspected this was not how self-confident lovers talked, but it might well be how prospective spouses grew closer.

He finished with Sorcha's hooks and soldiered on to deal with tapes, laces, and the rest of the whatnot that trussed women up like songbirds in whalebone cages. She stepped out of the froth of skirts and petticoats in only her shift and black silk stockings. Those she slipped off, revealing slender, muscular legs, the sight of which sent Bernard into a reverie of appreciative gawping.

Her ankles were perfection, and she was right to pity the husband who'd failed to caress those elegant feet.

"They are legs, Bernard. I've had them all my life. I suspect you claim a pair of your own, though I've yet to see the direct evidence."

"An oversight to be remedied immediately." Bernard shrugged out of his coat and passed it to Sorcha.

She dealt with the clothing, hanging hers in the enormous carved wardrobe in the corner, folding Bernard's over the back of the chair at the escritoire. He sat to pull off his boots and rose with a sense of having passed the point where any sermon ever composed in the entire history of human endeavor could aid him.

Instead, words passed along by his father—by the man who'd selflessly and lovingly raised him—came to mind.

The lady risks her life every time she admits a man to her bed. Be worthy of the trust and honor she reposes in you, young man. Nothing less than best efforts, every time, or you'll eventually regret your selfish slacking to the bottom of your soul.

Peculiar words for a vicar to pass along to his son, but then, Papa had been a truly kind man and neither a paragon nor a hypocrite.

Sorcha paused in her folding and draping with Bernard's shirt in her hands. "I have pictured you up in the bleak wilds of Yorkshire, translating away the winter evenings, reading learned tomes first thing in the morning. You have a studious quality that I like, but without your shirt..."

Without anything save his breeches. "Yes?"

"I believe the phrase is: He leads an active life."

And once again, Bernard had occasion to pity Lord Barclay. "The wood does not chop itself. The horse does not take himself for a hack. I generally left the coach for my mother's use up north and still prefer to travel on foot here in London. Some of my best sermons were composed while out rambling the countryside."

He undid his falls, though why thirteen fiendishly complicated buttons were necessary to hold up a flap of cloth, he no longer knew. Bernard knew very little, in fact, except that he desired Sorcha madly and loved her more madly even than that.

He stepped from his breeches and draped them across the vanity stool. "Shall we to bed, my lady?"

She finished with his shirt, did a proper job of folding his breeches, and frankly stared at the evidence of Bernard's inchoate desire.

"Bed soon. First, might I have a look?"

The moment verged on hilarity, but was also too tender, too trusting, for humor. "Look all you like." What need had any man of sanity when Sorcha wanted *a look*?

She looked. She touched, tentatively and then more boldly. By the time she had Bernard sprawled on the bed and praying for fortitude, she was also smiling like the cat who'd been given the keys to every dairy in the shire.

And Bernard was smiling too.

CHAPTER ELEVEN

The part of Sorcha housed in her body lay in a thoroughly rumpled bed, her back warmed by the muscular expanse of Bernard's chest. His patience had risen to new heights in the past hour, while Sorcha's appreciation for the outer bounds of physical ecstasy had undergone cataclysms and revelations.

The pleasure two people could bring each other was orders of magnitude greater than she'd imagined, provided one of those people was Bernard and the other was a woman he was intent on pleasuring.

He was a walking wonderment of inventiveness, an inspiration for fancies too intimate for words, but not too intimate for deeds behind a locked door in a sunny, private bedroom.

Some part of Sorcha not of the body purely floated, bobbing on a sea of warmth, lassitude, and relief. She wanted to point and shout and laugh: *I was right.* MacPhee was wrong. The bond between a man and a woman could be the consummation of a friendship deeper than affection, desire beyond words, and amazement of the body, mind, and soul.

She could love and be loved. She could aspire to joy rather than lecture herself about the privilege of hard-earned contentment. With

Bernard, she even looked forward to the spats and disagreements, because they would have them honestly and respectfully, without sulks and pouts and sneering insults.

"My lady is awake." Bernard's hand trailed over her hip. The caress wasn't suggestive or even possessive, just a pleasurable stroke of his palm over Sorcha's flesh.

"How can you tell?"

"My mind heard yours stirring."

"Something else is stirring." Nudging gently at her backside.

"If I don't get out of this bed—when leaving present company appeals to me about as strongly as all the labors of Hercules combined with the tribulations of Job—you will soon be astir as well. The children will think we've been kidnapped by river pirates."

She caught his hand and kissed his knuckles. "I want to tell you, 'Don't leave me, don't leave this bed,' but I am also aware of all the times I felt very differently about a conjugal interlude. That I long for you to stay is delicious."

Also a tad bewildering. The yearning for his continued company wasn't exclusively carnal or even dominated by desire. Wrapped in Bernard's arms, nothing between them, Sorcha felt safe and at peace. Deeply happy and whole.

When had she decided that life was a battle to be endured? Weapons always at the ready, sentries on alert?

Bernard patted her hip. "You wanted the marital bed to yourself, did you?"

"Desperately, especially after Jordy was born, but Barclay wanted more sons... The accoucheur opined that ninety days was the most any healthy woman should need to recover, and I had had an 'uneventful delivery.' I wanted to murder the man where he stood."

Bernard climbed over her, caging her on all fours, though Sorcha remained on her side.

"I'm sorry. It's for you to say how much time you need. I am a firm believer in spacing children and keeping their numbers manageable. There are herbs, you know, and French letters, and times when conception is more or less likely."

And there were men like Bernard, who withdrew, found their pleasure without risking conception, and regarded that as a simple courtesy rather than an imposition.

"I've heard other women referring to those measures, but all I know of them is what my old governess managed to impart." And none of that had been any use when Lord Barclay had decided to favor his wife with his pawing.

Bernard rested his cheek against hers. "I suspect I will still be composing sermons when I am an old man haunting the pubs in the City, reliving the glory days when I actually ran my own enterprise. My years as a vicar have left their mark.

"You were married to his lordship for seven years," he went on. "You became a mother twice over, a lady by courtesy, and then a widow. I would never want you to ignore that part of your life or feel you could not discuss it with me. Some portion of your spectacular fortitude was forged during that season. Those experiences matter to you, so they matter to me."

He settled over her, a whole-body embrace, and she needed that from him. Seven years was a long time, but Bernard was right—those years hadn't been all bad, and they were behind her.

"Will you tell me about your mother someday?"

He sighed and eased away to his back, though he took hold of Sorcha's hand. "Mama was a serpent. *Is* a serpent, rather, because wherever Lady Josephine Huxley dwells, she must disrupt others' peace and interfere with their happiness. She describes her meddling as consideration for the less fortunate, who—not being her ladyship—aren't as gifted when it comes to knowing what's best for them. And through one astonishing coincidence after another, what's best for others is generally no good for them at all but soundly benefits Lady Josephine. She was an embarrassment and then a menace, and I am the worst of all possible sons because I am glad she has sailed for the Antipodes."

Sorcha took a turn blanketing her lover. "Might she return?"

"Lord Lorne will see her prosecuted for hanging felonies if she tries. Should that fail, the secondary line of defense is to commit her to an asylum for hysterical females. She has caused more harm to innocent people than you can possibly imagine. Destroying the dreams of young lovers was her particular specialty, and no, I do not accord her any lenience because her own youthful dreams where Lord Jerome were concerned came to nothing. Lord Jerome, as far as I am concerned, had a lucky escape."

From Bernard, this was a tirade. Sorcha cuddled down to his chest and listened to his heart. Slow and steady.

"I want to know what she looks like, Bernard. If she did come back, she'd try to wreck your happiness and possibly mine and the children's. You must find a likeness, or draw one, and we will show it to the staff. We'll explain that she's a mentally unbalanced former parishioner, and any sighting of her is to be reported immediately. Do the same at your office and with your domestic staff."

Bernard's kiss was sweet, leisurely, and thoughtful. "Sound advice. You don't think I'm fanciful to be so skittish where she's concerned?"

Well, yes. Maybe a little, but then, meddling matrons were two a penny in Mayfair. "I am skittish, too, in many regards. We learned to be skittish for reasons."

Sorcha remained draped over her lover, breathing in synchrony with him, desire humming along as a pleasant ache.

"We should get up," she said, moving not one inch. "Showing you the house doesn't take half the afternoon."

Bernard trailed a hand over her back. "I am loath to leave this bed, but I will treasure the memories we've created today, just as I treasure all the time we spend together."

Gallant, and honest, an attractive combination. "You don't view me merely as a good set of hips." Not the riposte his lovely little speech merited, but an inordinately comforting truth.

"Let it be said that your hips could inspire me to odes and panegyrics. Notwithstanding the aforesaid, you don't view me as another randy vicar to be dismissed when he's provided a predictable service."

Stupid, stupid boardinghouse widow. Sometimes Jordy's word was the right one. "Nothing about the service was predictable, Bernard, and I treasure all of the time I spend with you too."

He seemed to subtly relax at that pronouncement. Sorcha pushed off him, climbed to his side, and looked at the clock. One hour of her life, and yet, everything had changed, and for the better.

The uncertainty was still there, but muted and marginally appeased.

"The sight of you..." Bernard muttered, flipping back the covers and slogging to the opposite side of the bed. "Your braid is still tidy. This should qualify as some sort of miracle. My thoughts will never be tidy again, and I am hard put to care. One should get dressed..."

Sorcha loved his muttering, his magpie mind, his lean, muscular back. She loved him, and this did not terrify her nearly as much as it should have.

They assisted each other to dress, and Sorcha had just shoved the last pin into the coronet she'd fashioned with her braid when a piercing scream rent the air.

Bernard, tidily attired, cocked his head in the midst of smoothing the last wrinkle from the bed's quilt.

"That is Bridget," he said, "and she's setting up quite a racket."

"She's terrified rather than angry," Sorcha said as the screaming went on. "Hurry, Bernard. She's never screamed quite like that before."

Bernard was out the door in the next instant, Sorcha right behind him.

~

"Sorcha, for pity's sake, tell that child to cease her caterwauling. Bridget, quiet this instant." Cousin Coraline's hand drew back.

Bernard caught her by the wrist, his grip firm enough to be effective, and manners be damned.

"We can't find Jordy," Bridget bellowed. "Tell her, Cousin Bernard. We must find Jordy."

"And you," Bernard said, dropping Coraline's hand and kneeling before Bridget, "were making exactly the sort of noise that would have summoned Jordy from hiding, if he's able to heed your call. Correct?"

Bridget sent a fulminating glower at Coraline. "Cousin Coraline said we mustn't holler, because ladies don't raise their voices, but I am not a lady, and we can't find Jordy. If he thinks I need help, he'll come *no matter what.*"

Bernard took Bridget's hand and rose. "Sound logic. Jordy is a loyal brother, and he would come to your aid if he was able to. Who saw him last?"

Sorcha, waiting at the top of the terrace steps, remained silent, though Bernard would not have given much for Coraline's chances had Bridget been slapped.

The older girls stood in a half circle around Bridget, while Gilchrist and another young woman—the Greer governess, perhaps—remained halfway up the steps, looking worried.

"We were playing hide-and-seek," Jessica, the youngest Greer daughter, said. She hadn't yet put up her hair, and Sorcha apparently regarded her fondly. "Annette was *it*. She counted to a hundred and started searching. She found me first because I am not very good at hiding."

"You don't even try," Annette said. "Eglantine takes too long to hide, but she tries. Elise excels at hiding."

Elise, the third from the top, was in that awkward phase between putting up her hair and letting down her hems.

"You never look high, Annette. You will search at your feet forever, but you don't look up."

Coraline made an impatient motion with her hand. "This discussion profits us nothing. The boy will come out when he's good and ready to, and setting up the hue and cry has only encouraged his foolishness. I say we serve lunch and ignore this stunt."

Bernard was puzzling out how to tell a lady to cease her clueless prattling when Sorcha came slowly down the steps.

"Imagine, Coraline," she said, "that Annette had gone missing, or Jessica, Elise, or Eglantine. Would you call it foolishness to search for them? Jordy likes to *win*, to earn the attention of others through impressive performance or charming humor. He would never think it sporting to frighten his sister by disappearing."

Sound logic, such as the mother of a boy or any sensible female who knew Jordy in more than passing might reason.

"Mama's right," Bridget said. "Jordy wouldn't scare me for fun. That's not sporting."

"We should search for him," Eglantine observed. "Brigands might have made off with him and be holding him for ransom."

Brigands and ransom doubtless would figure in her next poem. "I agree with Eglantine," Bernard said, which provoked Coraline and Annette to scowling, while Jessica and Eglantine appeared surprised. "If Jordy is in distress, the sooner we find him, the better."

"He's not in distress," Coraline retorted. "He's being exceedingly inconsiderate and immature."

Gilchrist looked ready to bring down the Wrath of the Clans for that bit of calumny. Bernard did as he'd often done when a committee meeting was reduced to chaos by one intransigent member.

"We'll conduct an all-hands search of the premises," he said. "What were the bounds of the game?"

Coraline, who likely had little experience with being ignored, twirled her parasol at a great rate.

"The house and carriage house were out of bounds," Jessica said. "The stable, garden, park, and the outbuildings nearest the stable were in bounds."

"That's the summer kitchen, brewery, laundry, and springhouse," Eglantine added, "but not the fishing cottage, folly, potting shed, greenhouses, kennels, chicken coop—"

"Eggie, you could just say the home farm is out of bounds," Jessica pointed out. "The home farm is too far away, and people work there, so they might give away a hiding place."

"This is all a waste of time," Coraline snapped. "The greater the fuss we make over Jordy's prank, the more likely he is to get above himself again. Annette and I will lay out the picnic blankets."

Bridget stomped her foot. "Stupid meat pies are not as important as Jordy, and *I am not hungry*."

"Really, Sorcha." Coraline closed her parasol with aggressive dispatch. "I don't know where you've been getting your nursery help these days, but your children need a refresher on their manners."

Sorcha's eyes narrowed in a manner that presaged eternal warfare. Bernard minutely shook his head.

The clouds gathering in the sky off to the south meant time was of the essence. "If Jordy is pulling a prank," Bernard said, "he'll be appropriately disciplined. If he's in peril, we cannot afford to misread the situation. We'll search in twos. Bridget and Annette, you cover the park and garden. Look for any sign of Jordy's passing. A stray marble, a bit of string for teasing the pantry mouser, anything. Elise and Lady Barclay, take the summer kitchen, brewery, and laundry. Miss Gilchrist, you and Jessica look around the back of the manor, and any window wells, cellars, or other hiding places accessible from the terrace."

"The manor was out of bounds," Jessica said.

"But the outside of the manor was not," Sorcha replied, "and Jordy loves to split hairs and play the lawyer. He might be stuck in a window well that he's not tall enough to climb out of."

"Eglantine," Bernard went on, "you're with me, and we'll focus on the stable and the springhouse. Meet back here in forty-five minutes, ladies, and howl like a demon if you find Jordy and he needs help."

"I can howl like six demons," Bridget said.

Annette shuddered. "I'm to help Mama. Bridget can search on her own."

"That young lady," Bernard replied, nodding at the Greer governess, "can assist Cousin Coraline to lay out the meal. You know the park, Annette. You've hidden there. You've searched there. Between you and Bridget, if Jordy has tripped on a root in the hedgerow and conked his head on a rock, you'll find him."

Annette seemed unconvinced, but Cousin Coraline held her peace. Bridget seized Annette by the hand. "Come *on*, Annette. You aren't a lady yet, so you have to help."

Annette sent her mother a pleading gaze, then trundled away with her self-appointed supervisor.

"Ellie, we have some searching to do." Sorcha and Elise headed off in the direction of the stone summer kitchen situated twenty yards down the path that led to the stable.

"Miss Jessica," Gilchrist said, "lead the way." Jessica trotted after Sorcha and Elise, then slowed her steps as Gilchrist followed.

"Cousin Eglantine." Bernard gestured to the stable path. He wasn't about to offer his arm to a perfectly spry adolescent. She fell in step beside him.

"Why search with me?" she asked as they left the garden. "I'm only good for reading books."

"You are a poet," Bernard said. "You notice details. You stand a little outside your family, as much an observer as a daughter or sister. If you were Jordy, where would you hide?"

Eglantine appeared to absorb his observations as neither flattery nor criticism, but factual statements, as Bernard had intended them.

"Jordy longs to be clever," she said. "Bridget is clever. She has nimble wits. Jordy isn't that quick. He's not slow, but he hasn't Bridget's mental reflexes. He'll make a fine duke, everybody will like him, and he'll be kindhearted and know how to make people laugh, but he'll have to work on his speeches before he gives them. He'll want a clever hiding place."

While her analysis of the sibling dynamic was astonishingly accurate, every child wanted a clever hiding place.

"Will he hide up high?" Visions of Jordy lying in a crumpled heap at the foot of some venerable tree threatened Bernard's composure.

"No. That is Elise's specialty. Jordy might hide somewhere Annette would be hesitant to look."

"Excellent notion. Somewhere dusty or dank or full of cobwebs."

"Yes, or mud or spiders. Nettie hates spiders, or pretends to. She's doing a lot of pretending these days. I wish she'd get married so we'd have some peace."

"She likely wishes she were married, too, provided her choice of spouse was a suitable swain." Bernard stopped before the empty stable building and surveyed the possibilities. The barn was two stories, stone below, wood up top, and in good repair.

"Nettie wants to marry a German prince," Eglantine said, "so that we have to back out of her presence. Even Mama tells her that's ridiculous, but Papa humors her and backs from the room sometimes, bowing with every step."

Eglantine sent Bernard a shy, sidewise smile, and Bernard saw a flash of Tallister Greer's charm. His good looks, too, moderated by Coraline's blond, blue-eyed coloring.

"Where would you hide, Eglantine, if you were Jordy, and you wanted Annette to lose the game?"

"Jordy is afraid of the dark, so he'll not hide below ground. Let's look in each stall."

The stable encompassed sixteen loose boxes, in addition to straight stalls. The far end included a saddle room, feed room, and a stall devoted to the storage of brooms, rakes, farrier's tools, and rugs.

The coach horses were at grass. The barn thus had the silent, stoic air of a sturdy structure left to take its chances with the elements. Dust was abundant, and that was fortunate.

"He's been here." Bernard pointed to a small footprint on the bricks of the aisleway. "Or some other child of about his size passed this way very recently." No dust within the tracks, but not much of a clear pattern either. Footsteps went in all directions, as if Jordy had peeked into every empty stall.

"Jordy!" Eglantine called in a surprisingly robust alto. "Jordan Dolforth, come out, come out, wherever you are! The game has been called for a picnic before the weather turns."

"Jordy!" Bernard used his heed-the-vicar-across-the-churchyard voice. "Come out. Annette has forfeited, and Bridget is worried for you."

They continued calling down the length of the aisle, going stall by stall. No handy footprints marked the far end, brisk breezes having swept the dust from the bricks a good dozen yards into the stable.

Not a sound greeted them. Not even the movement of a mouse or a barn swallow ensued.

As silent as the tomb.

"You'd best have a look up in the hayloft," Eglantine said. "Jordy might have borrowed a leaf from Elise's book after all, and Annette would hesitate to climb the ladder in her skirts, much less brave a dusty hay mow."

The ladder looked sturdy enough, but the hay mow was empty. Slats of light crossed the bare floor, which had been formed of rafters cross-bedded with saplings, the better to circulate air on a freshly cut crop. The saplings would give way under even modest weight now.

"No Jordy," Bernard said, returning to the lower floor. "We'd best have a look at the springhouse."

"Lots of spiders in any springhouse," Eglantine said with some relish. "Nettie would hate to look there. Spiders can bite, can't they?"

"A few do when threatened, but their bites are not dangerous." Bernard was reminded, though, that Jordy could not swim, and most springhouses sat immediately beside, if not half in, small ponds.

"All these buildings standing empty is a shame," Eglantine observed, exiting the barn opposite the end where they'd entered. "Papa says Auntie should have continued to rent the property, but Mama didn't want her to. I love Mirobello for the fresh air and quiet."

To Bernard, the quiet had become ominous. He stood in the entrance to the aisle and considered the yard beyond. The grass area revealed no footprints. If Jordy had considered hiding in the stable and discarded the notion, he'd backtracked out the front end rather than passing through and going out the back.

The springhouse and its pond sat in the fold of a small swale twenty yards away. The logical path would have been right across the stable yard. The grass wasn't disturbed in any manner that suggested recent foot traffic, but then, Bernard had only a rural upbringing to support his deductions.

"One moment," he said. "I want to have another look inside." He rifled the few old horse blankets still hanging in the stall with a dilapidated muck cart and rusty rake.

The feed room was probably the cleanest space in the whole barn. Three wooden bins, two with lids up, one with the lid down, lined the walls. Cobbled stone floor. Stout construction such as would deter mice, rats, and other vermin interested in poaching oats.

Bernard lifted the closed lid casually, thinking only that the bins would fare better for being open to the air.

"Jordy." The boy was crouched in the bottom of the bin, not moving. "Eglantine, we've found him. Yodel like a Valkyrie pursued by demons flying over a battlefield in hell."

Bernard lifted the boy from the dusty confines of the oat bin, and still, Jordy did not move.

CHAPTER TWELVE

Never had Sorcha seen a more welcome sight than Bernard coming up the garden path, Jordy perched on his back.

"Our young man chose to hide in an oat bin," Bernard said. "The lid came down and knocked him on the head. He seems right enough, if a bit groggy."

"Jordy." *Our young man.* Sorcha held out her arms, and Bernard passed her dusty little son into her embrace. Jordy barely fit on her hip anymore, but Sorcha managed. "Jordan Dolforth, I do believe you've had an adventure."

"Mama." He curled against her shoulder, as he had much earlier in life. "My head hurts."

Coraline glanced up from the array of picnic blankets, rose from beside a hamper, and came over to the garden. Jessica shifted from foot to foot beside Gilchrist on the terrace steps, and Elise, a purple iris in her hand, looked worried. Annette waved from the edge of the park, while Bridget pelted across the parterres as if in pursuit of the Scots Greys.

Sorcha moved to the bench beside the sundial and sat with Jordy in her lap. "Your head hurts, your face could use a wash, and you will never again hide in any oat bins. Does anything else hurt?"

He shook his head and sighed.

"All this drama over a game of hide-and-seek," Coraline muttered, hands on hips. "I daresay he would have rejoined us five minutes after we opened the first hamper. Children get into scrapes and are best served if they learn to get out of those scrapes on their own."

"Jordy got out of this scrape," Bernard said, "thanks to Eglantine's vivid imagination. She was able to put herself in her younger cousin's shoes and describe an ideal hiding place from Jordy's perspective. I do hope some appropriately inspiring verse results from the day's excitement."

While Eglantine, probably for the first time in her life, preened, Sorcha held her son and wrapped an arm around Bridget. Loyal sister that she was, Bridget had charged into the garden and budged up against Sorcha's side.

Jordy managed a weak smile. "I'm fine, Bridge."

He was not fine. He was subdued and hurting, also embarrassed. That Sorcha's son should suffer another mishap before his cousins, and in the same place where he'd come off a pony so ignominiously, meant Sorcha wasn't fine either.

Even the garden, with its soothingly formal parterres, gleaming crushed-shell walkways, and precisely placed pots of salvia annoyed her. The gawking cousins annoyed her, and Coraline—tapping her foot and looking impatient, then whisking herself back to the hampers—could have done with a smart rap on the head from the hand of the Almighty.

Bernard, doing his best to allay concern and hide his own annoyance, was by contrast justification for relief and gratitude.

"I hate Cousin Coraline," Bridget whispered. "I love Cousin Bernard."

"Coraline did not know what to do," Sorcha replied quietly. She risked mortifying Jordy past all bearing by kissing his temple. "She makes foolish pronouncements when she's at a loss." Also when she wasn't at a loss, and Annette was all but doomed to become exactly like her mother.

"Cousin Bernard is not foolish." Bridget didn't bother whispering.

Bernard was... a wonderment. He'd known what to do, from organizing the search, to finding Jordy, to deflecting Coraline's criticisms with praise for Eglantine.

"Coraline wants to be the queen," Jordy observed. "Queens are stupid."

Worse, Coraline hoped for her daughters to be queens of a sort. "Feeling more the thing?" Sorcha asked as Jordy sat up and moved to sit beside her. He was certainly sounding somewhat recovered, though Sorcha's heart was still thumping against her ribs nigh audibly.

"My head hurts awfully, and I'm hungry, and I want to wash my face."

"Notify *The London Times*. 'Boy seeks soap and water,'" Sorcha retorted, tousling Jordy's hair.

He yelped and flinched away. "Even my hair *hurts*, Mama."

Bernard, who'd apparently become the apple of Eglantine's eye, as well as the pattern card for masculine perfection according to Annette, disengaged himself from both young ladies and approached the bench.

"The wounded will now be carried to the infirmary," he said, turning, crouching down, and presenting his back. "Hop aboard, young man, and do not think of pulling my mane."

Jordy did not exactly scramble to comply, but he did grin as he accepted his piggyback privileges.

"To the herbal," Sorcha said, taking Bridget's hand. "A few dabs of arnica can't hurt and maybe a tisane of peppermint." To soothe a mama's nerves.

"Eww." Bridget made a cold-porridge face. "Poor Jordy. You should have let Annette find you."

"I thought she did find me. I heard footsteps, then somebody closed the lid of the oat bin on my head, and that hurt."

"Your head will heal," Sorcha said with a calm that was utterly feigned. "You will be right as a trivet in no time." She crossed the terrace, hand in hand with Bridget, annoyance escalating to fury. One of Jordy's cousins had injured him deliberately and then feigned ignorance of his location.

"What does that mean?" Bernard mused, sounding utterly unruffled as they passed into the house. "Right as a trivet? A trivet merely sits about the kitchen, waiting for the next hot pot to rest upon it. Why not right as a new lamb or right as a lapdog?"

"Right as a swimming unicorn," Bridget chorused, keeping up the game until they wound down the steps and through the kitchen to reach the herbal.

"Will it sting?" Bridget asked as Sorcha located a bottle of arnica and a clean cloth.

"Not in the least, and the scent is pleasant." She held the bottle so first Bridget and then Jordy could sniff the contents.

Bernard stood in the doorway to the herbal, arms crossed, shoulder propped on the doorjamb. To all appearances, he was slightly amused and slightly bored, though to Sorcha's eye, he was also slightly distracted.

Somebody closed the lid of the oat bin on my head...

Children could be so thoughtless. "Hold still," Sorcha said, gently parting Jordy's hair, then laying the back of her palm against his crown. Heat and swelling. "You will have a goose egg, my dear. Best not wear any crowns or top hats for the next few days." She tipped some of the tincture onto the cloth and dabbed gently along the edges of the rising bruise.

Jordy tolerated her ministrations while Bridget began opening bottles one by one and sniffing them.

"He shouldn't wear a helmet either," Bridget said. "Who shut you in the oat bin, Jordy?"

Sorcha kept dabbing. Bernard watched Bridget's progress along the lower shelf.

"I don't know. I heard footsteps, and I thought Annette had found me, so I crouched halfway down and held my breath, and next thing I knew, the lid clobbered me on the head. Then it was all dark, and I was stuck."

Bernard murmured in Latin. *Deus nos ad*-something.

"I screamed for you, Jordy." Bridget banged a cork lid onto a wide-mouth jar with her fist. "I screamed and screamed, and Cousin Bernard and Mama came, and we found you. Cousin Coraline didn't help at all. She's a lady."

"You're a good screamer, Bridge. I bet Cousin Coraline tried to shush you."

"Cousin Bernard shushed *her*, except he didn't say 'shush,' or 'be quiet,' or anything. Did you hear big footsteps, Jordy, or little footsteps?"

The question prompted Bernard to raise an eyebrow, while Sorcha busied herself corking the arnica and folding and unfolding the damp cloth.

"Not tromping," Jordy said. "Quick, like looking for me, but not looking carefully. Like a bird trying to find the way out when it's flown into the church by mistake." He made a rapid zigzag pattern in the air with his hand. "I'm hungry."

"Are you fit enough to walk back to camp?" Bernard asked. "Your noble destrier is weary."

"I'm fine."

He was still nowhere near fine. Jordy's irrepressible spirit had taken a knock along with his head. When he fully realized that one of his cousins had laid him low, he would be exceedingly troubled and probably furious.

"What is a destry-air?" Bridget asked.

"A steed," Bernard replied. "A charger, a horse of noble mien and weighty responsibilities."

"I want to ride a destrier!" Bridget commenced skipping a circle around the herbal.

"Let's be off." Sorcha resisted the urge to take Jordy's hand. "If the weather is kind, we'll have time for our picnic before rain arrives. I'd hoped we could stay longer, but the best-laid plans 'gang aft agley,' as Mr. Burns says."

Bridget ceased her cantering. "Please, Mama, not Mr. Burns. C'mon, Jordy. We'll share a blanket with Gilly, and the cousins will leave us alone."

"Jess isn't so bad," Jordy said, following his sister out the door.

Bernard looked ready to call them back.

"Let them go," Sorcha said. "We know the important part. Somebody closed that lid, Jordy suffered a blow to the head, and he'll make a full recovery."

"You consider this a prank?" Bernard asked, frowning down at her.

"I consider that Jordy has told us what he can, which isn't enough. I might plead youth on Jessica's behalf for such nastiness, but Jessica likes Jordy, and she's not given to meanness. The other girls are old enough to know better, and while they regard Jordy and Bridget as pests, they don't wish either child ill."

Bernard's expression became remote, as if he were listening to a hymn sung in the distance and couldn't quite recall the lyrics.

"Don't say it, Bernard." Sorcha started after the children.

"Don't say what?"

"Don't say, 'That leaves Gilchrist.' She would strangle anybody who sought to harm either child."

Bernard ambled along beside Sorcha, then politely followed her up the steps to the main floor. "I wasn't about to accuse Gilchrist, though we should ask her where she was while the children played their games."

Sorcha paused at the top of the steps. The children were already across the foyer and out on the terrace. "We can ask, but she'll have a reasonable answer and be mortally offended at our questioning. I need her, Bernard, and an insulted nurserymaid is one step away from giving notice."

"Very well. We won't question her directly. That leaves two other people, at least. The Greer governess, whom I have no reason to suspect, and Cousin Coraline, who did everything in her power to stop and then delay the search for Jordy."

He spoke so calmly, and for the first time, Sorcha resented his self-possession. "A gentleman does not speak ill of a lady, much less a lady who is a member of his family. You will embarrass Jordy if you insist on pursuing this, Bernard."

"A little boy for whom I am responsible was put in harm's way, Sorcha, and that displaces every gentlemanly scruple I ever aspired to."

Sorcha walked away from him, out onto the terrace. Bernard trailed her at a polite—prudent—distance.

"I love my son," she said, going to the balustrade. "He can be mendacious. For all we know, Jordy pulled the lid closed on himself and is making up this business of footsteps to preserve his pride."

"Jordy is afraid of the dark. He would not have pulled the lid closed on himself." Offered gently, but not apologetically.

Bernard was kind and polite and very dear, also capable of relentless determination that might in some context be called pigheadedness.

"I'm sorry, Bernard, but I cannot believe Coraline would do such a thing and then prolong Jordan's misery."

"Prolong his danger, Sorcha. An oat bin is designed to be as airtight as possible. Not quite up to Royal Navy standards, but solid. Jordy might well have suffocated in that oat bin."

No. No. No. And yet… Sorcha refrained from outright argument. Bernard was the last person to indulge in wild notions or to malign another without reason. He was upset, with some justification, and now was not the time to antagonize him.

"I promise I will supervise the children directly for the rest of the afternoon, Bernard. Would you do something for me?"

"Anything."

"Go back to the stable. Do as you asked the girls to do: Look for any signs that indicate somebody else was in that space. I will do likewise—smudges on gloves, dust on hems, that sort of thing. We will discuss this further, but right now, we are exchanging opinions when we might be discussing evidence. I will keep the children in sight while you investigate the supposed crime scene."

Give him something to do, give him time. He was a reasonable man who'd calm down soon enough.

"I understand." He bowed formally. "Your servant, my lady." Sorcha watched him bounding down the steps, all male vitality aimed at a worthy goal and wished she could turn the clock of her life back one hour to when she'd felt sweet and sleepy and safe in Bernard's embrace.

She was instead relieved to see his departure, and that did not bode well for anybody's foolish dreams.

"Coraline claims she was reading a book in the conservatory when Jordy was assaulted," Bernard said. "Gilchrist was on the terrace, chatting with the Greer governess throughout. One wants to shake Coraline and to blazes with her condescending dismissal of a potentially serious situation."

"I did wonder." St. Didier poured two drinks at the sideboard. "Your health." He passed one over, and such was Bernard's agitation that he did not refuse even for form's sake.

"And yours, St. Didier. Also little Jordy's. A more blameless child has not been born. What did you wonder about?"

St. Didier took a wing chair and gestured to its twin.

Bernard did not care to lounge at his ease in one of St. Didier's diabolically comfortable chairs. He would rather have downed his nightcap at one go, marched over to the Greer household, and put the fear of dissembling into Cousin Coraline. He'd had forty-eight hours to ponder Jordy's latest *mishap*, and he'd grown more upset the longer he ruminated.

Let not the sun go down on your wrath was all well and good for exhorting the Ephesians, but of no earthly use to at least one agitated Yorkshireman.

"One wondered," St. Didier said, "how you'd react when excellent manners, exquisite gentlemanly consideration, and polite discourse didn't resolve all difficulties. You cannot go about shaking other men's wives, Huxley. Behavior like that will get you called out, and Greer will be a passably good shot."

"While my own aim approaches perfection. Because Yorkshire suffers a paucity of leisure activities for unmarried parsons, I am also competent with a foil, épée, the Old Testament, the Gospels, and the Stoics. Lady Barclay wants to believe one of the younger cousins played a prank and did not realize the consequences of her actions."

She not only wanted to believe that, she did believe it, and Bernard was at a loss how to convince her otherwise.

"Huxley, compose yourself. Have a seat. Consume the brandy—don't merely hold it while you brandish your figurative fist at Coraline. Who else was present?"

Bernard sipped. He sat. He set down his drink. "I cannot be sure. Lady Barclay's coachman claims the lot of them—coachies, grooms, footmen from both households and all three coaches—went into the village to enjoy a pint and a pie and to collect the local gossip. Tallister Greer was not among our party, but I have no idea of his whereabouts. The Greer groom remained behind in case the family chose to depart, in which case he was to summon his mates. I haven't been able to question each man individually, though I'd like to."

"Right. Because every man in service knows that when some irritated toff comes around demanding answers to incriminating questions, the best strategy is always to peach on one's mates, to deliver up the good fellows one has worked with for years to the tender mercies of the beadle."

I am not a toff. "That is part of the reason I haven't asked those questions, though please note, the Greer groom is notably diminutive. A former jockey, and thus a man who leaves small footprints."

That much had been obvious about O'Malley from a distance. "While I am certain I could best Greer in a fair fight," Bernard went on, "I might not survive a mauling in the court of public opinion if I offend Coraline. She can start rumors that would wreck a business Camden spent years building."

She could also cast slurs on the widowed Lady Barclay, though she'd be careful about it, lest the talk redound to Annette's eventual discredit.

"I thought Coraline was trying to toss Annette into your lonely arms?"

"My arms are not lonely, and I will thank you to cease jesting. The whole situation vexes me exceedingly. Would you be averse to taking her ladyship and the children to Yorkshire? Camden and his baroness could accommodate half a regiment at the ancestral pile, and Jordy and Bridget will adore having playmates."

The subtle air of patient bemusement faded from St. Didier's expression. "Are you taking a bump on the head too seriously, Huxley?"

"Not simply a bump on the head. Last summer, on a similar outing to Mirobello, Jordy's saddle slipped, and he came off his pony. The pony was a hack sent out by the local livery, but the Greers were present en masse, with attendants."

St. Didier ran a finger around the rim of his glass. "I'd forgotten about the fat pony."

"The fat, round pony. Have you also forgotten about last week's bellyaches following Sunday supper at the Greers?"

"No, but children overeat, and bellyaches follow."

"Both children?"

St. Didier scowled at the fire. "You were an only child, Huxley. Afflictions in the nursery can be contagious or even competitive. One child is afraid of the dark, and suddenly, they all are. One child takes shortbread into dislike, and shortbread must be stricken from the menu, until the next child declares it to be the best treat ever."

I will never deliver another sermon in my life. "St. Didier, since when are you, who have no offspring, the oracle of the nursery? Both children cast up their accounts."

"The aroma of illness—"

"I removed Jordy from the coach, away from Lady Barclay and Bridget. He was sick outside the coach. *Aromas* didn't come into it." Fisticuffs well might, if St. Didier didn't cease his tut-tutting.

But then, St. Didier was on a first-name basis with Sorcha. He would naturally take her part.

"*You* removed young Jordan from the coach?"

"To be ill in front of his mother and sister would have mortified the boy past all bearing. Of course I hauled him from the vehicle. Bridget, by contrast, was horrified to think the neighbors had seen her indisposed. I should have anticipated that."

St. Didier frowned at his drink, took a taste, and rose to toss another square of peat onto the fire. "I see."

"What do you see?" Very likely, St. Didier saw a fool in love, which did not alter the facts at issue one iota.

"I see that I must organize my affairs such that I am available to escort her ladyship to a northern destination, the details of which I assume will not be disclosed to her family."

"That will be up to Lady Barclay. My recommendation would be to plan a trip to Scotland—summer approaches, after all—and to detour to Yorkshire indefinitely and discreetly."

"While you do what?"

Miss Sorcha and the children terribly. "Work. Ensure the Greers and their footmen, grooms, and familiars aren't heading north."

St. Didier finished his drink. "That is no sort of solution, Huxley. If you fear the child is in peril, for reasons nobody has yet disclosed to me, then you can't expect Lady Barclay to kick her heels in Yorkshire until the Greers magically decamp for darkest Cornwall."

Cornwall was far, far too good for the likes of Mr. and Mrs. Greer.

"Lady Barclay only need kick her heels in Yorkshire until the courts have officially appointed me as the children's guardian." Bernard had reached this conclusion while staring at a stack of correspondence that might have been written in the language of unicorns, so little did he comprehend or recall of it.

"Huxley, I am accounted a dull fellow. Please explain your thinking, and without reference to law Latin."

"Jordy has encountered several incidences of bad luck. A fat pony might maintain a trot if compelled to do so, but the creature was unlikely to run away with his rider when summer grass was to be had instead."

"True, but Jordy still could have been dragged a good way, stepped on, and otherwise banged about."

"He was banged about some, but suffered no lasting damage. The bellyache was gone within two hours—his second bellyache apparently, there having been a sour stomach at some point adjacent to the fall. This bump on the head will likely be healed within a week. The point is not to injure him, but to prove that he needs a competent guardian, and I am not the right party for the job."

"The saddle slipped last summer. You weren't in the picture."

"But Jordy was already without a guardian of record, the old duke having gone to his reward. Greer might have been nudging the present titleholder to appoint someone, preferably Greer, to that office. Cousin Coraline, all unbeknownst to her adoring spouse, might be trying to make that point. In the alternative, we accord the fat pony the status of an unhappy coincidence or an inspiration."

A gentleman was not supposed to pace, or Bernard would have worn a path in St. Didier's lovely carpet.

"If Greer was not responsible for the incident," Bernard went on, "he was still well aware of it. He might have concluded that repeated instances of Jordy coming to harm would reflect poorly on the duke's preferred prospective guardian. I am the problem, in other words, and if Chanderton can be made to view me in a dubious light, then Greer is the logical alternative."

St. Didier stared at the fire as if it were a chessboard with all pieces still in play. "Far-fetched," he said. "Fanciful, even, except that your theory explains the facts to a nicety. I agree that Coraline might well set these wheels in motion without consulting her spouse, or the two of them might be advancing this scheme together. Still, the whole theory has a castles-in-Spain quality to it."

No, it did not. It had a makes-perfect-sense quality.

"My theory," Bernard went on, "also encompasses Coraline recommending an agency that has provided only the most dubious of candidates for the post of governess. To the casual observer, Lady Barclay's nursery is not well staffed. Jordy's tutor, an aspiring scholar with few pedagogic credentials, is also connected to the Greer household. Entwhistle tutors the young ladies in French. To say that Jordy's studies are behind is a charitable characterization of where such a lively little boy's academics ought to be."

"I thought lively little boys and academics were sworn foes from time immemorial."

No vicar would survive long laboring under that assumption. "Jordy has a lively mind, a lively imagination. He sees sums as a game. He's a gifted mimic, which is half the battle with foreign languages. Nonetheless, if Chanderton should ask, any report of Jordy's progress would be discouraging."

St. Didier settled more deeply in his chair and steepled his fingers. "Because of the laggardly tutor and the lack of a suitable governess to date. Greer or Coraline could have engineered both situations. You have given this some thought. When presented with an instance of the Quality behaving badly, an examination of the relevant ledgers can be illuminating. Do you have any idea of the state of Greer's finances?"

"He has four daughters to launch and a wife determined to be fashionable. Might you look into the particulars?"

"You'd be better off asking your solicitors to do that. That lot hear things one wouldn't mention behind the door of a confessional."

Bernard schooled himself to patience for the thousandth time in two days. "If my solicitors, or the Huxley family solicitors, are seen to nose about the Greer family's finances, what do you suppose the gossips in the clubs would make of it?"

"Dear me. They will assume you intend to court the fair Annette, because Coraline has doubtless intimated as much—very discreetly, of course—to half the women married to the gossips. Right. You'd best leave the nosing about to me, though to be truthful, becoming Jordy's guardian shouldn't put Greer any closer to Jordy's funds. The courts are fussy about that."

Oh right. The courts. The courts were a reliable source of comfort to exactly nobody. "I beg leave to differ with you, but money might not be the primary motivator, St. Didier. Greer will become responsible for the heir presumptive to the Chanderton title. Coraline's status will rise as a result, and her daughters' prospects will benefit."

"Roundabout, but you are right: Guardian to the next duke would matter to Coraline and her sort. One does wonder what exactly went on in that Yorkshire parish of yours. All manner of intrigue, apparently."

The urge to pace was nigh unbearable. "Most of the mischief was engineered by, and intended to benefit, my very own mother. I was too willing to overlook Lady Josephine's machinations, too willing to pass them off as the annoying games of a hopeless busybody. Coraline has much of that Lady Busybody quality, and Greer's interests coincide with hers."

St. Didier slanted a puzzled look at Bernard. "These people are your family, Huxley."

"Precisely, and Lady Josephine is my *mother*. She committed multiple felonies simply to keep me from pursuing a new post."

"So she did. Is the brandy not to your liking?"

"This isn't the vintage that you served before."

"Gracious, a parson turned connoisseur. I'm impressed. I ran out of the other, and Fournier hadn't any of my usual preferences on hand. I'm left with the dregs of my cellar. He claimed he would soon be in a position to sell me the most exquisite brandy he had yet encountered in the whole of France. He was very jolly about it."

"Gallic exaggeration, surely." Bernard rose, leaving his drink unfinished. "One other consideration that you may attribute to my churchyard experience: If Greer controls the upbringing of the ducal heir, he will have indirect access to the funds required to raise that heir. Every pony Jordy outgrows must be sold. Every tutor hired on his behalf must negotiate wages. Presumably with Jordy's guardian."

Most definitely with Jordy's guardian, in fact. "If Greer was careful," Bernard went on, "he could make a packet off his ward without touching a penny of the boy's actual funds. I would be remiss if I did not mention as much. When one is in trade, the ledgers are never very far from one's awareness."

When one was in love, one's beloved was never very far from one's awareness as well. Bernard's imagination had never been so busy or so full of worrisome conjectures.

St. Didier got to his feet, taking both glasses to the sideboard. "If Fournier is willing to do business with you, Huxley, your prospects are looking up."

"So are Monsieur Fournier's. He'd never heard of your little family operation in the Charente department. I am not in the business of importing spirits. He is, and he understands that he owes this new opportunity to you. You will have a steady supply of good brandy at a bargain price. The French family will have more revenue, and Fournier will have both more revenue and some delighted customers."

"Why do that? Why pass along to an émigré an opportunity that could have been profitable for you?"

The question left Bernard profoundly weary. "The golden rule is the *golden* rule, St. Didier, applicable in all contexts, universally sensible and honorable without reference to creed or crown. I am no less answerable to my conscience in a business context than I would be in a cathedral. I could import that brandy, but I'd have to learn an entirely new line of products, deal with a supplier in a foreign country, and find customers in a competitive market. Better to do a fellow merchant a good turn and know that you'll be enjoying your preferred nightcap."

St. Didier took up the candle snuffer and doused the candelabra on the sideboard. "More vicars ought to go into business, methinks, though who would mind the flocks in their absences?"

"The Lord and Lady Busybodies would give it a good go. I'd best be off. Commerce waits for no man, and I've been absent without leave from my desk far too much of late."

"You're going to the office at this hour?" St. Didier sounded genuinely horrified.

The pull of unfinished business was relentless, also seductive. "I have an office at the town house. Camden bequeathed me that as well. I'll look over a few ledgers as a soporific and be that much less behind in the morning."

Though tomorrow morning, Bernard was to hack out with Sorcha, and not for all the ledgers in the City would he miss that appointment.

St. Didier set aside his snuffer. "Camden would tell you to take a good book to bed with you and forget the ledgers, but far be it from me to keep a man from his medicine."

"Camden hardly went to bed at all before his baroness got hold of him. Their reports of marital bliss continue unabated." Short, merry epistles that until recently had been more annoying than informative.

St. Didier led the way to the front foyer, which was illuminated by a single sconce.

"When I hear from Lorne at all, he seems to be very much in charity with the world. How is Lady Barclay taking all this potential family intrigue swirling about her son?"

"She is politely skeptical of my concerns, though not entirely dismissive." Bernard accepted his greatcoat, leaving it unbuttoned.

The evening air was cool rather than chilly, and a brisk walk was in order. "She has also given me leave to court her, though we haven't announced that to the family or the children."

Which was fortunate when Bernard and the children's mama disagreed pointedly on their present best interests.

St. Didier's expression was hard to read in the shadows. "You are to be congratulated, Huxley. Please believe I mean well when I also caution you to be careful." He passed Bernard his top hat.

"*We* will be careful. I am well aware that if Greer is trying to discredit me as a guardian, then for me to marry Jordy's mama is a long step toward thwarting his plans."

"If she'll marry you." St. Didier handed Bernard his walking stick. "I cannot imagine her ladyship enjoys the prospect of enmity within the family ranks. One should never presume on a lady's affections."

When had St. Didier learned that lesson and from whom? "One does not presume, but one does hope for the best. Good night, St. Didier."

"Be careful, and give my regards to her ladyship when next you see her."

He held the door, and Bernard passed into the darkness of the spring night.

CHAPTER THIRTEEN

The day was beginning with the balmy, cloudy weather that could descend into steady rain or clear off and usher in a beautiful spring day. Sorcha's mood was equally unsettled.

"Mr. Huxley." She nodded for the benefit of her groom, who trailed a few yards behind on an aging gelding. "A pleasure."

"Lady Barclay, likewise. Shall we enjoy your favorite path?"

Even the sound of Bernard's voice pleased her. The sight of him on his lean gray, the hint of amusement in his words as they played the polite games necessary in public...

I am in love. Sorcha relished the thought even as it worried her. Bernard had fallen curiously silent on the matter of Jordy's bump on the head, and his greeting was notably restrained.

"Mr. Huxley will see me home, Grimes."

"Very good, my lady." The old groom touched his cap and gave Bernard an admonitory glower. "Sir."

Bernard maneuvered his horse—Bounder—next to Sorcha's mare. "Rain this morning would have been disappointing, to say the least. How fare you, and how fare the children?"

The park wasn't crowded, probably as a result of the weather and also the advancing Season. In early spring, the need to see and be seen, to establish who was back in Town, and who had yet to make an appearance was paramount. As exhaustion set in and social calendars filled up, a morning hack became a luxury.

"I am well," Sorcha said, which was mostly true. "The children seem to like their new governess. Miss Gelling is imaginative, also firm and very good-humored. Gilchrist has given Miss Gelling a cautious vote of approval. Mr. Entwhistle has taken to hiding in his study."

They turned their horses onto the path that led along the Serpentine.

"Speaking of Entwhistle, what exactly do we know of his particulars?"

An odd gambit for a courting swain. Very odd. "I hired Entwhistle at a bargain. Coraline employs him to tutor her girls in French and Latin, though only Eglantine takes an interest in Latin. I had room to house him, Jordy was approaching the age when a tutor was needed, and Mr. Entwhistle was available."

"I fear he is no bargain, my lady."

Riding side by side with Bernard, Sorcha noted signs of fatigue evident only at close range. His eyes were shadowed, his mouth a little grim. While his turnout was pristine, the knot in his cravat was off-center, as was the golden pin securing the linen.

"Entwhistle is young," Sorcha said. "He doesn't cause any problems, and Jordy is accustomed to him."

"Jordy runs circles around Entwhistle, and Entwhistle spies on you. I grant you, matters have improved in recent weeks. Entwhistle simply lacks experience and probably deals better with biddable young ladies than with rambunctious little boys. He does take direction and seems to care about Jordy's progress."

"You want me to sack him." Coraline would find eleven thousand reasons to criticize a change of tutor. Sorcha wasn't keen on the notion either. "For a young man to lose his first official tutor's post could be devastating, and why should Entwhistle be any different from the entire houschold?"

Bernard held back the branch of a leafy maple dripping with a heavy dewfall. "What are you implying?"

"They all spy on me. They always have. Gilchrist's loyalty is trustworthy, but when she and I speak Gaelic, you can bet the whole neighborhood hears about it, as well as the duchess, Coraline, and probably the Mayor of London. When Jordy has a cold, when the fortune hunters make their annual trek to my parlor... I have virtually no privacy. I know that now."

Bernard adjusted his reins. "What fortune hunters?"

"The ones with pockets to let—those fortune hunters. Younger sons home from the war, widowers who find courting the diamonds and heiresses expensive and tedious. They all look in on me to remind me what I'm missing and to try to tempt me back to the altar."

The gray halted. "I am not a fortune hunter, Sorcha. Believe that if you believe nothing else."

Finally, the suitor had joined the discussion, albeit his tone was nearly priggish for a fellow who'd commenced his courting only three days ago.

"Your financial situation doesn't interest me, Bernard. What has put you in such an ungracious mood?"

"Bounder, walk on." The horse plodded forth. "'Ungracious' is an interesting description. Apt, for which I apologize. I am deluged at the office, concerned for you and the children, and have been to more Venetian gossip-breakfasts and at home gossip sessions, and card-gossip parties in the past fortnight than I hope to attend in my entire life. The duchess is plotting a ball at the end of the month, and I am to make my debut. One is tempted to dress in white and wear roses in one's hair. I suppose a fan embroidered with gamboling lambs would be too much."

He'd been neglecting his rest again. That explained much. "You poor dear. If you attend Her Grace's ball—and you must—then the hostesses will include you in other formal entertainments." Roses in his hair...

"My valet will be in alt. I never had a valet before I went into trade. He fusses about everything in bad French and laundered Cockney. This is not what I wanted to discuss with you in the very limited time we have together."

He'd wanted to discuss sacking Entwhistle for some reason. Sorcha had wanted to discuss nothing at all. To find a quiet clearing in the woods, dismount, and wrap her arms about the solid, wonderful reality of Bernard Huxley.

Granted, he wasn't at his most wonderful in his present mood. "What do you want to discuss, Bernard?"

"Jordy's bump on the head."

This again. "I share your concern—somebody treated my son very badly at Mirobello and then didn't own up to their bad behavior—but I don't see that the situation admits of any resolution. I will exercise caution when Jordy is around his cousins, but other than that—"

"Other than that, you can sack Entwhistle or, better still, quit Town."

Sorcha's mare shied as a gust of wind whipped a branch across the path. "Settle, girl." She patted the mare's shoulder, though how could the horse settle when the weather was so contrary?

"I realize my proposal sounds ludicrous," Bernard went on. "If anybody had told me that my own mother was tampering with my mail, subjecting my parishioners to extortion, and pilfering pin money from the local orphanage, I would have called that ridiculous too."

What had his perishing mother...? "Bernard, did you even sleep last night?"

He peered at the sky. "I think so."

His ungraciousness, his stubborn fixation on a bit of juvenile mischief, the lines grooving his mouth... One did not have to be a mama to understand the evidence.

"You need a nap, Bernard. You will come home with me, I will feed you a proper breakfast, and then you are to find your bed and deposit yourself therein until you've treated your temple unto the Lord to the rest it craves."

"I am tired, but I am also concerned that Coraline—"

"Not now, Bernard. You can be as concerned as you please—I have concerns too—but we will discuss them far more productively when you can put two sensible sentences together." Sorcha used her Mama-isn't-having-any-nonsense voice, and it seemed to do the trick.

She circled her horse in the direction they'd come, and—signs and wonders—when traveling toward home, the mare was much less susceptible to spooks and shies. Bernard's gelding toddled along, and Sorcha had to look closely to ensure Bernard wasn't asleep in the saddle.

"I am concerned," Bernard said as they approached the park gates, "that Greer or Coraline want me displaced as Jordy's next guardian. If Jordy's studies aren't progressing, if he's having too many mishaps and unexplained illnesses, then my competence is cast in doubt."

Two sentences, and they made sense in themselves. Sorcha decided to humor him, because that strategy generally applied when an overly tired male was in the picture. Then too, even when well rested, Bernard would not let a matter drop until he'd analyzed it to his satisfaction.

"Why would Tallister engage in such a roundabout scheme, Bernard? If he wants guardianship of Jordy, why not simply petition Chanderton directly or win me to the cause? Until a few weeks ago, you were unknown to me, while Tally and I are at least cordial."

This peculiar exchange was reminding Sorcha that, in some ways, Bernard was still unknown to her. She had learned the muscular contours of his bare back, knew the way his breath hitched when he found his pleasure, and could detect the particular gleam in his eyes when determination coalesced into one of his unorthodox strategies—flying dragons, swimming unicorns, card tricks.

But much of him—his romantic past, his upbringing, his churchly endeavors—was a terra incognita to her. His descriptions of his mother were frankly horrifying, and his shift from churchman to cit had been abrupt indeed.

"For all I know," Bernard said, guiding his horse into the street, "Tallister did approach Chanderton, or Chanderton signaled Tallister's unsuitability. Coraline might be moving her troops around without a word to her nominal commanding officer. I am using military metaphors outside the schoolroom. You are right. I am tired."

Not merely tired—exhausted. "We will talk later, Bernard, when you've rested."

"I should have a cot moved into the office."

"No, you should not. You should hire an assistant. Who are those two boys?"

"Which two—oh, the blond is Heevers. The shorter, dark-haired lad is Ipswich. I am being summoned. Kessler now dispatches them to nanny me about Town. Vexing in the extreme, but the boys have proven useful a time or two when I needed to send a message back to the office."

"You are spied on too," Sorcha said. "Welcome to Town life, Mr. Huxley."

"I don't care for it, though I care very much for present company. I've missed you. I meant to say that earlier."

"Glad to hear it." Sorcha had needed to hear it, in fact. "I've missed you too."

When they reached the mews, Bernard stumbled a bit getting off his horse. Sorcha summoned his junior nannies and consigned them to the kitchen. She sat Bernard down before a sizable plate of toast, eggs, and ham, and when he was doing justice to the meal, she sent an epistle off to Mr. Kessler, who needed to learn a thing or two about the proper care and treatment of his employer.

"Mr. Huxley's done fallen asleep, your ladyship." The first footman sounded both embarrassed and amazed when he found Sorcha at her escritoire. "Has the butter knife in one hand and a piece of toast in the other, sitting as upright as a bishop, but he's gone for forty winks, ma'am."

"Or more than forty." The situation would be comical, except that Sorcha did not feel inclined to explain to Coraline or the duchess why Bernard had been napping in Sorcha's breakfast parlor. "Have the coach put to. You can see Mr. Huxley home. Have a word with his staff about a firm hand being needed with people who work too hard. They were employed by Lord Lorne before he came into his honors. You will find them a sympathetic audience."

"Yes, my lady. Shall I waken Mr. Huxley?"

"We'll do it together." Less potential for talk that way.

Sorcha wanted to dismiss Bernard's maunderings about spies and schemes, but Bernard was, above all, sensible. Kind, patient, occasionally inventive, occasionally passionate, but also sensible. He wasn't given to mad flights.

He was utterly daft, though, if he thought Sorcha would remove the children from London over what could only be a nasty prank gone awry.

"I'm sorry, sir." Kessler looked pleased with himself rather than contrite as he stood across from Bernard's desk. "Her ladyship was very clear you were not to be disturbed. I must say you look a little more the thing for having taken a day of rest."

The allusion to the Sabbath was hardly subtle. Bernard had slept for eighteen hours and awoken feeling eighty years old and sleep-drunk. Also foolish.

"Her ladyship does not employ you, Kessler, and should a similar situation arise in future, I will expect you to recall that."

Kessler smiled, putting Bernard in mind of a beatific Father Christmas in the off-season. "His lordship used to holler something marvelous when we let him sleep. He never wrote his notes in Latin, though."

Very foolish. "Latin?"

Kessler settled into the chair opposite the desk and passed over a wad of correspondence. "I could have managed French, German, or even some Scots, but my Latin went begging decades ago."

Each page of the stack was adorned with notes in Bernard's own tidy hand, all written in Latin.

Reiectionem comiter mitte. Send a polite rejection.

In principio consenti, vitanda sunt specifica. Agree in principle, specifics to be avoided.

Statim singula pete. Ask for details immediately.

The business directions were sound enough. Some consolation there.

"Kinrade has fairly good Italian," Kessler said, "but he didn't want to guess. His lordship would mutter in German, I think it was. Might have been speaking Yorkshire, though."

Kessler was in good form. "Did you win the betting pool, Kessler?"

He sat up. "You know about that?"

I do now. "You all speculated about how long it would take me to work myself into a collapse, and not one of you thought to suggest that I voluntarily get some rest?"

"With all due respect, sir, you are a Huxley. Telling you something you do not want to hear would be a thankless and pointless task. The polite word for that quality is 'determination,' but stubbornness might apply as well."

By blood, Bernard was a Dolforth, which mattered not at all. He was a Huxley by name and upbringing. "Does the term pigheaded come to mind?"

"I wouldn't go that far, sir."

"Kind of you." Bernard began translating his Latin notes. "Might you hire me an assistant, Kessler?" Sorcha had made that suggestion, and she was right. She was wrong about the Greers, but to tell Lady Barclay something she did not want to hear... a useless business. *Negotium inutile.*

Thankless and pointless, in fact. Perhaps she'd be a Huxley one day too.

"Were you jesting about an assistant, sir?"

"The Latin has amused me. I am in complete earnest about an assistant. Find me a banker's wayward son, a restless curate with no vocation, a would-be fortune hunter ready to give up the game and work for a living."

"A discontented man?"

"A man motivated to make the best of what might be his last chance. If he knows Latin, so much the better. He should have charm if he's not to offend the clerks, and he'll want basic honor if he's not to offend me. The need is urgent, but discernment must take precedence over haste. Here." He handed the translated stack across the desk. "We can start on the morning batch next, but I have a luncheon appointment. Please send me Heevers and Ipswich."

"Of course, sir."

Kessler departed without further homilies, which was fortunate because Bernard needed no more preaching from any quarter. He'd been dangerously tired, stupidly tired, and all because Mayfair hostesses were entitled to look him over and count his figurative teeth.

"Entitled by whom or by what celestial decree?" he muttered, getting out his calendar. Meetings as far as the eye could see, evening *entertainments*—using the term euphemistically—and no time to spend with Sorcha and the children when those activities encompassed both his greatest pleasure and his solemn duty.

He gave Ipswich and Heevers their orders for the next week, plowed through the morning correspondence, and was out the door by the eleventh hour. Time enough to get home, change into riding attire, and make it to the park with ten minutes to spare.

Amazing what adequate rest could do for a man's productivity and sense of purpose.

"That's Cousin Bernard," Bridget said, standing on the picnic blanket. "His horse is gray, like a ghost."

Jordy was on his feet in the next instant. "Bounder isn't a ghost. He's a gelding. Cousin is trying to put both weight and muscle on him."

Such manly talk. "What does that mean?" Sorcha asked. "To put weight and muscle on a horse?"

"Grimes says that means to get the horse fit," Bridget replied before Jordy could admit he hadn't a clue. "Grimes also says Cousin Bernard is no sylph, but I don't know what a sylph is."

"A fairy of the air," Sorcha said, shading her eyes the better to watch Bernard's approach. Bounder was looking a bit less ribby, and the horse cantered down the path without laboring for breath. "I am no sylph either." Which Bernard seemed to enjoy about her.

Coraline had already started remarking on Bridget's unfortunate tendency to height, and Jordy was also tall for his age. Not a sylph, fairy, or gnome to be seen.

Bernard slowed Bounder to a walk, patted his horse, and pretended to hold up a spyglass. "Picnic off the port bow! The SS *Bounder* asks permission to dock in the royal harbor."

"Bounder isn't a ship," Jordy said, settling back onto the blanket. "Cousin Bernard is silly."

Better silly than spouting accusations and suspicions. "Imaginative. Permission granted by order of Her Majesty Queen Sorcha!" And to blazes with what the footman, enjoying a respite on a bench in the shade, thought of a lady raising her voice.

"And by Princess of the Unicorns, Bridget Catherine Marie Dolforth!" Bridget plopped on the blanket in an unroyal heap.

Jordy opened the hamper at his corner. "You lot are all silly, and I'm hungry, and now Cousin is here, so we can eat."

"Your Majesty, Princess Unicorn, Lord Jordy of the Picnic Feast, good day." Bernard swung off his horse. "No eating until diplomatic protocol has been observed."

"If I had a ring, you'd have to kiss it." Bridget flung a curtsey at him and sat back down with a bit more decorum. "Annette knows all about being a princess, and that's what she says."

Jordy opened the second hamper. "You don't have a ring, and Annette is stupid."

Bernard ran up his stirrups and loosened Bounder's girth. "Young man, is that any way to greet an ambassador returned to the royal court from the distant and perilous purlieus of the City?"

Jordy held up a silver flask with the Dolforth coat of arms engraved on it. "What's perilous about the City?"

"A question for the ages, young man. We haven't enough crossing sweepers, to begin with. *Hazards* everywhere as a result. Noxious miasmas rise from the very streets, and solicitors occupy every third building." Bernard extracted a length of rope and a stake from his saddlebag and picketed Bounder a few yards off. "Please keep a sharp eye on my dragon, or I'll have a long walk back to my office."

To Sorcha's sharp eye, Bernard had regained his balance. He was spontaneously entertaining the children with his imaginative flights, moving with energy, and back on his mettle.

Bless Mr. Kessler, who'd acknowledged Sorcha's note with a few words of polite understanding.

"We have tarts," Jordy reported, still nose-down in the hampers. "Also meat pies, oranges, a cheese-and-ham pie, and chocolates."

Bernard lowered himself to Sorcha's side. "I have a prodigious appetite for all delicious things. Leave me at least two chocolates, or I'll toss you into the Serpentine by your boots."

A governess would have missed the look Jordy aimed at Bernard. Bernard might have missed it, and even Sorcha wasn't certain what that expression portended—fear, annoyance, anger?

"I can't swim," Jordy said. "If you toss me into the Serpentine, I will drown, and then I will come back and haunt you to death, even if you hide in the City where nobody will ever think to look for you."

Bernard passed Sorcha a plate. "Tell me, Jordy, would you like to come see the City with me some pleasant day?"

Bridget wiggled over to Bernard's side. "I want to see the City. I want to see the Tower too."

"We already saw it," Jordy retorted. "The Tower, that is. We saw the lions and hyenas, and they stink."

Sorcha put two slices of the cold ham-and-cheese pie on the plate, along with some beef tarts and an orange. Jordy ought not to be tired, and his mood hadn't been this sour in some time.

"I was too little when we saw it," Bridget replied. "I don't remember the Tower, but I don't want to see it with you if you are going to be such a grouchy old swine, Jordan Dolforth."

Jordy wrinkled his nose and snorted like a pig. Bernard sent Sorcha a quizzical look. Lord Jordy of the Picnic Feast was in a notably foul humor.

"Jordy suffered a significant bump on the head," Bernard said to nobody in particular. "This can put a fellow inexplicably out of sorts, make him crotchety even. Jordy, I would never throw you into the Serpentine. The authorities would arrest me for it, and the ghost of Queen Caroline would haunt me in truth. It's her lake, you know."

"Which Queen Caroline?" Bridget asked, which allowed Bernard to prose on about the Georgian succession, the good queens, and the history of London, all while Sorcha filled plates and wished that Lord Barclay had bothered to picnic with his children even once.

They would not have recalled such an occasion, but Sorcha would, just as she'd take with her into old age the image of Bernard cantering across the grass and blathering on about royal harbors and the City's abundance of horse droppings.

"We brought kites," Bridget said when she'd devoured the one chocolate she'd been allotted. "Mama said there's a decent breeze, though how can a breeze be decent? A breeze is a breeze."

"Kites?" Bernard affected a puzzled look. "I don't believe we have kites in Yorkshire. Somebody will have to explain these kites to me."

Jordy took the bait. "The kite is like a little sailboat for the air, without much of a ship, and you run with it on a string, and the wind grabs the kite, and up it goes. For a time, anyway. Sometimes it won't go up, and sometimes—"

"It crashes down." Bridget took up the instruction.

The children soon had Bernard charging down the nearest declivity, launching their kites while they bellowed encouragement. The breeze ruffled his hair, the horse watched the situation with a placid eye, and Sorcha knew a joy so sweet as to be nearly painful.

Thank goodness the suitor was back in evidence. That other fellow, the overly protective, overly tired guardian, was poor company.

Bernard turned over the kite-launching task to the young footman, whom Sorcha knew to be a dab hand with a flying dragon, and returned to the blankets.

"You got my note," he said, helping himself to another chocolate.

"You demanded a chance to redeem yourself after nearly falling off your horse at our previous rendezvous. One could not deny such a heartfelt petition."

"I've missed you. Did I say that part aloud last time or only think it?"

"You said it. I said I missed you too."

He bit off half the chocolate and passed Sorcha the rest. "I missed you all over again in my sleep. Mr. Kessler is your sworn vassal, and he's hiring me an assistant. Am I pigheaded, Sorcha?"

"Yes. I am familiar with the quality, having a touch of it myself."

"Yours is a mild case, though. A gentleman is compelled to keep the record accurate in that regard. I have also taken a look at my calendar, your ladyship. I would like to consult you regarding some regrets that must be sent if I am to retain my sanity."

Sorcha was seized with an impulse to push Bernard onto his back and kiss his precious sanity right out from under him. This Bernard was too kissable. That other fellow... Sorcha hoped she'd seen the last of him.

"Regrets, Mr. Huxley?"

"My social calendar is intolerably full. I am to attend at least two, sometimes three, different affairs in an evening, and the duchess's ball looms as an unparalleled ordeal."

"I'll give you my supper waltz."

Bernard closed the lid of the hamper. "You should make me work for it, Sorcha. I'm courting you, after all."

"Court me quietly, please. I want to enjoy myself before Coraline gets wind that I have designs on you."

As soon as the words were out, Sorcha regretted them. She most definitely had designs on Bernard, though the thought of remarrying —even him—was taking some getting used to. A lot of getting used to.

Mentioning Coraline, though, admitted a serpent to the garden of flirtation.

"Designs upon my humble person? My lady, I am flattered past all bearing, and I will most assuredly stand up with you for any and all available supper waltzes. Jordy isn't feeling quite the thing, is he?"

"He's been subdued all week, but then, Jordy has always been something of a clown. If this is my baby boy growing up, I suppose I must learn to accommodate the change. Does a bump on the head truly affect personality?" And where had Bernard learned that?

"A concussion can. Spend enough time in enough sickrooms, and you come across all manner of arcane medical facts. When might you be available to consult regarding my social calendar?"

He held out another chocolate to her. The last of the lot.

Sorcha took it, bit it in half, and passed him the remainder.

"You finish it," Bernard said. "The look of you savoring your sweet is treat enough for me."

He offered that confession in all seriousness. Sorcha finished the chocolate, chewing slowly while Bernard regarded her almost bashfully.

To share a picnic like this... Sorcha was on the point of saying something sentimental and honest when she spotted a trio of riders emerging from the trees.

"What?" Bernard followed her gaze. "Drat and perdition. What are they doing here?"

Annette, Eglantine, and Entwhistle approached, their horses moving at a shuffling walk.

"Come by after supper tonight," Sorcha said. "We'll review your calendar then."

"You are managing me," Bernard replied, gaze on the youthful threesome. "Preventing me from working late. My thanks for that. Time for dear old Cousin Bernard to do the pretty."

Over on the hill, the children and the young footman had paused in their kite flying. Bernard rose and offered Sorcha a hand up, which she accepted and then dropped.

"Ladies, Mr. Entwhistle," she said. "Good day. Nice weather for an outing."

"Oh, it is," Annette replied. "Mr. Entwhistle opined that one could practice French on horseback, the better to acquaint oneself with equestrian vocabulary, and here we are."

She was on the same aging mare, but she sat the horse more confidently, and the feathers brushing her shoulder were at a jauntier angle.

"Ladies." Bernard bowed. "Entwhistle." A nod. "You mustn't let us keep you. The children will be flying their kites all afternoon if possible."

Annette shaded her eyes, perhaps the better to look fetching on her horse. "Oh, I hadn't noticed. Is Jordy quite recovered from his little misadventure?"

How like her mother she sounded, and Sorcha did not consider that a compliment. "He's fine. Mr. Entwhistle, you may expect him in your study in an hour or so." Though since when had Entwhistle been out *teaching French* when it wasn't his half day and without notifying the employer in whose household he dwelled?

Bernard's suggestion that Entwhistle should be sacked reared its head.

"Cousin Bernard," Annette said, "I have just had the most marvelous idea. Eggie is dying to stop at some musty old bookshop, where I refuse to be seen. You can escort me home and spare me the ordeal of the bookshop, while Mr. Entwhistle can escort Eggie. They can even practice their Latin."

When had Annette become so... so shameless? Sorcha half hoped Bernard would put her in her place, but she knew his manners wouldn't allow that.

"If you'll wait while I take my leave of her ladyship, I can accommodate that request, Miss Greer, provided you understand that time is of the essence. I cannot add any calls or stops to our itinerary."

Eggie looked pleased with that riposte, while Mr. Entwhistle sat upon one of Sorcha's geldings, fiddling with the horse's mane.

"My lady." Bernard bowed over her hand. "Good day, and thanks for the meal. I see the children are back at their kiting, so I will ask you to make my farewells to them."

Sorcha curtseyed, half amused, half annoyed at Annette's interruption.

Had Bernard not spiked her cannon, the little minx would have dragged him to every hat shop and glovemaker in Mayfair and tossed in an impromptu call on Lady Bloomton for good—or bad—measure. Gentlemen that he was, he'd have sauntered along at her side, while the matchmakers whispered and the gossips discreetly pointed and nodded.

Bernard gathered up his horse and left in company with the young people.

Sorcha hiked up the hill and demanded a turn launching the red dragon kite.

CHAPTER FOURTEEN

"We have hill races in Yorkshire." No way to start a conversation, but Bernard was quite out of small talk. "After fifteen minutes in Annette's company, I felt as if I could have scaled sheer vertical inclines at a dead run and gone for miles at high altitudes thereafter. A gentleman ought not to say such things."

Sorcha closed the door behind him, kissed his cheek, and led him to the library's reading table.

"And yet, I still account you a gentleman in every particular. Did she chatter?"

To be greeted thus, with a sympathetic smile and a kiss, was stupefyingly sweet. "Annette chattered, and giggled, and chattered some more with occasional odd sounds sprinkled throughout, probably meant to resemble French. 'Dear Cousin Bernard, might we stop for an ice?' '*Cher Cousin* Bernard, we approach the very best confectionery in all of creation.' 'Bernard'—she addressed me simply as Bernard before we'd traveled three streets from the park—'might you not relent for one teeny-tiny little stop at the pie shop?'"

"You stood firm?"

"Even in the face of her French. 'Chair Coo-soon'? Whatever

could that mean? When I denied her importuning, I felt like I was both a bully and being bullied. No wonder Coraline is so anxious to see Annette married. If Annette's sisters imitate her example, the bachelors will flee Mayfair for the Continent."

Sorcha took the place at the head of the table. Bernard held her chair, then seated himself at her right hand. She was in wonderful good looks, all serene and amused and kissable.

"I am whining." He gazed around the library, noting the open curtains, though the view looked out onto the darkening garden. One could sit with one's intended in a shadowy garden... "Whining is unbecoming. I beg your pardon. How has your day gone?"

"Do you know, my husband never once asked me that?"

Bernard risked a stroke of his fingers over the back of her hand. "I am asking because I want to know. I can tell you I sat at my desk this afternoon grateful to attend to my work rather than endure hat shops and cousinly presumptions." He'd also sat at his desk wishing he'd been able to linger in the park.

"My day has been peaceful," Sorcha said. "The children tired themselves out chasing dragons through the sky, and Gilchrist and Miss Gelling could not be happier. Why did you suggest I sack Entwhistle?"

Bernard hadn't had to suggest it. Sorcha had leaped to the accurate conclusion all on her own. Entwhistle made him uneasy, but that was hardly evidence against the man.

"My primary complaint is that he lacks the imagination and experience to keep up with a lively little fellow like Jordy."

Sorcha rose and tugged the bell-pull three times, then resumed her seat. "That wasn't your only complaint."

"This has been on your mind?"

"Jordy isn't himself of late. The bump on the head might be to blame, but today was not Entwhistle's half day, and there he was trotting about with Annette and Eglantine. He and Jordy have been having great fun with sums, though that was your idea, not his. Why did Coraline sing Entwhistle's praises when he's less than adequate for the post?"

Not quite the same thing as admitting that Entwhistle was a spy, or even that he had divided loyalties. Nonetheless, Sorcha was worried—perhaps a good thing—and managing the whole burden of that worry on her own.

Definitely a bad thing. "We would not have left Mirobello without Jordy, Sorcha. I would have mustered the whole village to join the search, and we would not have relented until he was safe. As it is, we located him after less than ten minutes of concerted effort."

"*You* found him."

"With Eglantine's assistance, yes."

Sorcha held out her hand, and Bernard laced his fingers through hers. Serious talk, indeed.

"Bernard, I suspect Jordy is afraid. This is pointless, of course. He's merely a little boy growing up in the normal fashion with a normal complement of scrapes, bruises, tummy aches, and falls. Nonetheless, when I mentioned the Duchess's Day at Chanderton, he announced that he didn't want to go. Jordy loves Duchess's Day. We all do, even the staff."

"What is the Duchess's Day?" And if the Greers were in attendance, Bernard might have to come down with a roaring case of the Vicar's Lament, a mysterious ailment known to strike on fine spring days, curable by fresh air and proximity to an unbaited fishing pole.

Jordy and Bridget could suffer a touch as well. The young were not immune simply because they hadn't taken holy orders.

"Two days before the ball, Her Grace of Chanderton opens the Chanderton seat to family and neighbors, and we gather for a grand picnic. The village has a fete in the morning, and the afternoon is for playing pall-mall, paddling around on the lake, stuffing ourselves with good food, and ambling about the park. We toddle back into Town the next morning fortified for the ball and quite in charity with Their Graces."

"And Jordy does not want to participate?" Bernard liked the

sound of this outing, but for the possible guest list. "I take it the Greers attend?"

"Of course. Your brother might even turn up."

Bernard was growing very curious about this brother of his. "I've written to him. Her Grace gave me his direction. No reply yet."

Bernard wanted to meet his brother, and a family gathering was the ideal place for that. He did not want to attend Duchess's Day. Rather, he did not want Jordy and Bridget to attend if the Greers were on hand, which they were sure to be.

The matter wanted thought. He extracted a small folding calendar from his pocket and laid it open on the table. "How many of these irritations can I delete from my calendar without being banished from Mayfair altogether?"

Sorcha leaned nearer, bringing with her a hint of jasmine. "You are in demand, Bernard. Any other bachelor would be flattered."

"This bachelor fell asleep at his beloved's breakfast table. Not well done of me. I have been reminded that I need sleep. Ergo, some of this,"—he waved a hand over the calendar—"must go. Lorne explained to me that I will be approached in the clubs with discreet inquiries regarding investment opportunities, but I must first pass muster with the hostesses."

She drew the calendar toward her. "Then you can send all the regrets you please to Lady Bloomton. My gracious, she is entertaining as if… Well, she does have three daughters and a horde of nieces and goddaughters to launch."

"Forget all about hill races. I will soon be flying high above London like an errant dragon. Do I send regrets because the family is well fixed and avoids commerce?"

"You send regrets because they are not well fixed. They cannot be a business asset to you, and you cannot be a social asset to them." Sorcha rose, went to the desk, produced a gum eraser from a drawer, and returned to the table. She began delicately eliminating Lady Bloomton from Bernard's social life.

"Will she be offended?" he asked.

"Exceedingly. She might even treat you to the cut direct, though even for her, that would be imprudent. You can also send regrets to Mrs. Culver, though she's a perfectly gracious hostess with no unmarried daughters. Her challenge is her sons. One of them ought to marry well, but they are both inveterate scamps. If they approach you about investment opportunities, they are looking for unrealistic returns."

Three more outings fell to the gum eraser. With each rubbing-out, Bernard felt his heart and mind growing lighter. Sorcha excised several more hostesses from Bernard's calendar, and he began to feel positively jolly.

All that time to spend with Sorcha and the children. All that time to train an assistant, whose earnest labor would free Bernard yet still more to spend time with his loved ones...

"You have an objection?" Sorcha paused with the eraser poised above yet another wasted evening.

"No objection at all, except... Would any of these entertainments appeal to you?"

Sorcha beamed at him, favoring him with the smile he classified as her Highland Houri expression. Full of mischief and warmth.

"Mrs. Culver's card party. The high sticklers aren't invited, the play is modest, and the company is often hilarious. Her sons are witty, and their friends are witty. The elders get into the spirit of the evening—you would be surprised at how Their Graces of Moreland can banter when the duchess is inclined to flirt with her spouse—and the buffet is magnificent."

"Will you come with me?" Bernard's question was far from casual.

Sorcha added a note to the calendar. "I believe I shall. The proceeds go to charity, of course, and Mrs. Culver ensures there are proceeds and that they truly do go to charity."

"Might you choose another outing we could share?" In for a penny...

Sorcha set down her pencil and rose to pull the drapes closed. "I know what you're about, Bernard. I'm flattered."

He got up and started on the curtains at the other end of the room. "What am I about?"

"You are courting me. Therefore, we must be seen together in public. That is doubtless how it works in Yorkshire, but it wasn't true for me here in Mayfair. I'd dance the occasional dance with Lord Barclay, we hacked out together a few times, but I danced and hacked out with any number of bachelors. One did as one was told."

One had regrets about that, apparently. "You are in charge of yourself this time around." And reluctant to exchange her freedom for the bonds of matrimony. Bernard closed the last of the drapes, which left him standing two feet from his *beloved.*

That was the word. That was the exact, right word. "How would you like to be courted, Sorcha?"

"Affectionately?" She crossed her arms and became fascinated with the calendar sitting open on the desk. "Quietly?"

Bernard plucked an idea from the growing pile of insecurities weighting his heart. "Sincerely?"

"Yes." Her chin came up. "Sincerely, not for show. The time with you at Mirobello was... was..."

A woman could torment a man with an uncertain silence, but Bernard waited for Sorcha to decide what Sorcha wanted to say.

"I hadn't known, Bernard. I hadn't known such intimacies were possible. I had hoped, and my hopes looked laughable after a week of marriage to Barclay. Now I hope again, and this disconcerts me."

The urge to take her into his arms was nigh blinding. "I am not Lord Barclay, may he rest in whatever peace he deserves, and you are not that biddable, bewildered girl."

Sorcha took a step closer. "You are not the unfailingly considerate, correct vicar either, are you?"

"I am not." Heaven and Cousin Camden be thanked.

She wrapped her arms around his waist and gave him her weight, wholly, completely. A wonderful gift of woman, warmth, and trust.

Bernard held her, glad beyond telling that he was no longer that vicar and never would be again.

"We'll attend Mrs. Culver's card party," Sorcha said, her cheek against Bernard's shoulder, "and Her Grace of Moreland's musicale. If Lord Valentine plays—and he'd hardly refuse his own mama's request—then you will think angels ought to have keyboards rather than harps."

Bernard held her as a thousand wishes fluttered through his mind, none of them having to do with angels. He wished that they were already married. That servants all went to bed before nightfall. That the vicar in Yorkshire had known such joy awaited him in London.

Sorcha eased away, took his hand, and led him back to the table. A soft tap at the door had her dropping his hand and admitting a footman bearing a tray.

"On the table please, O'Leary," Sorcha said. "Don't bother returning for the tray this evening."

"Very good, my lady. Sir." He bowed and decamped, cutting a fine figure in his livery.

"O'Leary was with you in the park today?" Bernard asked.

"He was. My next younger sister employs his older brother. Kevin hails from the Isle of Mull, and he wanted to see Town. He's a hard worker, and the children adore him." She lifted the lid from the plate on the tray and revealed a cold collation—meat and cheese—while a basket held bread wrapped in snowy linen. Another basket held an abundance of cinnamon biscuits.

Food. Wonderful, simple food. "Lady Barclay, I am compelled to confess the highest adoration for you and your cook."

"You skipped supper. I prefer not to deal with peckish males. Cider or tea?"

"Cider, please. You'll join me?"

They fell to, not much discussion needed. *Pass the salt. Excellent ham. Another slice of cheddar?* When Bernard's tummy was as happy as the rest of him, he topped up their glasses of cider and used his libation to salute his hostess.

"My thanks for the feast and congratulations on hiring one of your own."

Sorcha paused while buttering a slice of bread. "Kevin?"

"He speaks the Erse, does he not?"

"He does. It's his native tongue, in fact."

"And he was recommended by your sibling, and he's connected to your greater family by his own fraternal ties. He'll be loyal to you all the rest of his days for giving him a way to leave home—he's a younger son, making his own way—and Gilchrist will enjoy having him about."

"They do seem friendly. I hadn't realized that I'm such a domestic genius. Have another cinnamon biscuit."

Bernard had two more. They put him in mind of the duchess—delicate and rich.

That thought was uncomfortably sobering. "For the Duchess's Day," he said, "let us agree that one of us will keep Jordy in sight at all times. If he thinks we're exercising extra vigilance, he might be more at ease."

Bernard would be more at ease, for reasons that would spoil the mood entirely.

Sorcha added a slice of cheese atop her buttered bread, folded the bread in half, and took a bite.

"This brings us back to Entwhistle, whom you'd like to see replaced."

"He is barely qualified as a tutor, though he may have plenty of scholarly inclinations. He's somewhat beholden to Coraline and Tallister for his bread, and he does watch the goings-on in your household."

"Jordy gets along with him."

Not a detail. "What would you think of adding Bridget to the afternoon study sessions?"

Sorcha munched another bite. "That would appeal to Bridget. Entwhistle's job would be easier because Bridget goads Jordy to exert himself. Jordy has a gift for languages—his Gaelic is better than Bridget's—but Bridget can recall facts and figures like a parrot."

Sorcha knew her children. Not something every aristocratic mother could say. Then too, Jordy had come to no harm under his mother's roof.

"Perhaps sacking Entwhistle isn't necessary. Include Bridget in the tutoring sessions and suggest to Miss Gelling that she monitor Bridget's attendance. She will bring needed experience to the pedagogy, and Bridget will inspire Jordy to apply himself. When summer arrives, you can give Entwhistle his conge and a glowing recommendation."

"I still don't want to put him out of a job, Bernard, but we needn't cross that bridge just yet. For now, Bridget's schedule changes, Miss Gelling will keep an eye on Bridget's participation in her new lessons, and we will keep an eye on Jordy at Duchess's Day. My guess is he will be equal parts insulted and reassured."

Sorcha was making reluctant concessions. Bernard could hear the hesitance in her voice, see it in her diffident air. She put down her cheese sandwich half eaten.

"I meant what I said about my supper waltz, Bernard."

"Good. Courting you sincerely does not mean courting you exclusively behind closed doors, my lady, as delightful as those endeavors have been."

He would have suited deeds to words, except that the door opened the moment he finished speaking.

Entwhistle stood in the corridor, looking flummoxed. "Beg pardon. Did not know the library was occupied. I was just going to find myself a book..." His gaze fell on the decimated tray and the half-consumed glasses of cider. Nobody had been holding hands or standing inappropriately close to anybody else, but the impression was still one of cozy informality.

"Come back in a quarter hour," Sorcha said. "You can have the whole library to yourself, though you should know, Entwhistle, that I'd like to try including Bridget in your afternoon sessions with Jordy. She's certainly his academic equal, if not his superior. Miss Gelling will see that she gets off on a good foot with you."

Bernard rose and brought the basket of cinnamon biscuits to Entwhistle. "Help yourself. Wouldn't want them to go stale in the larder." He smiled politely, the better to make the little sneak squirm.

Entwhistle took one sweet, then another. "Thank you, sir. Sorry to interrupt, your ladyship. I'll look forward to including Miss Bridget in our lessons. Master Jordan will enjoy showing off his Latin to her." He nodded awkwardly and withdrew, biscuits in hand.

When Bernard brought the biscuits back to the table, Sorcha helped herself to one as well.

"Don't say it. He spies on me. He has an office full of books, but he could see light from the library windows before we closed the drapes and came to investigate."

"He has been with you for months. He might well be a spy and an incompetent tutor, but we have no proof that he's a threat." Neither did they have exculpatory evidence.

"Give me your handkerchief."

He passed over a clean square of plain linen.

"Of course he isn't a threat. We are making much ado about nothing where Jordy is concerned, though now I sound appallingly like Coraline." She wrapped three biscuits in the handkerchief. "We will have a fine time at Duchess's Day. All will be well, and we can cease jumping at shadows."

Better to jump at shadows than be set upon by footpads. "I hope you will allow me to partner you for a few hands at Mrs. Culver's card party. I suppose I'd best be going, lest the corridor monitor return to chaperone us."

He rose, stashing the sweets in his pocket and collecting his much-amended calendar. "Thank you, Sorcha. I almost look forward to offending Lady Bloomton with my regrets."

"You will survive her censure, I assure you. Many have." Sorcha rose and walked with him to the door. "You are not to return to the office, Bernard."

She was giving him orders. Surely he could be encouraged by that? "I could not possibly return to the office. I have dreams I must dream, and that requires a decent helping of slumber."

He tarried long enough to enjoy kisses only verging on torrid. Before passion relieved him of all sense, Bernard parted from his beloved.

As he trotted down the front steps and resisted the urge to blow kisses at his beloved's front door, Bernard mentally added an item to his schedule: procure a special license from the good fellows at Doctors' Commons.

He'd start that process in the morning, very first thing.

He and Sorcha were agreeing to disagree where the children's mishaps were concerned, but they were disagreeing civilly. Then too, what mischief could befall small children in the midst of their own family and a horde of neighbors?

~

"Duchess's Day comes around again," Coraline said, passing the invitation over to Tallister. They had long since established separate bedrooms, but Tally often shared breakfast with her. Annette and Eglantine had taken to enjoying trays first thing in the day, and the younger girls had eaten an hour ago and been shepherded to the schoolroom by their governess.

This private hour with her husband had become a fixture on Coraline's schedule and, usually, a pleasant one.

"Trooping the Dolforth colors." Tallister glanced at the invitation and set it aside. "Weren't you and the girls just off in the country with Sorcha and Huxley?"

Once upon a time, Tally had been much better at dissembling. He well knew of the outing to Mirobello. He likely knew to the minute how long Jordy had gone missing and how Eglantine had figured in the boy's rescue. Tally's valet would have apprised him of that much.

"We enjoyed a couple hours of fresh air, though the day was marred by some drama. Jordy chose to hide in an oat bin and suffered a knock on the head when the lid came down on him. Cousin Bernard located him with Eglantine's assistance, and as far as I know, the boy is fine. More tea?"

"Please. Is this why Annette has been gracing us with fulminating silences and pensive frowns? Her younger cousin became the center of attention and Eggie the heroine of the piece?"

Tallister had many faults, but an unobservant papa he was not. "Perhaps, or perhaps Annette is simply very young and prone to moods. She came home from the park yesterday on Cousin Bernard's arm, so to speak. She was by turns ecstatic to have won his escort and wroth that he wouldn't accompany her to any of the shops."

Though in support of Tally's point, those flights and dips in Annette's moods did seem to be growing more dramatic, if such a thing was possible.

Coraline added sugar and milk to Tally's tea, then poured out for herself.

"Do you encourage her fondness for Cousin Bernard?" Tallister asked.

"Annette claimed Eggie and Entwhistle would tarry for hours at the bookshop, which is likely true, and there was Cousin Bernard having to kick his heels while Sorcha's children flew kites with the footman. He was probably relieved to have an excuse to quit the park and go about his day. You will come with us to Chanderton, won't you?"

Tally stirred his tea, though it needed no stirring. "Would not miss it. Richard will make an appearance. His one reliable concession to family ties. I don't believe he and Huxley have met. Should be entertaining."

Coraline had not planned for Richard to be on the guest list. Annette despised him, and he was none too fond of her. "Thank you for the warning. How is Richard getting on these days?"

"As illegitimately as ever." Tally set down his tea and took a slice of orange torte from the plate in the center of the table.

"Tallister, be serious. If Richard is rackety in the wrong direction at the wrong time, he could make things very difficult for our girls."

"I have listened at every available keyhole, my dear, for news of Richard and any interesting on-dits regarding Cousin Bernard. The usual wags have little to say, though I've already seen a bet on the books that Annette will be married to her handsome cousin before she makes her come out."

"Was the sum at issue respectable?"

"A hundred pounds."

The wager was probably five pounds, and Tally was being kind. "I cannot approve of Annette's name being bandied about in the clubs."

"But you would not mind seeing her married to Cousin Bernard. I honestly do not think they would suit."

Neither did Coraline, but since when did suiting come into it? "Bernard Huxley is legitimate, unlike Richard. He is ordained. He's received everywhere. He's solvent. He enjoys the status of heir presumptive to a wealthy barony, and his mother's family sports an earldom. Annette could do much, much worse." And Cousin Bernard would be understanding about the settlements, lest he embarrass his own family.

Tally took a bite of his torte and sent Coraline the sort of considering perusal that meant he was truly paying attention and wanted her to know it.

"Annette will come right," he said. "She is your daughter, after all, and the duchess will take a hand in her presentation. If Nettie is nigh unbearable these days, that's to be expected. This spring is the bad dress rehearsal before the wildly successful opening night next year. Put your mind at ease, Corrie dearest. We shall contrive and triumph in the end. Nettie has her heart set on marrying a handsome prince."

Once upon a time long ago, Coraline would have been fortified by such a display of paternal optimism. The theatrical metaphors were appropriate, coming from Tally, who was nothing else if not a born thespian.

"Tallister, what are you up to?"

"Coraline, you wound me. I am the same doting father and husband I have always been. If I'm keeping closer watch on the talk in the clubs, it's because secrets have a way of not remaining secret, and whatever Cousin Bernard's connection to Annette becomes, we want to be the arbiters of its terms, don't we?"

Tally was prone to attempting interfamilial blackmail. He'd searched in vain for any little scandal that might have reflected poorly on the present duchess, and when he'd tried to extort money from Richard over some seditious drunken ramblings, Richard had laughed in his face.

"Tallister, I esteem you above all other men, but please do not embark on any schemes where Cousin Bernard is concerned."

Tally munched another bite of torte. "Have you schemes of your own in train, my dear? Best tell me, if so. We wouldn't want to work at cross-purposes."

So he *was* up to something. That would not do. "The only scheme I have embarked on is the presentation of our oldest daughter to Society on the best-possible terms. That her dowry remains distressingly modest is a situation for her doting papa to remedy."

Coraline expected either sulking or an outburst—Tally was always going on about economies and the burden a younger son faced—but instead, he finished his torte, rose, and kissed her temple.

"You may rely on me to do all in my power to aid your ambitions, dearest Corrie. I always have, and I always will. I'm off for a stroll through St. James's. Even at this unlikely hour, one can hear the most interesting news. Fencing at Angelo's, lunch at the club, a hand of cards thereafter, and hack at the fashionable hour. Enjoy your day."

He'd visit his mistress at some point during that exceptionally unbusy day. Coraline did not begrudge him his pleasures—four daughters were enough—but she'd heard nothing in his recitation about addressing the situation with Annette's funds. Blackmailing Bernard Huxley might accomplish that end, but recruiting him as a son-in-law would put his whole fortune much closer to where Coraline wanted it.

Nothing said the two objectives were mutually exclusive. Coraline helped herself to a slice of torte—her second, it was quite good—and mentally wished her spouse the best of luck.

CHAPTER FIFTEEN

"Not to be rude," Richard said, trailing his fingers in the water, "but what are we doing in this ornamental boat, on this ornamental lake, on Duchess Lilly's ornamental day?"

Bernard pulled hard on the oars. "I thought two brothers deserved some privacy as they grew acquainted for the first time. This is the best I could do on short notice. Even your voice is similar to mine."

"You look like me, but for that blond hair." Richard sounded as puzzled as Bernard felt. "The same wavy hair, you wear it in the same style, but yours is more Nordic, I suppose."

"Yorkshire summers, and my mother was fair."

Richard lifted his hand and shook droplets in Bernard's direction. They occupied a rowboat built along the lines of a modified punt. Shallow draft, shallow sides, made for navigating a shallow lake. The water fixture was probably six feet deep at the center, and it was to the center that Bernard piloted the boat.

"Are condolences in order?" Richard asked.

"You know they are not. Mama is en route to, or has arrived at, the Antipodes. She is an arrogant, meddling busybody who very nearly stole bread from the mouths of orphans. What of your mother?"

"Blessedly enjoying her celestial reward. I hope she's ringing a perpetual peal over our mutual father's head."

Bernard let the boat drift. They were as far from the dock as they could get and likely scrutinized by every cousin, neighbor, footman, and truant village child within thirty yards of the shore. Seen, but not overheard.

Sorcha stood by the duchess on the terrace of the fishing cottage —a modest structure boasting a mere six bedrooms—while Bridget and Jordy capered around a smiling O'Leary and dodged in and out of assorted other youngsters. The crowd ranging along the shore lounged on blankets, played at horseshoes and pall-mall, and sat about chatting in lawn chairs. A tableau of ease and relaxation, while the mood in the boat was...

Tentative. Not hostile, but wary perhaps.

"You are angry with Lord Jerome?" Bernard asked.

"You aren't? He played your mama false, the way I heard it."

Very odd to have a conversation with one who sounded, looked, and gestured so like oneself.

"Mama's family played her false. She set out to compromise his lordship, and her parents decided they would rather have decent settlements for her than an angry ducal son-in-law. A baron's younger son was found to escort Mama and her improved settlements to the altar, and she has been inflicting her revenge on the world ever since."

"What do your maternal relations think of you now?"

Annette and Eglantine emerged from the fishing cottage. Both wore straw hats sufficient to keep the sun from half of Kent. Annette also carried a parasol that she twirled incessantly.

"Is this how brothers talk?" Bernard asked. "I honestly don't know my maternal relations that well. Mama kept her distance from them. The present earl is my cousin, or first cousin once removed. How do you go on in life?"

"Well enough," Richard drawled. "And you?"

Bernard rocked the boat violently, and Richard grabbed for the gunwales with both hands.

"Huxley, are you mad?"

"I am out of patience. We will not be given a moment's peace once we're back among the family throng, and I would like to get to know my brother. I am not the author of your miseries, nor are you the author of mine, if any misery I have ever had. Might we not be at least cordial?"

"We shall be cordial," Richard said, gaze on the lady cousins. "Dolforths are always cordial. We look alike, Huxley, but you are a legitimate bastard. I am the other kind. My mother's family hadn't the standing to find her a handy younger son to tidy up loose ends in the person of yours truly. Your path has doubtless had its challenges, but so has mine."

Bernard had surmised as much, but that Richard would admit it was progress. "You attended university?"

"Cambridge. Took a first in Latin just to show the ignoramuses that I could, but Latin doesn't go very far toward paying the tailor. Annette needs a dunking in the lake, if you ask me. She's grown far too impressed with herself, and Coraline isn't rectifying the situation."

Bernard gave the oars another pull, lest the boat drift back toward the dock. "You are cordial with our cousins?"

"I am now. For a while, I was intent on sowing wild oats all over Mayfair. Not done. Had to slink off to Lisbon. Did me good. Learned my way around the Port and Madeira business, and I'm modestly successful at it, which is fortunate. Chanderton was about to put me on permanent remittance. I decided to grow up instead."

Footmen carried two more little boats to the dock from where they were propped on the side of the fishing cottage. Each boat was gently lowered to the water and lashed to a stout cleat. Perhaps a regatta might follow, in which case Bernard would choose Sorcha for his captain.

"Do you enjoy being in trade?" Bernard asked.

"Love it. You?"

"Growing to love it," Bernard said slowly. "I knew I wasn't cut out for the Church, but one does as one is told when one is raised in a vicarage. Religious life can be pleasant and meaningful, but it's also..."

"Yes?"

"Boring at times. Grueling, draining. People expect unfailing compassion and endless interest in their little tribulations, along with forgiveness for their shortcomings and tolerance for their stumbling, while directing very little of same back at their shepherd. After a few years, I found it all tiresome."

"While trade is not tiresome. Frustrating, challenging, and occasionally exhilarating, but not tiresome. Lilly said I'd like you. I wanted her to be wrong."

"Shall I tip the boat to oblige you?"

"Chanderton would blame me, and Cousin Coraline would demand that I be banished again. Hers was the loudest voice demanding that I be sent away, and I don't care to be banished again. Tally does not have his womenfolk under control, but speaking of which, you are to be appointed guardian of Sorcha's little heathens."

"They are far from heathens, but yes." Another push on the oars kept the boat in the middle of the lake.

"Take the wrong line with those children, Huxley, and you will find yourself with a very sore head aboard a schooner bound for Portugal. Are we clear?"

Bernard respected people who did not mince words. People like Richard and Sorcha. "You're fond of Jordy and Bridget?"

"I absolutely am, and I am beyond fond of her ladyship. Sorcha spotted me some of the ready when I was in everybody else's black books. She never said a word to that jackass of a husband, never even told Lilly. Dipped into her pin money or her own funds and refused to charge me interest."

On the dock, Annette was dragging Eglantine down the planks toward a boat. Jordy and Bridget continued to play fox and geese among the milling herd, while Sorcha and Her Grace were in conversation with some diminutive granny who barely came up to Sorcha's shoulder.

Coraline and Tallister were nowhere to be seen. Bernard would have preferred to keep them in sight.

"Sorcha hasn't said anything to me about making you a loan." Bernard picked up the oars and maneuvered the boat toward the dock. "I will do my absolute best by the children. They are both very bright and easy to like." Easy to love.

"You like their mother, too, don't you?"

"Very much. Why?"

The old lady had Sorcha by the arm and steered her around to behold the Chanderton family seat on its majestic rise half a mile away. Eglantine, meanwhile, had flounced back to shore from halfway down the dock, leaving Annette twirling her parasol like mad and stomping after her.

"Why do I suppose you and Sorcha are in charity?" Richard mused. "Because a man doesn't loll about on picnic blankets making sheep's eyes at a lady unless he's smitten, Huxley. In the middle of the day, Hyde Park is all but deserted, so I doubt the gossips saw you, but I did."

"You were on reconnaissance?" Spying. Was a brother permitted what a tutor was forbidden? Bernard suspected the answer was yes.

"I was hacking out at an hour when fashionable Society isn't on hand. I very nearly ran into Nettie and Eggie and their nanny-scholar. I recognized Nettie's mare in time to avert disaster. What is she doing with our Jordy?"

Annette had seized the boy by the elbow and was half dragging, half marching him down the dock. She hopped into a boat none too gracefully and hauled Jordy into the same little vessel. Some people were laughing and pointing, but Bridget ran to her mother, turning Sorcha around by sheer dint of yanking her skirts, and pointed to the boat, which Annette was rowing away from the dock.

Jordy sat in the prow of the boat, looking pale and thunderous.

Sorcha bellowed for Annette to cease her foolishness, and Bernard began rowing with all his might.

"Nettie must make a spectacle of herself," Richard muttered. "If she's like this now, she'll be a flaming terror by next spring."

"The boat is taking on water." Bernard pulled on the oars as if his life depended upon it. "Nobody checked to see if the bilge plug was tight."

Richard yanked off his boots, stashed his pocket watch in one of them, and wrestled out of his coat. "Spare me from maidenly drama, but thank heavens the lake is only about five feet deep that close to the dock."

"A boy can drown in five feet of water if he doesn't know how to swim. I'm for Jordy. You get that infernal female to shore, and don't let Sorcha near her."

Annette commenced wailing.

Bernard abandoned the oars, divested himself of his boots and coat, and dived flat for the sinking boat.

"I don't even know what a bilge plug is," Annette caterwauled.

Sorcha gave the girl credit for stamina. She hadn't ceased bleating since Richard had pulled her from the water. All the way across Chanderton's park, across the back terrace, and into this little informal parlor.

"I will have a lung fever soon," Annette went on. "See if I don't. Jordy should have looked to see that the plug thing was where it was supposed to be."

Having flung that accusation for the third time, Annette gathered her damp blanket around her shoulders more closely.

"Lower your voice," Coraline snapped before Sorcha could put the matter more bluntly. Across the parlor, Bernard perched on a window seat, Jordy in his lap. Sorcha's son was swaddled in Bernard's jacket. Richard stood at the door, perhaps blocking any attempt by Annette to flee in hysterics.

"Annette, why did you insist on putting Jordy into that boat?" Sorcha asked.

"Because I'd look pathetic rowing about all on my own. If I was seen to give my younger cousin an outing, I would appear gracious and like a good sport. Mama, I'm cold. I want Papa."

And to think Sorcha had been married when she'd been nearly as young as Annette. "Jordy did not want to sail with you, Annette. You disregarded his wishes, put him in harm's way, and terrified me and Bridget."

The duchess had collected Bridget and involved her in a game of pall-mall. Bridget had been last seen smacking the devil out of her ball and to blazes with wickets and courses.

"You frightened me as well," Bernard said, managing to make the admission sound dignified, though he was barefoot, disheveled, and wearing somebody's pink shawl.

"Make it unanimous," Richard added. He'd found a dry jacket somewhere, but that only made his appearance more bedraggled. "Nettie, word of your foolishness will spread all over Town, and you will have a reputation as a hoyden before you've attended your first ball."

Coraline rounded on him. "Hardly fair, Richard. Nettie merely got a soaking because the boats were not adequately maintained. You, by contrast, set out to drag the family name through the mud and nearly succeeded."

"Old business, Coraline." Bernard sounded *quite* stern. "Annette ignored Jordy's protests, and he deserves an apology for that disrespect."

"I did not want to look foolish," Annette said again, though she was finally modulating her volume. "I wanted to appear good-hearted. When did that become a crime? I am good-hearted, most of the time. A normal boy would have appreciated a little outing on the lake."

"I am normal." Jordy, too, managed a certain dignity despite his hair sticking up and his bare toes peeking from the bottom of Bernard's coat. "You want to *look* gracious, Nettie, but you aren't gracious, and that makes you a liar. You are scared nobody will marry you and you will be an old maid."

Coraline drew herself up as if preparing for a peroration on rude little boys and respect and all manner of righteous irrelevancies.

"Annette owes Jordy an apology," Sorcha said. "If the boats were not properly maintained, that is a matter for His Grace to address, and we won't resolve it in this room. For my part, Annette, you are never, ever to impose your will or judgment on my children again. A choice of sweet, which card to play, or whether to participate in a game is their decision, not yours. Are we clear?"

Coraline might not care for that scold, but she held her peace.

"Yes, Auntie. I never want to see Jordy again."

Bernard shook his head when Jordy doubtless would have concurred.

"Apologize to Jordy," Sorcha said, "and we can be about finding everybody dry clothes."

"And do it properly," Bernard added. "None of this 'I'm sorry you ended up in the boat which I happened to dragoon you into bodily against your wishes in front of half the shire, and I'm sorry you got a soaking when my own soaking was so much more mortifying.'"

Annette addressed the parquet floor. "I am sorry I took you along, Jordy. You did not want to come with me, and I should not have insisted. Mama, I am exhausted by my ordeal. Might I retire for a nap?"

Coraline ushered her unrepentant chick from the room, doubtless to harangue Annette at length, all the while blaming Jordy, Richard, or even the duke for Annette's dunking.

"Tiresome girl," Richard said. "I'm off to change. Bernard, I have sufficient extra wardrobe that I can kit you out. We appear to be of a size, oddly enough. Come by my room when you have located your boots. I can escort Jordy to the nursery too."

Sorcha did not want to let her son out of her sight, but Jordy would resent her for hovering, and Richard was a favorite with Jordy.

"Off you go, Jordy. Gilchrist will order a hot bath, and you will not grumble about it. She'll also order you a posset, which you must at least attempt to sip."

Gilchrist would ensure the posset did not go to waste.

"Yes, Mama. I never want to go boating again, and especially not with *her*."

Bernard set the boy on his feet, then knelt to face him. "Annette was just as frightened as you were, Jordy. She's wearing yards of skirts and petticoats that got sopping wet and dangerously heavy. She can't maneuver all that freely in her fashionable attire even when it's dry. She's also not very tall, and despite being close to the dock, the water was nearly over her head. Had Richard not come to her rescue, she could have suffered a very unfortunate fate indeed."

"She still shouldn't have put me in the boat. She grabbed me around the waist, and I wanted to punch her, but I'm not allowed to punch girls, and I can punch boys only if they hit me first."

Bernard smoothed a hand over Jordy's cowlick. "Instead of all this punching—about which you are quite correct—why not focus on learning to swim? I will happily teach you when the weather is warmer, and we can start in shallow water. Shallow enough that you can stand up in it."

"Will you teach Bridget too?"

"That is for your mother and Bridget to decide, but let us agree that your swimming lessons will begin as private instruction. I can also teach you to float and to tread water."

"Will we have to swim in the Thames?"

What had prompted that question?

"We will not. The water is foul, to put it delicately. For now, consider the offer, enjoy your bath, and gather your thoughts. Gilchrist will want to hear your firsthand account of this adventure on the high seas."

Richard held out a hand. "Let's have a word with Cook before we head upstairs, shall we? A biscuit or two might restore this able seaman's humors."

They tramped off together, both barefoot and damp, prepared to forage in the fashion of intrepid explorers the world over.

Bernard closed the parlor door. "I want to hug you, but I am sodden. Consider yourself well hugged."

"The same to you." Sorcha took a second, dry window seat, and Bernard joined her. They weren't quite touching, and he smelled of wet linen and lake. Still, his presence comforted.

"I could spank Annette," Sorcha went on, "but I also understand how awkward this year is for her. She should be at a finishing school, where she'd at least make friends with her peers. Being in the schoolroom one day and attending at homes the next is confusing."

"But," Bernard said, "if Annette is sent off to Switzerland or Shropshire, or wherever fashionable girls go, then the other three would expect the same sort of launch, and I doubt Tallister can afford that."

Sorcha dearly, dearly wished she could lay her head on Bernard's shoulder. "You will teach Bridget to swim, please. I know how, thanks to a hot spring on my uncle's estate, and some older cousins. When Jordy went under..."

Only the duchess physically holding Sorcha back had stopped her from leaping into the water, skirts and all.

"Jordy wasn't in much danger, Sorcha. He was within a dozen yards of the dock. If I hadn't reached him, somebody else would have. The water was shallow enough that swimming didn't have to come into it."

"You are admitting that this is a plain-and-simple accident?" Sorcha's relief was inordinate. Given how Bernard had reacted to routine bellyaches and a game of hide-and-seek gone awry, he was being blessedly reasonable.

"I don't know if Jordy suffered an accident, a mishap, or mischief, but Coraline and Tallister would be loath to jeopardize Annette's reputation by presenting her with an opportunity for public histrionics. Jordy was in that boat solely because Eglantine refused to join her sister at the last moment, and nobody could have foreseen Annette's behavior thereafter."

"I missed that part. You are applying logic and reason. Good of you. I just want to hug my little boy and wrap him up in cotton wool." Or to take him on an extended outing to Scotland, but Sorcha could hardly say that. Not to Bernard. "I'd best rescue the duchess from Bridget's dubious company."

"Bridget needs to see Jordy back on his mettle," Bernard said. "I should change into dry attire, or I will be a present-day scandal."

"Thank you. Your vigilance did not lapse, while I grew distracted. I am endlessly grateful that you were there and thinking quickly."

"As am I. I like Richard, by the way, and he likes you."

"Good. He's matured into a thoroughly estimable gentleman. Siblings should be friends, if at all possible."

Bernard rose and held out a hand. Sorcha took it and was glad for the assistance. She hugged Bernard briefly, despite sodden clothing and lake stink.

"Come to me tonight?" she asked.

He stepped back, his smile sweet and naughty. "If I must climb drainpipes or creep down a chimney to do it, flying dragons will not keep me away."

They parted at the panel that opened on the footmen's stairs, Bernard being in serious deshabille. Sorcha went to relieve the duchess, troubled by the day's events, but also comforted by Bernard's assessment of them. He was protective of the children—not a bad thing—and when rested and fed, he was also reasonable.

For her part, Sorcha was positively delighted with the thought of Bernard's company in the still watches of the night.

CHAPTER SIXTEEN

Commerce moved *forward.*

Bernard enjoyed that aspect of trade. Goods were put under contract, money changed hands, shipping commenced, followed by delivery. In the alternative, goods were rejected, a rousing debate ensued, or custom was lost to a competitor. Mercantile activity was unceasing and always with a sense of goals to be accomplished. Very unlike the liturgical year, which trotted out the same texts, feasts, and themes season after season, with little apparent improvement in the human condition to show for it.

Courtship had a goal, certainly, but Bernard had lacked a sense that he was making progress toward it. The card party had been enjoyable, as had the musicale, but other than hacking out with Sorcha twice, he was no closer to using the special license than he'd been the day it had arrived.

Sorcha's invitation to climb figurative drainpipes thus loomed as a rare opportunity of which the most must be made. Bernard rose from a tub of warm water, toweled off, and decided that before he could contemplate that happy challenge, he must consult with Jordy, whose day had gone poorly.

A sinking boat was a very serious sort of mishap, if it had been a mishap at all.

Bernard found Gilchrist in her favorite place at the window, while Jordy occupied a chair by an empty hearth.

"What are you reading?" Bernard asked Jordy after properly greeting Gilchrist.

"Stupid poems. Gilly says they will calm my nerves, but I can't understand some of the words, and my nerves are not calm."

"Yon little besom took two sips of his posset, sir, and wouldn't have any more. He will not nap, and he doesn't want to play soldiers."

"What about a hand of cards?" Bernard asked.

Jordy shut the book. "We looked. No cards in the nursery."

The boy's hair was almost dry. He was in clean clothes, and keeping him immured in the nursery was likely asking for trouble.

"What do you say to finding Bridget and challenging her to a game of pall-mall? She's had some practice this afternoon, and I can be the referee."

Gilchrist muttered something that sounded vaguely prayerful.

Jordy shot to his feet. "Let's find Bridge. She was with Auntie Lilly, and she looked mad when you carried me up to the house."

"We might find your mama at the same time. Gilchrist, we'll be at least an hour. My thanks for serving yeoman duty on a trying day."

Gilchrist marched for the door. "You mind Mr. Huxley, young man. I know you had a bit of a difficult afternoon, but you'd best find your good manners soon and keep them handy." She patted Jordy's shoulder and disappeared into the corridor.

"What did you and Richard find to nibble on?" Food being a reliable conversational gambit with even young besoms.

"Biscuits. Cinnamon biscuits because the duchess favors them. Cousin Richard favors them too."

"How many?"

A hint of a grin. "I'm to say two, because nobody will believe I had only one. Richard said I might have three because I must keep up my strength in the face of public tribu... tribu-something."

"Tribulation. Means great affliction, oppressive troubles. You appear to have dried off quite nicely."

They trundled along the corridor. When they reached the head of the staircase, Jordy paused, a look of longing crossing his features.

Bernard picked him up and put him on the banister. "Hold on all the way down, young man, or I will face a few tribulations courtesy of your dear mama."

Jordy went flying all of fifteen feet to the next landing. He scrambled back to his feet. "Did you slide down banisters when you were a boy?"

"Of course. My cousin dwelled in a very large manor near the vicarage, and we couldn't expect the maids to polish all the woodwork on their own, could we? No sliding to the first floor, though. Those are public rooms, and the dignity of the house must be preserved."

"That's what Richard said. Richard is my cousin, like you are."

Bernard saw no need to dissemble. "He's my half-brother, albeit the connection is mildly scandalous. We probably don't speak of it outside of family, though the resemblance to Chanderton is strong in both of us."

They reached the back terrace, and sounds of merriment drifted up from the lake.

"You won't make me get into any boats, will you, sir? Richard said I needn't go boating again."

"I agree with Richard, though rowing is good exercise. I would like to show you exactly what went amiss with the boat you and Annette shared."

Jordy stalked down the steps. "I hate her. I know I mustn't hate anybody, and I mustn't say that I hate her, but she's not a lady yet, and she would not listen when I said to put me down."

The boy needed to air his grievances to somebody. "And nobody made her listen. I am very disappointed in Annette as well."

They reached the garden, a lovely formal expanse separated from the park by a bowling green at the bottom. A dozen adults and several adolescents lounged about the edges, calling encouragement or awaiting a chance to throw.

"Let's cut through the rose garden," Bernard said. "Nothing blooming yet, but the path to the lake is shorter." Not as full of people bent on nosy small talk.

Perhaps Jordy's irritability was catching.

"Not the roses," Jordy said, stopping short. "I hate roses."

What on earth? "Not even if you can ride past them on your loyal steed?"

Jordy sat on the bottom step. "You can't jolly me along, Cousin Bernard. I want to find Bridget, but I don't want to see Annette, and she *loves* roses. She thinks roses are *romantic*."

Bernard was torn between impatience with a small boy's stubbornness, amusement, and the certain knowledge that, today at least, Jordy was entitled to his sour mood.

Bernard perched beside the boy on the hard stone steps. "Do you even know what 'romantic' means?"

"Kissing and being silly and tricking a man into marrying you. That's all Annette thinks about."

"Some people like to be married."

Jordy picked up a rock and pitched it at an urn of red salvia. "Nobody should have to marry Annette. Cousin Richard says I must not be so wroth with her—she got a soaking too—but she stinks, and she wants us all to treat her like a princess when she can't row a boat or stop chattering."

Even for an aggrieved little boy, this was bitter sentiment. "I can show you exactly what went amiss with the boat, and it wasn't Annette's fault. You are angry with her for more than the boating incident, I take it."

Another rock hurled at the hapless urn. "She isn't nice, but she wants everyone to think she's nice. Cousin Coraline isn't nice and doesn't care if we don't like her. Cousin Tally is nice, but he doesn't care either. He's nice because that's easy for him."

An insightful summary as far as it went. Somebody had been

brooding. "Before you damage your aunt's urn, let's get down to the lake, shall we?"

"We'll find Bridget and Mama." Jordy rose, rubbed his backside, and headed down the crushed-shell walkway.

"The other way is shorter." The other way was also free of potential new acquaintances.

"I don't care. Roses are the dumbest flower. Annette smells like roses and lemons, and roses are stupid."

Jordy had nearly shrieked his opposition to even passing through the rose garden. Down at the bowling green, a few heads turned toward them, and Bernard realized he wasn't dealing with a boy who was merely angry or tired or too full of cinnamon biscuits.

Jordy was on his last nerve and seeking the only ally he truly trusted.

"We'll avoid the roses," Bernard said. "And then I have a few questions for you while we look for Bridget."

They braved the gauntlet at the bowling green, which turned out to be a few greetings and smiles. Bernard waited until they were in the middle of the park—seen but not overheard again—and put his question as casually as he could manage.

"Jordy, if you think back to the day you hid in the oat bin, you said you heard light footsteps, like a bird trapped in a church."

"They sounded run-run-run-stop. Like when a bird flies around, then perches on a rafter, then takes off again."

"You offer an excellent description. What else do you recall? About the aromas you detected in the oat bin, for example?"

Bernard did not want to lead the witness, but Jordy had said that Annette 'stank' and had described the peculiar combination of lemons and roses that she apparently favored.

Jordy picked up his pace. "I hate her, and she's mean."

"Jordy, your opinions are your own concern, but you are speaking ill of a lady in your family. Why would you, a gentleman to your little bones, be so rude?"

He stopped and stared mutely at his boots, and Bernard understood the impossible conundrum Jordy faced. If he truly, truly spoke ill of Annette—accused her of specific crimes rather than casting general contumely in her direction—then he would not be a gentleman in his own estimation, much less that of his elders.

Bernard sat in the grass, legs crossed. "Let's look for lucky clovers."

Jordy adopted the same posture. "Annette shut me in that oat bin."

"One surmised as much but had no evidence. You recognized her scent?"

Jordy brushed a hand over the lush grass. "In the herbal. Bridge was sniffing each bottle, and she held out some for me to sniff. The lemongrass bottle made me realize that stinky old Annette had been in the stable when I got knocked on the head, though I didn't figure that out until later. She also runs like that—flit, flit, flit—then stops and holds up her hands as if she's just remembered something important."

What an eye for detail he had, but then, he was monitoring his enemy's maneuvers. The whole war might depend on...

Military allusions outside the schoolroom. *Steady on, Huxley.* "I'm sorry," Bernard said. "Annette has much to answer for, and her behavior put you in an impossible situation. You could not peach on her, and you could not keep your distance from her. What's a fellow to do?"

"Will Mama be mad?"

"She will be very mad at Annette." Possibly a little angry at herself. "The nonsense will stop, Jordy."

He sighed mightily and stuck a clover flower in his mouth. "Annette made me fall off that pony too. She rode the pony first and changed the saddle for me. She fixed the girth before I mounted, but she didn't *fix it*. She unfixed it, then laughed at me when I came off. Bridget says I'm right. Bridget rode the pony before Annette did, and the saddle was snug then."

Nasty, dangerous business. Annette, who was no sort of equestrienne, likely hadn't realized how dangerous. "What she did wasn't in the least funny."

"Will you tell Mama?"

Jordy clearly didn't want to be the bearer of troublesome tidings. "I will, and rest assured that your mother will brook no more foolishness where your safety or Bridget's safety is concerned."

"Mama was very fierce with Annette, wasn't she?"

"Between us gents, I thought your mother was far too lenient, but she makes allowances for the fact that Annette is facing a challenge for which she does not feel prepared." For which she, in fact, *was not* prepared.

"Tricking a prince? He won't be a very smart prince if he marries Annette. Can we find Bridget now?"

He might be a smitten prince of the lowly variety. Bernard had presided at all manner of nuptial ceremonies, and there was no accounting for the path Cupid's arrows could take.

"We will find Bridget, and your mother, and you will have a grand time whacking the stuffing out of a wooden ball. Makes a very satisfying sound when the mallet connects with its target."

They chatted about the rules of pall-mall until they spotted Bridget riding her pall-mall mallet like a stick horse around the edge of the pitch. Sorcha watched from a bench in the shade of a stately maple.

"Bridge!" Jordy yelled and waved. Bridget dropped her mallet and waved back. Sorcha left her bench. She looked of a piece with the rural scene, sturdy, sure of herself, happy to see her darling firstborn.

She would not be quite so happy when Bernard gave her a full report. He struggled with the impulse to gather them all up and retreat to Yorkshire, where the only family he had put no demands on him, and young ladies did not become obsessed with impressing all of Society in an annual public courting contest.

"Did you drink your posset, Jordy?" Bridget asked.

"Two sips. It was awful. Where's Annette?"

"Not here," Bridget replied. "Eggie and Jessica are reading on their blanket. Elise is sailing toy boats with the other girls."

Sorcha cocked her head at that report. "And are you also watching Cousins Coraline and Tally?"

"No, but Cousin Tally went for a stroll around the lake with some girl. They are there." Bridget pointed quite rudely to a couple meandering along a few hundred yards across the water. "Cousin Coraline might be in the tea tent with the *ladies*."

"You would do well in commerce," Bernard said. "You notice details and can recall them."

"Our Bridget will do well in Society," Sorcha added, "and in the schoolroom and everywhere in between. Jordy, would you like to take a turn at pall-mall?"

Jordy eyed the pitch, which was set up as a course meant to be challenging. "Do we get to smack the ball as hard as we can?"

"You call those practice shots," Bridget replied, quite confident of her expertise. "You can take as many of those as you want. Aunt Lilly said. Then you have to hit between the wickets and smack other people's balls and go in the right order. It's complicated. Mama knows the rules."

Mama also fortunately knew how to discreetly thwart the rules. Bernard was fondly beholding his favorite rule-bending lady when he spotted Annette swanning down the path from the house.

"I want to go home." Jordy looked anywhere but at his cousin in the distance. "I don't feel well, and I want to go home now."

"Jordy, what's wrong?" Bridget sounded more concerned than annoyed.

"Nothing is wrong. I just want to go home."

"Annette has apologized," Sorcha said gently. "You will have to face her sooner or later. If you'd rather it be later, we can go for a walk around the lake."

The boy looked ready to bolt hotfoot for Wales.

"Jordy," Bernard said. "She can't hurt you again. You have your family right here with you, and we won't let any harm befall you. You and Bridget take some practice shots while your mama and I have a chat on the bench."

Sorcha's brows went up, but she let Bernard's suggestion stand.

Jordy looked from his mama to Bernard and ultimately at Bridget. A silent exchange took place between the siblings while Annette twirled her white parasol over by the boathouse, and Coraline beamed determinedly at her oldest daughter's side.

"I like the mares' paddock," Bridget said. "The foals are wonderful, and the mamas don't mind if we visit them. Let's go see the mares and foals."

Brilliant girl. Jordy nodded. Sorcha looked puzzled.

"The mares' paddock it is," Bernard said, offering his arm to Sorcha, and away they sauntered. Bridget skipped along beside her brother, the picture of a carefree little girl on a pretty spring day.

Over by the water, Annette and her mother joined the women taking tea under the white tent. The lake itself was a flat blue mirror of the sunny sky, and two rowboats made a lazy progress across the surface.

The very picture of a lovely day on a lovely estate in lovely company.

And yet, pictures, as Bernard well knew, could be deceptive.

"Has Eglantine always been a reluctant sailor?" Bernard asked.

To Sorcha's ear, his tone was casual—too casual. "In fact, she has. She claims if God had meant ladies to travel across water, then ladies would have webbed feet. Eggie has some queer notions, and her opinions can become quite fixed."

"Then Annette well knew her sister would not get into that boat."

Bernard's voice, always so rich and resonant, held an edge that contrasted with the peaceful scene in the mares' pasture. The mamas munched the lush spring grass while foals slept in the sunshine, gamboled about, nursed, or nosed at the grass beside their mothers.

The little ones grew so quickly. This batch, mere weeks old, were already steady on their feet and challenging one another to mock battles.

"Jordy!" Bridget called. "I'll race you around the paddock. On three!"

They counted together and pelted off along the fence line. The mares watched, but only one raised her head, and even she did not stop chewing.

"You've been questioning Jordy, haven't you, Bernard?"

Sorcha took the sketching bench conveniently placed on a slight rise beside the paddock. Bernard remained on his feet, gaze on the children, who'd slowed to a jog.

"Jordy has been keeping a confidence out of a misguided attempt to emulate gentlemanly behavior. The burden grew too much for him, and yes, I did put a few questions to him."

"Please have a seat. If we are to engage in a disagreement, I don't want you looming over me."

The Scots in Sorcha's voice was gaining an upper hand. She mentally counted to ten in the Erse and waited for Bernard to do as she'd told him to.

"Please hear me out, Sorcha. Jordy has recalled that Annette changed saddles for him the day he came off that pony. I gather the girls had been riding aside, while Jordy would, of course, ride astride. He is quite certain she left the girth too loose."

Old business. Why must Bernard be so concerned with old business? "The grooms assured me the saddle had been properly adjusted."

"Are we to believe a lot of grooms—who could have been sacked for allowing Annette to meddle with the saddles—over Jordy?"

Though Bernard posed a question, he was making an accusation. Barclay had resorted to the same tactic. *Would Madam have me believe her allowance is inadequate? Is it the case that my wife prefers the Scottish wilderness to English civilization?*

Two people could pose questions. "Jordy has taken Annette into dislike, Bernard. Unfortunately, she makes that easy. Why has Jordy decided to point a finger at her, months later, over an incident better forgotten?"

"A gentleman does not speak ill of a lady, especially a lady in his family."

Sorcha snorted as the children slowed to a fast walk. "Jordy has been insulting Annette roundly for the past fortnight."

"General aspersions. He kept more specific criticism to himself. When he was hiding in the oat bin, he heard a tread that exactly matches Annette's flitting gait. He also detected that peculiar scent she prefers, a muddied blend of lemons and roses."

"And again, he told you that only now, a good fortnight after it would have been relevant. Annette drenches herself in attar of roses to try to hide the scent of the lemon rinses her mother insists she use on her hair. I agree that the aroma is distinctive, and Jordy is clever enough to discern that and pin guilt on Annette accordingly."

Bernard sat forward, forearms braced on his thighs. Why must he be so attractive when he was determined to be so vexatious?

"They are looking for lucky clovers," he said.

The children, on the far side of the paddock, were on all fours in the grass, slowly crawling about. Looking for luck, while Bernard apparently thought he'd come upon some relevant truths.

"Children will play pranks on one another, Bernard. I mean you no insult when I note that you have no children. You had only the one cousin as a companion growing up, and you and he rubbed along well. That is often not the case in larger family settings."

He scrubbed his palm across his face and glanced back at her. "I doubt these pranks, as you call them, are exclusively the work of a child, and as to that, Annette expects to take Mayfair by storm in less than a year. That is not the aspiration of a child."

"That is her mother's aspiration. Annette has no choice but to support it."

Bernard sat up. "My mother had choices. Had somebody confronted her at the age of seventeen and held her responsible for her various schemes and pranks, a lot of innocent people might have been saved a lot of pointless misery."

Real bitterness colored that observation. Real pain. "Bernard, I am sorry your mother was a disappointment, but she is *halfway around the world*. Are you perhaps confusing old ghosts with present difficulties?"

He rose, went to the fence, and commenced pacing. "Sorcha, why won't you even entertain the notion that this situation requires a resolution?"

Sorcha stood as well rather than be literally talked down to. "The resolution is to move forward, Bernard, and keep a close eye on matters where the children are concerned. You could send your mother to the ends of the earth. I am stuck three streets from Coraline and Tallister and three streets from Their Graces. The Dolforths have the authority and power to separate me from my children. If I must appear to ignore Annette's foolishness to placate the Dolforths, ignore it, I will."

The same bay mare who'd inspected the children's progress lifted her head to peer at Sorcha.

"Sorry," Sorcha said, moderating her tone. "I do not mean to be contentious, but you have little proof. Please recall that these people can also ruin your businesses, Bernard, and they will do it while chatting pleasantly with their acquaintances over tea."

He gave her the same sort of inspection he'd turned on her once before. Both penetrating and distracted, as if he was seeing a version of her she could not recognize for herself.

"When we joined the Greers for Sunday supper," Bernard said, "Tallister went into the kitchen to fetch the ham. He made a little production out of bringing it forth and laying the platter on the table. My own father was prone to the same ritual, half in jest, half as symbolism for a papa's role as provider. Tallister could have meddled with the children's servings of raspberry fool. The two youngest were given smaller portions, and both children had bellyaches."

Sorcha scuffed her boot over the grass, when she wanted to scream. "Bernard, I esteem you greatly. You are an estimable fellow in many regards, and I do admit the need for some caution."

He nodded. "Now comes the part where you give me a verbal birching. If it matters, I don't merely esteem you, I love you, and I love those children. I do think a trip to Scotland is in order, for you and the children. The sooner you depart, the happier I will be."

Unfair. Unfair and just like him to say the hardest part at the hardest moment. "If you love me, you will not tell me what to do, Bernard. Chanderton remains the ultimate authority over my children unless and until a new guardian is appointed. Even then, he is the patriarch and a peer. Even the courts will show him great deference. That is the reality I face. His Grace nearly had an apoplexy when I hired Gilchrist without his permission."

A lump had caught in Sorcha's throat. She ignored it. "I did not endure the courtship and marriage Barclay subjected me to, did not endure Mayfair's tender mercies toward a blameless Scottish girl, just so you—who doesn't know one hostess from another—could come along and make a scandal out of a squabble. I will be careful, Bernard, but that's all I can promise, and being careful means treading softly with those who could make my life and the lives of both my children hell."

Jordy and Bridget rose and began climbing the paddock fence.

"I understand your reasoning," Bernard said, sounding damnably self-possessed. "I am asking you to choose between a semblance of peace, which you have crafted at great cost over a period of years, and certain conflict with people you might not be able to best. I am offering only my humble self as an ally. Not the best odds, but consider this, please: I have not raised a brood of my own children, though I have been responsible for any number of boys boarding from time to time under my roof. I also was a boy, Sorcha, an often unhappy, bewildered boy."

He was about to deliver the worst blow. Sorcha watched the children scramble into the paddock and blinked ferociously.

"Go on. I must fetch those children before the horses take exception to a visit."

"Sorcha, the greatest harm to Jordy thus far is not a passing bellyache or a rap on the head or even a dunking in the lake. It's that he doubts your commitment to his welfare. He knows you love him, but in his little-boy mind, it's already a strong possibility that you value placating the Dolforths more than you value his dignity or respect. He hasn't the words to express that, but you've seen his sullen and difficult mood in recent days. Your child needs you, and I fear you will disappoint him, albeit with the best of intentions."

How the gently pleading note cloaked an accusation designed to haunt even the best parent. *Your son needs you...*

"Bernard, I will do what I can to keep the combatants in their separate corners. Modest measures will keep Jordy safe until Annette finds other matters to absorb her attention. Hurling accusations now will cause a rift that will hurt Jordy far more than a bit of bruised boyish pride."

A weak defense. Jordy's pride was sorely battered, as Sorcha's had been all but destroyed in her first Season.

Sorcha was casting around for conciliatory words, for common ground, when the bay mare went on alert, head up, not chewing. She swished her tail at the small human intruders who'd breached the fences of her citadel.

"Jordy and Annette are not combatants, Sorcha. They are cousins. When we are dead and gone, they will still be cousins, and that should count for something positive. Instead, we leave them a legacy of distrust and disrespect, which appears to be the real glue holding Mayfair Society together. They deserve better. Jordy, leave the foal alone!"

Bridget was intent on crossing the pasture, while Jordy had

tarried to approach a foal curled in the grass. The bay mare's ears were back, her tail swishing from side to side as she trotted across the grass.

Bernard was over the fence in a single athletic bound. He'd been standing a few feet from Sorcha one moment, then his hands were on the top rail, and he was on the other side of the fence.

"Please call your son," he said, jogging off toward the mare. "Halloo, Madam Horse! I'm over here! Ignore the boy, he's no threat, and I am much bigger and noisier."

The other mares were showing concern, moving to stand between Bernard, who was trotting around and waving his arms, and their babies.

"Jordy, get out of that field now!" Sorcha yelled. "The mares don't like you meddling with their babies."

"C'mon, Jordy!" Bridget bellowed, picking up her pace. "Race you to the fence!"

Jordy stood rooted to the spot, apparently torn between the foal, who continued to regard him placidly from its bed on the grass, and the need to appease parental authority.

Bernard scooped the boy up and jogged away from the foal. "Sorcha, make some noise, please. Move about, distract the ruddy mares."

"Over here, ladies!" Sorcha thundered as she marched along the fence and shook her skirts. "Have ye no' had visitors afore? We mean ye no harm. We only came calling to admire yer weans!"

Bridget clambered over the rails. "They are lovely, wonderful babies," she called. "We would never, ever hurt them."

Bernard handed Jordy over the fence, then vaulted after him in another athletic bound.

"We're out!" Jordy called, sounding vastly pleased. "Sorry, mares!"

Sorcha dropped to her knees and hugged her son. "You idiot. You foolish, foolish boy. That mare meant business, and she was bigger and faster than you and determined to protect her baby."

Jordy tolerated the embrace and then wiggled away. "She scared me. I didn't know mares got all fierce like that."

"They do," Sorcha said, rising. "They don't like surprises. They don't like strange creatures sneaking into their paddock to possibly take their babies away."

The lump was back in Sorcha's throat.

Bernard ruffled Jordy's hair. "What have we learned from this, my brilliant little scholars?"

"Stay out of the mares' paddock," Bridget said, "unless you want to be kicked."

"Mama can make quite a racket," Jordy added. "She *yelled* at those horses."

Bernard offered Sorcha his arm. "So she did, and the mares were distracted, and all's well. I, for one, am a bit peckish after all this excitement. Let's inspect the buffet, shall we?"

Amiable and authoritative, and Sorcha was both resentful and grateful. Bernard had once again been gallant, putting himself at risk of harm without a moment's hesitation. Chanderton himself would not have done that. Tallister, Coraline, Lilly... At best, they would have shouted at the children and then criticized Sorcha for her lack of vigilance.

A quarter hour later, Sorcha was busying herself with helping the children choose one small portion of a sweet to tide them over until supper while Bernard fetched glasses of lemonade.

"If you'll excuse me," Bernard said when the children were settled on a picnic blanket. "I would like to have a word with my brother. My lady, I will see you at supper. Children, good day."

The words were pleasant, the demeanor congenial, and yet, the distance Sorcha felt between them was real too.

For the best, perhaps, but even as she had that thought, Sorcha knew it for a lie.

She wasn't about to whisk her children up to Edinburgh without any explanation to the duke, but she wished she and Bernard had not quarreled. She wished even more that she'd chosen her words more carefully and that Annette was safely married to some doting German prince.

"Mama, are you looking for cloud beasts?" Bridget asked, setting aside an empty plate. "It's a good day for cloud beasts."

The sky was lovely, full of puffy white clouds against a serene blue canvas. "I am watching for flying pigs." Though such signs and wonders were unlikely. Unless, of course, Annette caught the attention of a Continental royal.

CHAPTER SEVENTEEN

"Annette." Bernard took the place beside her at the tea table, having waited half an hour for the girl's mother to abandon guard duty. Sorcha could not forbid him to address his own cousin, though she had given a very good account of herself in a verbal sparring match.

Painfully good, and Sorcha wasn't even half wrong in her reasoning. Her intransigence broke Bernard's heart—no moonlit drainpipes for him, not tonight, probably not ever—but it had also inspired some cogitation on the subject of females who felt they had few options and little support.

Such females, such *people,* could be led into poor choices, such as, for example, marrying an ass like Lord Barclay, or bullying a small boy who'd done nothing to deserve the abuse. Sorcha would not appreciate the analogy, but Bernard took some small comfort from it.

"You've recovered from your swim?" he asked.

Coraline had decamped, perhaps to heed the call of nature, the call of the buffet, or to attend to the thankless patrol duty of a wife with a handsome husband loose in polite society.

"A gentleman would not tease me," Annette said, "but yes. I am quite recovered. I am a capable swimmer, as it happens. Papa taught us, but Mama says we mustn't mention it. One cannot actually swim in proper attire. Jessica is part selkie, not that she'll need that skill when she's married."

Bernard did not particularly like Annette, but he increasingly understood why Sorcha pitied her. "Was it your papa who suggested you take the boat out today?"

Annette's prim visage shifted. They sat in the shade afforded by the tea tent, little company about. The rest of the ladies had apparently taken their refreshment and gone back to other entertainments, leaving Annette alone and uncertain.

"Papa? He does fancy the sight of pretty young ladies at the oars. He'll tell anybody that. Duchess Lilly took a boat out earlier with Mrs. Edgars, and Papa said Her Grace made a very fetching sight, all feminine beauty and repose, gliding along in the sunshine. Mama agreed with him. I do know how to row a boat, Cousin, if you're about to offer me lessons. Eglantine does not know, but she should have come with me anyway."

"Because she'd have made a pretty picture too?"

"Because she is my sister, and taking a boat out by myself would have looked pathetic. The duchess had a companion on the water. Nobody goes boating alone. It's not sociable. Jordy should have been a good sport and come along when I asked him to."

Asking hadn't come into it. "Jordy cannot swim."

Annette took a sip of tea that had to be tepid at best. "I know. Auntie Sorcha was wroth with me when I was already unbearably mortified to have required Richard's aid. Richard is odious, according to my mother, and Jordy has recovered perfectly well."

Said a bit plaintively.

"Annette, would it relieve your mind to know I have no intention of proposing to you?"

She inflicted upon him a startlingly adult perusal. Frank, dispassionate, unimpressed. "Mama says you'd 'do.' Papa concurs. He doesn't agree with Mama outright, but he doesn't argue. Papa would argue if he disagreed. He picks his battles with Mama and humors her otherwise. For me, he'd gainsay Mama if he believed we wouldn't suit."

She scooted about on her chair. "My children can inherit the earldom," she went on. "That title can be preserved through the female line. Mama has quoted the letters patent for me."

Annette was avoiding his question—more proof that the girl was drowning in expectations she could not manage.

"A Scottish earldom would be very prestigious," Bernard said. "You might even someday be a countess in your own right." He was goading her, testing the theory that Annette was easily and often goaded.

"I might, but then there's *Jordy*, ruining *everything*. If he were a girl... but he's not. Papa says I'm not to wish Jordy harm, that Jordy can't help it that he'll be the duke and the earl and all the other things, but even Papa admits the unfairness. Here I am, with three sisters to lead into good matches, and there's Jordy, a title dangling right over his hard little head."

Papa doubtless admitted the unfairness at every opportunity when he and Annette had no audience.

Bernard called on years as a vicar, when judgment of others had been forbidden to him, and every confession had to be met with kindness and understanding—or a credible facsimile thereof.

"Annette, Jordy knows you thumped the lid of the oat bin down on that hard little head."

"He can't know. He can't have seen..." She fell silent, and pink flooded up her neck and across her cheeks.

"He knows, and you know, and now I know too. You must promise me, on the hope that you make an excellent match, that you will never again menace your younger cousins. Jordy knows it was you who failed to take up the girth on that fat pony last summer. He said nothing until now because he didn't want to tattle. His silence has apparently only encouraged you." Jordy's silence and Tallister's dubious paternal sympathy. "You must stop."

"Why does Jordy have to inherit everything? It's not fair."

"He won't inherit everything. He will inherit whatever is entailed with the Chanderton title, which, I can assure you, will include mostly acreage and debts. He very likely won't see much of his mother's wealth. He won't be able to touch your settlements. He will have no ability to—"

"I barely *have* settlements," Annette snapped. "That's the problem. If you offered for me, I'd have to accept. You haven't a title, you are in trade, you aren't even legitimate, I most assuredly don't even want to kiss you, and Mama says..."

She picked up her tea cup, peered at the dregs, and set it down with a sigh. "I don't dislike you, Cousin, but I hardly know you, and you are a serious sort..."

"Also doddering, and I occasionally deliver impromptu sermons. I'm stodgy. I know. Can't be helped. Whatever else is true, Annette, I will not offer for you. You are lovely and comely and all that is bound to turn a bachelor's head, but my sentiments toward you are purely cousinly and always will be."

Her sigh was worthy of Mrs. Siddons at her die-away best. "I should be mad at you. Please convey your unavailability to Mama. She regards you as the solution to the whole problem of what to do with me."

"You should be angry with your mother, whose own consequence will rise and fall based on the match she can secure for you." Bernard was certainly displeased with Cousin Coraline. "You should also be angry at your father, who has apparently done nothing to augment your modest settlements. You should not, for one moment, direct your wrath at little Jordy."

She took the table napkin from her lap, balled it up, and pitched it onto the table. "I know. I don't hate him, but he can be a brat, and I apologized for the boat, and that wasn't my fault."

"Very well done of you, to apologize. Now that you've hit that practice ball, see if you can muster up the courage to apologize for the other instances of cruelty." Not pranks, not jokes, not teasing. *Cruelty*. Dangerous cruelty, in fact, despite Sorcha's need to believe otherwise. "Listen to your better angels, Annette, not to those who remind you constantly of what can never be yours and would only make you unhappy anyway."

"That's what Eggie says. She says Lilly is a duchess, but not a very happy one. Lilly was supposed to have sons. Mama says it's not Lilly's fault, because none of Uncle Chandy's duchesses have ever conceived."

"And none of that is our concern, is it? Work out your apologies to Jordy and find a time to pass them along when no adults are around. He will be gracious, I assure you."

Bernard used Annette's own word—*gracious*—to drive home the point.

He could not remove every impediment to the children's safety and happiness, but he could blunt the weapons that had already been turned against them. Sorcha would doubtless disapprove, but he'd likely earned her eternal enmity with the day's earlier argument.

He'd left the Church, where he'd spent ten years of his life, without anything like the ache that the thought of parting from Sorcha caused.

She wasn't wrong. She knew Mayfair, the Dolforths, and peerage family politics far better than Bernard ever hoped to, and she was safeguarding her offspring and their future to the best of her ability.

"You won't tell anybody?" Annette said, folding her table napkin into a neat, if wrinkled, triangle. "I should not have picked on Jordy, but I get so mad... A lady never yields to temper. I had to stitch that on a sampler once."

Burn the damned sampler. "I am in the habit of respecting confidences. You are entitled to your frustrations, Annette—much is expected of you—but your aunt Sorcha would remind you that if Jordy does eventually become the duke, you will want his kind regard. You might have some trouble finding him alone for the next while, but be patient and persistent, and the right moment will arise."

She smoothed her fingers over the abused napkin. "Is this how an older brother would talk to me? A little bit scolding, a little bit consoling? I've always thought that if Mama had had a son, then she and Papa would not always be so anxious. My brother would be Uncle Chandy's heir, and everything would be as it should."

How many times had her parents burdened her with that wish? "Any older brother of yours would be much wittier than I am and better-looking too."

"Now you do tease me. Has it been a quarter hour yet? Mama said I was to find her in a quarter hour unless a suitable bachelor decided to keep me company."

Leaving Annette like a staked goat to face the perils of the social wilderness all on her own. Though, to be fair, Coraline would doubtless come swanning back—

"There's Mama. What do I tell her?"

"I was assuring myself that your impromptu dip in the lake had no lasting ill effects. Good day, Annette."

Coraline stopped a few feet from the table, raised both hands, and clapped gently. "Cousin Bernard, none the worse for your ordeal, apparently. You must sit with us at supper—another buffet—and tell us how you're finding your first outings in Mayfair. I understand Sorcha dragged you to the Moreland musicale. An excellent affair, if a bit tedious for those not musically inclined."

Bernard rose and bowed. "Madam, I have been assuring myself that Annette is also none the worse for her mishap. I regret to report that my evening meal is already spoken for. I don't suppose either of you has seen my brother recently?"

Coraline's smile became a bit feline. "Richard is making a pest of himself to Sorcha. She is inexplicably tolerant where he is concerned, though I do apologize for my jaundiced view of the man. That you have a connection to him is no fault of yours."

Annette sat mutely, staring at her empty tea cup.

"I am not yet well acquainted with my brother," Bernard said, "but I both like and respect the man based on what I have learned of him. If we are to be eternally judged for the mis-steps we make early in life, few of us would merit much esteem."

For that brief homily, he did not chastise himself even a little.

"I sought the company of the broodmares," Richard said, "but had to revise my destination when I saw the ladies already had callers. Were you and Huxley arguing?"

Sorcha nearly pitched him into the lake for that question, not because Richard deserved a second dunking, but because the day had gone from all wrong to hopeless and then to...

Brokenhearted. That's what Eglantine would have called the heavy, despairing feeling in Sorcha's chest.

"A gentleman never argues with a lady, Richard, and Bernard is the most honorable gentleman I have ever met."

Sorcha had consented to this stroll around the lake because sitting still was beyond her, and Richard had offered. Why must he look so much like Bernard?

Ten yards ahead, the children were engaged in some sort of skipping competition. Skip ten steps, walk ten steps, then skip with the other foot in the lead, as if they were cantering horses.

"Huxley will argue with you if the matter at issue is serious enough. He nearly capsized our little boat when I attempted to twit him. He's not the twit-able sort, and I must say, I like that about him."

Bernard was the sort to make his points with imaginary dragons, real evidence, and the most luscious kisses...

No more of that for you, lassie.

"Annette has apparently been bullying Jordy," Sorcha said. "Jordy confided the particulars to Bernard, and Bernard is ready to launch the Battle of the Nations to see the matter resolved. He proposes to undertake this... this... campaign for truth and justice when every gossip in Town is watching his smallest move, and Coraline is making the opening maneuvers in her own battle to see Annette married to a prince."

The skipping competition shifted to a backward-walking race.

"Annette is a minx in the making. Somebody needs to put the fear of scandal in her, or she'll end up married to a shepherd on some Scottish island. She's too immature to be grateful for even a shepherd's devotion."

"The Western Isles are beautiful." Were the Antipodes beautiful? "I am not stupid, Richard." Muddled, yes. Sad, upset, and frustrated, but not stupid. Then too, stupid and pigheaded were very different propositions.

"I think you are very bright, but also tired. The Dolforths are exhausting, though they are relatively few in number. They bring with them the eyes and ears of half of Society, and not the nicer half."

"You are a Dolforth." Sorcha was a Dolforth, though only by virtue of a marriage long over.

"I changed my name to Dolforth by deed poll when I attained my majority. Please recall that I was a Wolfinger for the whole of my minority. How did you leave it with Huxley?"

"He wants me to take the children north for a repairing lease, but Chanderton will never allow that, and then Lilly will get her oar in, and Coraline will start showering me with advice, and I have had enough of being told what to do, Richard. More than enough."

The backward-walking game had ended, and the children were trooping along. Bridget looked about five minutes away from asking for a piggyback ride.

"Was Huxley telling you what to do, then? Raising his voice, threatening, sneering?"

"Bernard is not Barclay. I know that."

"Let's skip some rocks."

I do not want to skip any rubbishing rocks. "Jordy! Bridget! Cousin Richard says he can make a rock skip five times!"

The children came gamboling back, and Richard set them to collecting a hoard of perfect skippers.

"Bernard is not Barclay," Richard said quietly, "and you are not stupid. Has it occurred to you that Annette might not be the only threat your children face?"

"Yes, it has. They might face the threat of being separated from their mother, for example. They might face the threat of harsh tutors, nasty governesses, and hours of copying Proverbs until my children come to resemble imps of Old Scratch because they have taken Scripture into such dislike. They might face cold porridge and days without sunshine, birchings without number, all the prescribed ingredients for a successful childhood among the English aristocracy."

Richard picked up a perfectly smooth, round, flat rock. "Barclay is dead, Sorcha. If you are not careful, you will become as rigid, opinionated, and thick-witted as he was. You owe Huxley a fair hearing. Keep to your present high dudgeon of maternal ire, and ten years on, you will be praying that Coraline doesn't sabotage Bridget's come out. Let Annette and whatever accomplices she has treat Jordy poorly now, and you are inviting them to strike again. I find it interesting that Huxley, who was raised with every advantage, should understand the schoolyard realities encountered by the realm's friendless bastards."

He handed her the rock and bent to admire another near-perfect specimen Jordy had found. This necessitated an assessment of Bridget's assembled arsenal and some practice throws.

When Sorcha took her shot, the rock bounced six times before disappearing into the depths of the lake.

"Well done, Mama!" Jordy crowed. "Mama is the best skipper!"

"I'm going to grow up to be a champion skipper like Mama," Bridget said, tossing her rocks one by one into the water. "C'mon, Jordy. I'll race you to the stump."

"Such energy," Richard said, once again falling in step beside Sorcha. "Are you wroth with me for taking Huxley's part?"

"A little. I suspect I am also angry with myself. I am most assuredly angry with Annette."

"Good. I don't truly blame Annette for being such a brat. Coraline sets impossible expectations on the girl, and Tallister does nothing to curb his wife's ambitions. Chanderton keeps a shuddering distance, and Lilly abides by Chanderton's wishes. She could get the old boy to lend a hand, but she's too busy pouring his tea and handing him his spectacles."

"Barclay threatened me with an asylum, Richard. He raised his hand to me a few times as well. You criticize Lilly to me at your peril. She is managing as well as she can, and I will not participate in the gratuitous character assassination society finds so amusing."

They walked along in silence while the children panted their way back from the stump.

"I'm sorry, Sorcha. I knew Barclay was tiresome. I hadn't realized he was awful."

"I didn't want anybody to realize. I didn't want to admit it to myself. He was awful."

"And you were stuck in a purgatory not of your own making. At least when I was sent off to Lisbon, I knew I'd landed myself there. I daresay you've consigned Huxley to something like a personal purgatory, and you, my dear, aren't looking any too cheerful either. Are we about to be importuned for piggyback rides?"

Will this rubbishing day never end? "They are getting too old for that. We'll walk slowly and take our time, but Jordy has had enough piggyback rides for one day, and I am honestly not up to carrying Bridget all the way back to the house."

Much whingeing and wheedling ensued, but Sorcha stood firm, and Richard supported her decision. They walked slowly. They sat on benches along the way. They paused to look for clovers, but the children returned to the house on their own tired feet.

"Will we see you at supper?" Sorcha asked when Richard would have parted from them on the back terrace.

"You well might, but I'm off early tomorrow. Some fellow named St. Didier has begged the favor of a call upon me. His note said Bernard would vouch for him, but no details. One is intrigued, and off to Town at first light."

"I know Leopold St. Didier. He's received everywhere. His family held a title that reverted to the crown a generation or two back. He has means and standing on his own merits."

"Then he's not inviting me to go adventuring in foreign climes, and he's not a competitor looking to pay me a fortune for my business. Life is a series of disappointments. If I don't see you at supper, sweet dreams."

He bowed and strutted off, and even his walk put Sorcha in mind of Bernard.

Sorcha did not anticipate sweet dreams. She anticipated a night of troubled sleep in a solitary bed, if she slept at all.

CHAPTER EIGHTEEN

Bernard made himself dress for supper—informal, thank the duchess—and descended to the back terrace at the appointed hour. He wasn't expecting Sorcha to ambush him as he emerged from the house.

She made a fetching picture in dark green velvet, an aubergine shawl about her shoulders. Her posture was militant, though, and Bernard thus offered her a bow rather than a less formal greeting.

"I'm sorry," she said, speaking quietly. "You are trying to solve a problem that won't go away just because I want to ignore it. I did not express myself as civilly as I ought, and I apologize for that."

He had to repeat her words in his mind to make sure he had the sense of them. "You are apologizing? To me?"

"Don't sound so surprised. I am never at my best in Dolforth territory. That is no excuse for sounding like my late husband, thinking like him, and acting like him."

Bernard accompanied her to the balustrade. A few other guests were strolling the garden, though the terrace was blessedly deserted.

"What has his late lordship to do with the present difficulties?" Bernard asked.

"He's like your mother, Bernard. He haunts me, but I can at

least be aware of when his ghost walks. He used to pretend to entertain a topic with me, when all the while, he was building his arguments against me, preparing little darts of ridicule or husbandly authority. If those didn't work, he'd resort to threats and shouting."

The prospect from the balustrade was lovely—the formal garden in neat parterres, the park lush with spring grass, the lake a placid feature in the distance. Lovely but tame. Completely devoid of the ancient wildness of the Dales, not so much as a hare daring to grab a bite of clover.

"You aren't wrong," Bernard said. "You know these people better than I ever care to, you do have to keep the peace with them, and you have managed to accomplish that without anybody's help for some time. You are also right that my mother is halfway around the world. I am haunted by the notion that had I been willing to admit that my efforts to manage her were inadequate, had I sought allies, I might have been able to put her on that boat years earlier."

"You wanted to banish your own mother?"

He nodded. "The North Pole would have done nicely. Very unvicarly of me. I would not face that truth until it was nearly too late."

He expected Sorcha to pat his arm or maybe kiss his cheek, murmur a platitude or two, and walk away. She'd apologized for becoming heated at the mares' pasture. She wasn't relenting on the whole topic of the children's safety or the need to hold responsible parties accountable.

"Bernard, you aren't wrong either. You said Tallister might have doctored the children's sweets at Sunday supper. I dismissed that claim, but you should know Coraline expects her cook to run an organized kitchen. The individual dessert servings are set out in advance, and you were correct that the smaller portions would have been clearly evident."

He risked a glance in her direction. Sorcha's features were composed, though she looked a bit tired around the eyes. "You've been thinking about this."

"I owed you a fair hearing, and what you got was an inquisition. I've been thinking about the incident with the pony too."

"Annette has admitted to loosening the girth on Jordy's saddle. She also admitted to smacking him on the head with the lid of the oat bin."

Sorcha stared hard at the distant lake. "She *admitted* to intentionally harming my son?"

"Annette has promised to mend her ways, but, Sorcha, I do believe that, to some extent, Annette has also been a victim. She claims she had nothing to do with the boat sinking today, which means somebody else had a hand in matters."

"You suspect Tallister. I'm listening."

Bernard schooled himself to give as factual a recitation as he could. As more people emerged to enjoy the garden, he described a girl made terribly insecure by her mother's criticisms and ambitions, a girl desperate for her father's approval and easily goaded by his suggestions and flattery.

"You have advised sympathy where Annette is concerned," he concluded. "I could not initially see your point, but having spoken with Annette and observed her at some length, I tend to agree with you."

"I'm not feeling very sympathetic toward her now."

Sorcha was sounding quite Scottish. Gratifyingly Scottish.

"She will apologize to Jordy when the moment is right, but please recall that she, too, was in that sinking boat. The lake is shallow enough that she was likely not at serious risk of harm—she told me she knows how to swim—though somebody thought it acceptable to mortify the girl before half the shire."

Sorcha gathered her shawl about her shoulders. "You are suggesting Tallister is growing desperate."

"Bold, certainly. He all but commanded Annette to take a boat out, knowing full well Eglantine would draw attention to the situation by refusing. Annette seized on Jordy to save face. To one who knows her well, that was her predictable next move."

"I will never forget the sight of my son in a sinking boat, Bernard. Chanderton won't believe a word of this, and he's the only person with sufficient authority to put a stop to it."

Sorcha was angry. She was also thinking strategically, bless her and her Highland temper.

"Chanderton might be the only single person who could hold Tallister accountable, but we have other options."

"In Yorkshire," Bernard said, "I made the mistake of thinking that Mama was my cross to bear, my problem to manage. She menaced the whole parish, but her mischief was never spoken of in public. Her victims were ashamed, everybody else too intimidated by the thought of the harm she could do. We all struggled along in silence until Lorne arrived and took a different tack."

"I've avoided Tallister," Sorcha said. "I wanted no grist for gossip, as charming as he can be. I simply didn't trust him. But then..."

"You've trusted nobody, for reasons. Tallister has asked to meet me here at midnight."

"You cannot possibly..." Sorcha turned her back to the garden so she and Bernard were nearly face-to-face. "You intend to oblige him."

"I will meet with Tallister," Bernard said, "though I will not oblige him. I was hoping you might give me the benefit of your thoughts on a few particulars."

Sorcha rearranged her shawl again and managed to gently flap a length of silk tassels across Bernard's forearm.

"Are you asking for my permission, Bernard?"

The question was fraught. To relegate Sorcha to the position of advisor would be to offer her disrespect, and yet, Bernard meant to confront Tallister, the sooner the better.

"I am asking for your help," he said. "Asking you to allow me to try to rout the rascal, which I cannot do on my own. I need your help, Sorcha, and I am asking for it."

A pair of footmen wheeled out a punchbowl on a tea cart. Another footman followed up with a tea cart full of glasses. Richard emerged onto the terrace, looking dapper and cheerful, as he greeted the footmen by name.

"You are right," Sorcha said. "You cannot defeat Tallister on your own, just as I could get nowhere with Chanderton on my own. Nowhere with any of these self-important, sophisticated, ninnyhammers who compose most of polite society. What do you have in mind, Bernard?"

He could have kissed the nearest drainpipe. Instead, he gestured toward the steps. "Let's admire the park, shall we? Perhaps Richard would like to stroll with us."

"Anybody else?"

"That will be for you to say."

He'd plucked the right answer from a dozen that might have had the opposite result. Sorcha took his arm and led him to the steps.

"I'm listening, Bernard. See that you listen to me as well."

"Of course. I will always listen to you, on that you have my word. The challenge as I see it is to beat Tallister at his own game, a game at which I am a newly fledged tyro, but at which you excel..."

The full moon cast ribbons of silvery light on the lake, a nightingale sang his little birdie heart out in the home wood, and Tallister Greer congratulated himself on a successful day that was about to exceed all bounds.

Coraline would be in alt. Annette would be enormously relieved. The problem of Bernard Huxley would be resolved to Tallister's satisfaction, and even Sorcha would get most of what she apparently wanted.

He sauntered over to the balustrade, where Huxley was pretending to admire the shadowy garden.

"Greer." Huxley neither bowed nor nodded. "Good evening. What was of such moment that you had to summon me with a cryptic note?"

Good heavens, the fellow must be nervous or dyspeptic. "We're not to indulge in chitchat? Huxley, you surprise me. I thought chitchat was an eleventh commandment for rural parsons."

"The usual ten suffice, as best I recall."

Arrogant bumpkin. He hadn't so much as looked at Tallister. No bow, no handshake.

"Very well, plain speaking it shall be. Marry Annette, and I'll let you become guardian of Sorcha's heathens, provided you assist with dowries for the younger three. You can have all the time and proximity to Sorcha you please. Coraline will be delighted, and Chanderton can go about his business without having to do battle with Sorcha over every tutor or puppy."

A sensible proposition from every perspective. Then too, Huxley would treat Annette decently in the ways that mattered. Not a detail.

Huxley took out a gold watch and peered at its pale face. "I am Chanderton's preferred candidate for the post of guardian, I already enjoy a friendly welcome under Lady Barclay's roof, and I do believe that Coraline's earthly joy is more a matter for you to address than for me." He snapped the watch closed and returned it to its pocket. "You should also be aware that Annette harbors no interest in becoming my wife."

A cit must be allowed his attempts to bargain, however futile those efforts might be. "Annette harbors a vast interest in escaping her mother's household. Show the girl a bit of consideration, buy her a decent riding horse, and she'll fancy you madly."

"I see. Annette gets a horse and a husband out of your scheme. I have managed quite well thus far without a wife, and I like the horse I have. Why should I accede to your wishes, Greer? And do be succinct. The hour is late, and my day has been long."

A father of four girls and a man married to Coraline developed vast stores of patience. "You are a vicar turned jumped-up huckster, so I will keep the explanation simple. You get to keep running your little businesses, which I could send into bankruptcy with a few words in the right ears. You can run tame in Sorcha's household, as you've been running tame. You will have the considerable social consequence of my dear wife to call upon and a wife of your own whom you can easily manage."

Huxley yawned and stretched, rudeness upon poor manners. "And if a wife I can easily manage doesn't appeal to me?"

"Huxley, is this really necessary? I understand pride better than you might think, so a bit of posturing on your part is understandable. Do you want to see Jordy and Bridget plagued by more mishaps and bellyaches? Annette truly resents the boy. All that the situation needs is a few pointed reminders of what Jordy's existence costs her, or some teasing suggestions about how she might plague him."

Tallister felt some pity for the lad, though with no brothers to toughen him up, Annette's pranks were nearly doing him a service.

"Annette does what she's told, bless her," Tallister went on, "and she thinks herself quite independent all the while. Has a touch of her mother's gullibility, does my Annette. And you dismiss the charms of a biddable wife out of ignorance. Barclay had his hands full with Sorcha, and that is not a prospect any sensible husband relishes."

Huxley was quiet, probably grappling with the realization that he'd underestimated his opponent sorely.

"Did you put Annette up to menacing Jordy?" he asked.

The light was beginning to dawn. Excellent. "I wouldn't describe the situation that strongly. She governs her impulses very well when her mama is on hand, but when Coraline is through dunning the girl for perfection, Annette must vent her spleen. Coraline doesn't understand this about her own daughter, but I do. Mother and daughter are more alike than either realizes."

Huxley straightened away from the balustrade. "A wife given to nasty and dangerous pranks has no appeal, Greer. If you'll excuse me..."

He began ambling back toward the house.

"Huxley, do you relish the thought of your businesses in ruins? Ridiculous to think a vicar could manage thriving enterprises. Perhaps nobody will blame you for wrecking what your cousin took years to build. Richard might make a place for you in his offices, but you'd best learn Spanish and Portuguese first."

Huxley paused but didn't bother to fully face the author of his future. "You don't move in commercial circles, nor are you respected in them. I am not inclined to submit to your threats, but I will instead make a few of my own."

Give the man credit for tenacity, albeit tenacity born of utter ignorance.

"Don't bother. You either marry Annette, or I will see to it that Lady Barclay's reputation makes the sewers seem fragrant by comparison. You will admit that I can command the appropriate audience to effect that result. She's dismissed any number of eligible suitors, she never *took* with polite society, and she hasn't bothered to improve her diction. I can bring her down overnight, and then she will have you to thank for the fact that Chanderton and I allow her to see her children only at Yuletide and only with appropriate supervision."

Huxley came about slowly, somehow looming large with the house as a backdrop. "To separate Lady Barclay from her children would be cruel to her ladyship, who is an exemplary parent, and to the children who love her dearly. I appreciate that you are desperate, Greer, and that you have no allies and dwindling means. I do have allies, as do the children. Ladies, Richard, if you'd join us please?"

Tallister recognized the tread on the steps leading up from the garden. He also recognized the particular swish of skirts that presaged his wife in a howling temper.

"Huxley, you cheated!"

Huxley's teeth gleamed in the darkness. "I was advised to play by your rules instead of my own. Sound guidance, as it happens. Your Grace, Cousin Coraline, Lady Barclay. I'm sorry to have subjected you to the night air."

Bernard noted with some gratification that at the sight of the ladies, Tallister went as pale as moonbeams.

Then he drew himself up and attempted an affronted sniff. "Coraline will understand that I was only supporting the goal she sought to win. You're well heeled, Huxley. God knows you're well-heeled. Annette would know no want as your wife."

Christian duty might require Bernard to put out Tallister's lights before his babbling further inflamed uxorial ire. The trio of women, escorted by Richard, formed a half circle that pinned Tallister to the balustrade. The drop was only about a dozen feet. Otherwise, Bernard would have suggested they move the discussion indoors.

"Tallister," Bernard said, "if you had asked me to assist with dowering your daughter, I would have gladly made a contribution. Thanks to Dolforth funds, I am more than capable of aiding family interests. In fact, I will provide that aid because the girls will need it."

Coraline, standing between Sorcha and the duchess, stared at Bernard, which was fortunate. She was less likely to murder her husband if she was distracted by the thought that Annette might carry some resources into the battle of the ballrooms.

"Very... very sporting of you," Tallister said. "Now, if that's—"

"Tally." The duchess spoke softly. "Shut your mouth."

"Her Grace," Bernard went on, "will sermonize and lecture and otherwise prevail upon Chanderton to assist, and I am sure Richard and Lady Barclay will come to the aid of your daughters as well. That said, I will not marry Annette, and I will never allow her ladyship and the children to be bullied and harassed by the likes of you or the boring, philandering, idle Society that you refer to as polite. Never again."

Bernard had managed not to shout, but he did grasp for the first time why certain preachers were tempted to a fire-and-brimstone delivery. Some matters demanded memorable emphasis.

Tallister half-turned and adopted a heroic pose, gaze upon the lake in the distance. "I do hope my efforts will not be misinterpreted.

I sought to spare my daughter the humiliation of multiple failed Seasons, and, Coraline, surely you understand—"

"I do *not* understand, Mr. Greer." Coraline's voice cracked like lightning as she marched up to her husband. "You preyed on our daughter, manipulated her when she was vulnerable and uncertain. You insult her and me before others. You are apparently responsible for the poor girl being humiliated today in front of dozens of onlookers. She could have come to real harm, just so you could scare the boy —again. You have failed me, Tallister Greer. You have failed your children. You are a disgrace to the notion of husbandly responsibility."

Coraline had a temper. Well, well. Sorcha was smiling slightly, while the duchess was simply goggling.

"That's fine for you to say, Corrie," Tallister retorted, "but you haven't exactly been my devoted helpmeet and boon companion. Spending us into the River Tick despite my every plea to the contrary. Putting ridiculous notions in Annette's head. Swanning about as if I'm made of money when, Coraline, I am made of obligations and no way to meet them."

Coraline shoved him hard in the chest. "What about your obligation on Little Dalrymple Street? Does she qualify as a *help*"—shove—"*meet*?" Shove, shove.

Tallister smoothed a hand over his breastbone. "She hasn't qualified as anything for more than three years. For pity's sake, if you're going to spy on your husband, make a proper job of it."

"If you two keep this up," Bernard said, "Chanderton himself will be down here asking questions, and I, for one, will happily oblige him with honest answers. Tallister, I suggest you gather up your family and enjoy a summer in Scotland. The young ladies should know their paternal relations."

Coraline drew away from her spouse as if he reeked of spoiled cheese. "I would not get into a coach with that man if he begged me on bended knee."

"Then have him ride up on the box," Sorcha said gently. "We are offering you a chance to regroup, Coraline. Both you and Tallister have become too attached to fanciful plans and too determined to make those plans come true through any means. You both claim you want only what's best for your children, and you are both being mendacious. We will not give you another chance to set matters right. *I* will not give you that chance."

She spoke evenly, no malice in her words, only a sort of implacable resolve.

"The air grows chilly," the duchess said, taking Richard by the arm. "Time for me to seek my bed. Please acquaint me with your travel plans, Coraline. A departure in the next fortnight will spare you the crowded turnpikes that characterize the Season's conclusion."

Richard offered a general bow and decamped with the duchess.

"I'm tired," Sorcha said. "Exhausted, in fact, and don't think I've forgiven either of you. You might have made my life so much easier, and you couldn't be bothered. Instead, my son has been bullied and put in harm's way because of you. My daughter has been terribly upset on her brother's behalf. You are fortunate that I refuse to retaliate by withholding my support from your offspring. Stay in Scotland as long as you like."

She took Bernard not by the arm, but by the hand.

They left the Greers in the dark, separated by several feet, a growing silence, and an entire lake full of regrets.

~

"How did you know Tally was rolled-up?" Sorcha asked as she and Bernard made their way through the darkened house.

"I had him followed. Kessler gave me the idea. He set Heevers and Ipswich to chasing me around Town, reminding me to eat, reminding me to keep this meeting or not be late for that one. Walking my horse." Bernard paused on the landing, his gaze on the next flight of stairs. "I would like a piggyback ride."

"I am weary too. Perhaps we're suffering battle fatigue." And yet,

Sorcha was also wonderfully relieved. The relief was creeping around the edges of her awareness, as gray light in the east presaged a brilliant day. "What did Heevers and Ipswich learn?"

Bernard started up the steps. "That Tally wastes most of his time. He strolls about Knightsbridge, idles around the book stalls in Bloomsbury, and assiduously avoids Bond Street or St. James's proper."

"Staying out of sight of his creditors?"

"Out of sight of friends and acquaintances as well. A man who will not seek refuge in his club is a man who is likely behind on his dues. I gather by the unwritten laws of Mayfair that is a black letter felony."

"Certainly an indicator of shaky finances. I knew Tally's means were limited. I did not think him..."

"Drowning," Bernard said as they approached Sorcha's door. "Coraline buying out the shops, insisting on a full staff from the most expensive agencies, filling Annette's head with dreams of princes and titles. As a new husband, Tally probably counted on Coraline having a son. Even had that son been the Chanderton spare, the child would have been insurance policy enough against ruin."

"Drat the rubbishing title. Next, you will have me feeling sorry for Tally. That, I refuse to do." Sorcha opened her door and stepped through. "My maid sleeps in the maids' dormitory. She claims all the best gossip is to be had from the other maids. Do come in."

Bernard hesitated, looking bashful and serious. "If I come in, Lady Barclay, I will be hard put to comport myself with strictest decorum."

How she loved his voice, loved his honesty. "That's fortunate, Mr. Huxley, because I feel a protracted bout of mad passion about to befall me, and occasions such as this are not to be squandered."

He stepped over the threshold and closed and locked the door. "I truly am tired, Sorcha, and probably not at my best."

"It's after midnight, the day has been interminable, and we've weathered the Battle of the Dolforths. I won't be at my best either,

Bernard, but right now, if all you do is hold me, I will count the day a victory."

He did hold her. At some point after both parties had properly rested, a bout of mad passion also ensued, and the night saw victories for love and pleasure.

Bernard and Sorcha explained the fact of their betrothal to the children during the coach ride back to London. An earnest discussion ensued regarding appropriate names for any siblings who might join the family. Jordy argued for Draco, while Bridget pointed out that a girl might prefer to be named Pendragon.

As it happened, both names were pressed into service eventually, with Richard being named as godfather to the first, despite the complications that good fellow was experiencing elsewhere in life.

But that, of course, is a tale for another time!